A GREEN AND
ANCIENT LIGHT

A
GREEN
AND
ANCIENT
LIGHT

FREDERIC S.
DURBIN

SAGA PRESS

LONDON SYDNEY **NEW YORK** TORONTO NEW DELHI

FOR MY AUNTS, AND UNCLE LES,
WHO BELIEVED FROM THE BEGINNING;

FOR EVANGELINE, WHOSE BOOK THIS IS;

AND FOR JULIE, ALWAYS.

SAGA PRESS
AN IMPRINT OF SIMON & SCHUSTER, INC.

1230 AVENUE OF THE AMERICAS, NEW YORK, NEW YORK 10020

remember the plane hurtling above the village. It left a trail of thick gray smoke, and its engine roared and coughed. Grandmother and I were working in the garden, digging potatoes. We could see the plane was an enemy fighter, part of the squadron we'd heard earlier as it growled north, heading up the coast. Now alone, skimming the mountain slopes, the plane dove toward us like a sorrowful, stricken angel. I was on my feet by the time it careened right over our heads. Its shadow made the sun above me blink.

Grandmother uttered a reproachful sound, her digging-fork across her knees as she tipped back her hard brown face, shielding her eyes from the glare. She didn't spring to her feet as I did. Nothing about the war ever made Grandmother dash to the window or pace the floor or otherwise put herself out. She didn't watch caravans, and she pretended not to listen to bulletins on the radio; she clucked her tongue when they interrupted the orchestra broadcasts, though she never actually switched them off. But neither did she stop snapping beans or darning socks. And I never saw anyone draw her into speculation on how things were going for the troops.

We could see the enemy insignia on the wings, and a row of bullet holes ran the length of the fuselage. There was an explosion; black smoke billowed. The engine sputtered out entirely, and flames rolled back over the cockpit. I dashed to the corner of the house to continue watching. With an eerie silence, the plane cleared the orchards and the front street; it missed the fishing boats in the green harbor, and it missed the rocks. Out where the sea deepened to blue, it smashed into the waves, throwing up a tower of spray.

I turned to look at Grandmother. My eyes must have been wide, and I think my mouth was open. My feet were tugging me into the side yard. Grandmother began scratching in the soil again, with a little grunt that meant, "Well, that's that."

But seeing that my knees wouldn't bend, my feet wouldn't be still, she said, "Go on, then. Run down and see." There was no disapproval in her tone. She was talking to a nine-year-old boy for whom a great many things were intriguing: moths on the screen, moss, the squirming life beneath rotted logs, and planes that fell from the sky.

Quite a crowd had gathered on the front street: people on bicycles, fishermen knee-deep in piles of nets, three sisters from the abbey clutching their rosaries and looking paler than usual—and of course children from near and far, wriggling over fences, pounding along the dusty lanes—everyone pointing and talking at once.

"It exploded," someone said. Indeed, a last, thick plume of black smoke hovered over the waves, at the end of the gray swath across the sky. "I thought it was coming right down on the street!"

"Rattled the cans on the shelves," said Mr. B——, the grocer. He had white hair and black sideburns, which seemed to me the opposite of how most men's hair turned white.

"Woke me up from a nap," said someone else. "I was sure they were dive-bombing the cannery!"

"Don't like it this close. Don't like it at all."

"Nothing left of that plane. Went straight to the bottom, I guess."

"He's a goner. That's no way to die, theirs *or* ours."

A woman in a green print dress kept smoothing her hair, as if the wind from the warbird's passing had left her in hopeless disarray. Two boys jabbered about how they'd thought the plane would hit the boats. They glanced at me but were more interested in the plane for now; children in the village generally seemed curious about me, but we rarely crossed paths—boys my age kept busy helping their elders on the docks or in the vegetable gardens, and I wasn't out of the cottage in the evenings when they might have been free. I wasn't opposed to making friends here, but mostly I missed my two closest friends back home.

The wind picked up, scattering the smoke. A little yellow dog ran through the crowd, barking and wagging its curly tail.

Climbing over the low stone wall, I stepped out of my battered shoes and padded across the wet sand, right to the water's edge between piers. At this end of the village, the land sloped down gently to the shore, and there were no cliffs. The sea-smell washed over me, huge and fishy and humid, with that dank hint of all that it hid, ancient wrecks and monsters that made whales look like minnows. Gulls screeched, riding the wind currents. Beside me, a tiny crab scuttled across a rock, and a raisin box bobbed, its sides puckered and bleached nearly white. Sand oozed between my toes; a wave rolled in, and soon my pant legs were drenched to the knees.

I could look right out through the harbor mouth to where the plane had gone down. There was not a sign of it now. Only the waves rose and fell, their edges dazzling in the light.

I won't tell you my name or that of the village where I spent that spring and summer when I was nine. I won't because you should realize there were towns just like it and boys just like me all around the sea—and in other countries beyond the mountains, and all over the world. We awoke in our nights to the growl of trucks, the barking of loudspeakers. (I was one of the fortunate, for whom the guns were a rumble in the distance.) The men in our families were soldiers now, regardless of what they'd been before; many were already dead. The women worked in factories, in hospitals, or stayed at home to care for the very young.

And then there were those like me: too old to be carried about, too young to work or fight. We were sent off to the countryside where no one thought bombs would fall. We came to know our relatives, old people who had known our parents in another time. In my case, it was only for the late spring and summer, while my mother was getting used to a new job and my baby sister was a newborn. (Schooling in those years was haphazard. Sirens interrupted classes. High-school boys went to war, and classrooms became factories where girls sewed. A season later, my elementary school closed entirely for two years.) I might have been of considerable help to my mother; I was old enough for that. But my father felt strongly that it was time I got to know my grandmother.

It is a strange thing to spend your days with a person connected to you only by the link of someone you both hold dear, but the young one they knew is not quite the same as the older one you know. It's like talking to someone through a hedge. Now and then, you see an outline, the edge of a face between leaves. You can only walk along in search of a gate.

On the table beside my bed at Grandmother's cottage, I kept a framed photo of the four of us: my papa in his Army captain's uniform, his eyes alight with kindness, one arm around my mama and one hand on my shoulder; my mama, cradling my newborn sister, holding her so that her little face showed, Mama's face inclined as if she'd only just managed to turn her gaze toward the camera as the shutter opened. And there I was, looking uncomfortable in my school coat and tie, my hair sticking up though my mama had just combed it down. I looked at the picture so much that spring and summer that I knew every shadow in it, every wrinkle of clothing; I could see our faces when I wasn't looking at it. In the picture, both my parents were smiling as if there were no cares in the world.

I loved the letters Mama sent me here, warm and full of the hugs and kisses that embarrassed me in public but that I was glad for in writing. She would give me reports on the castle—Papa and I had built a castle out of wood, complete with turrets and a drawbridge, and I had painted it all; it sat on a table in my room but was too big and delicate to bring here. So, my mother would write to me about the weather over the castle, about the feasts they were having in the great hall. She tried to tell me about the knights and their quests, but she didn't understand that part very well. It was all right. I was always happy to hear that the King and Queen were well, that no enemies had invaded. I wrote back to her and to my father, though I knew it took longer for mail to reach him. Grandmother didn't read the letters I wrote or the ones I received. "That's your business," she said, which was a new arrangement for me, that I might have "business" apart from that of the grown-ups around me. She taught me once what to say at the post office, showed me the jar where I could find coins for posting letters, and after that, I was on my own.

I missed my parents, but I had stopped crying for them in the dark hours. After a few weeks in the village, our city began to feel like a distant dream. I knew it was real, that if I rode the train again, it would be there, and its bricks would become the reality once more, and this village would be the dream. One person, I'd come to understand, was actually many people—people of different ages, people who lived in different surroundings; these people all had the same name and knew something of each other, but they lived entirely separate lives.

It was a wondrous village Grandmother lived in. I was used to straight, level streets, advertising signs and honking cars, puddles and dodging bicycles and people who hurried along with blank faces. There was more sun in Grandmother's village, and ordinary life seemed half like a festival. People stopped to talk when they met, setting down their shopping baskets. There were benches everywhere that seemed placed for this purpose, often roofed by trellises of flowering vines. Many shops had open fronts all day, the wares spilling out and piled in the street.

I'd never seen streets like these! They wandered as if a great wave had washed up through the village, its water coursing among the buildings, finding a thousand ways eventually back to the sea; and these runnels had left magical sand that had hardened into cobbles, flint paths, and lanes of hard-packed earth. At its end farthest from Grandmother's house, half of the village climbed a cliff, so the streets there would turn without warning into steep stairways. There were no posted names, no numbers on doors or lanes. People would emerge from gates beneath ceilings of vines, from doors set right into the rock, and I always wanted to crane my neck and peer past them, sure I might glimpse stairs winding down to kingdoms under the ground where the light came from jewels in the walls.

Down at the cliff's foot, the sea had carved out high-rimmed basins and caves where the waves rushed in through narrow mouths, flooding the rocks with surges of foam. Grandmother had led me there in the first week, and we'd watched the scurrying crabs, our faces wet with spray, our ears half-deafened by the sea's roaring. "People have drowned here," Grandmother yelled beside me, her grip fierce on my arm. "Do not ever come back here alone. Do you understand?" I nodded, sensing how important it was to her. She'd wanted to show me these merciless sea-basins before I discovered them on my own.

A day or two after the trip to the cliff's foot, I learned Grandmother's other sacred commandment, but this one she didn't warn me about. It happened like this.

I'd made my first trip alone to the post office, mailed letters to both my parents, and was feeling quite happy with myself as I returned toward her cottage down the main street, which at our end of the village was wide and mostly straight. I kicked a series of pebbles, overtaking one and kicking it ahead of me until it bounced too far aside, then choosing another. As I admired the dense, round tops of some orchard trees, I came alongside Mrs. D——, whom I knew to be Grandmother's friend. Mrs. D—— had a round face like a china plate and small, sparkly eyes. She laughed pleasantly and often, and she had a way of asking one question after another, so that you could get only about half an answer in for each question and you wondered whether she was even listening. As I got near Mrs. D——, I saw that she was carrying her wicker basket from the shops and a parcel besides, and remembering my manners, I offered to carry them for her. She lived not far from Grandmother's, and on the way.

"What a gentleman you are!" she exclaimed, gladly handing them over. They were both quite heavy. "Just like your father. Oh, he was a fine boy, and he is a fine man, and it's no accident, because you come from fine stock!"

"Thank you," I said. I'd only ever heard "stock" in reference to cows, and I wondered how it was that our family had come from cows, or what exactly Mrs. D—— meant.

"Are you settling in? It must be so different for you here, so quiet, and none of your friends about, just us old folks, and our funny ways, our speaking—it's the sea-speech. We sound like the gulls, I suppose, like the waves all rolling, one into another. Mumbling like the ocean. The city-folk say they can't make pails or pitchers out of what we say. Can you understand the people?"

"Yes, ma'am," I said, supposing that a "Yes" answered more of her questions than it didn't.

"And as smart as white gloves!" she cried proudly, patting my shoulder as if I'd won the races. "But of course you would be a smart one, your father's son, and M——'s grandson. Sharp as shears, the whole family! I must tell you, I'm honored to call your grandmother a friend! And a wonderful friend she's always been."

I nodded and smiled, readjusting the parcel.

"But how about *you*; I want to know more about *you*! What do you like about our village? Aren't the flowers pretty? We take great care with our flowers! 'You can grow them beautiful only if the heart has good soil'—that's what we say!"

She paused expectantly, but I wasn't sure how to answer. I wasn't entirely convinced the question had much to do with me at all.

"The flowers are very pretty," I said. "And I love the trees. The mountains—it's all so green. It's like the woods go on forever."

Mrs. D—— looked taken aback, which surprised me. "H'm. Well, yes. The woods go on, but they're no place to be. There are wild animals, and worse things."

"Worse things?" I was suddenly much more interested.

Her sparkly eyes looked away from me, up toward the endless ranks of the treetops on the mountainsides. "I'm sure your grandmother doesn't want you going up there, and she'd be a fair sight better than me at telling you. But it's best not even to think very loud about the forest. Where the sun doesn't go and the salt breeze can't blow away the cobwebs, no good can happen, and that's a fact. Witch-weasels and sickle-winds, and old Mr. Clubfoot with his hollow back—lots of no good in the woods." She shook herself like I'd seen a friend of my mother's do when eating a pickle. "Enough of that! You're safe down here. 'Mountains for woods, and houses for people.'"

I nodded, thoroughly intrigued. It was clear to me that Mrs. D—— thought the woods were every bit as deadly as Grandmother told me the sea-basins were. Grandmother's caution made perfect sense to me, but I believed the best of trees. I wondered at how anyone could be afraid of any gathering of peaceful giants that grew from nuts over decades or centuries with such patience, such purpose. Granted, I had never been into a deep wood. But this one above the village called to me.

Mrs. D—— dove back into her comfortable nest of topics. "Did you have a garden in the city? Nearly everyone has a garden here! 'A house without a garden is a rock in the sand.' I'm sure you help M—— with her garden, don't you?"

"Yes, ma'am." I was learning to answer quickly, in the instant that Mrs. D—— took a breath.

"Hers is one of the loveliest in the village, and she uses every inch of it so well, the moss and the shade and the sunny stretches! A greener thumb I've not seen. And always a marvel, always some changes every year. We old folks are set in our ways, but your grand-mother has a young heart, a *young* heart, I've always said, like the princess in the old story that sees the world new each morning— do you know that one?"

"No, ma'am," I said. I'd thought I knew all the fairy tales, but I didn't know that one. Maybe the village folk had different ones.

"'Looking-glass, candle, moon on the sea'!" said Mrs. D——, and I supposed she was telling me a part of the fairy tale. But she raced on, as she always did. "We look forward each year, I can tell you, to what she'll plant where, what will sprout out of this corner or that! She must be planting now—are you helping her plant these days?"

I nodded, thinking of the hours Grandmother and I had already spent digging and filling hanging pots, filling window-boxes, trans-planting shoots from indoors to outdoors, opening envelopes of last year's seeds that Grandmother had carefully labeled.

"And what are you putting into those long boxes under the front windows, where the sun shines so nice?"

Without a thought, I answered. I'd learned the name from Grandmother, and I'd repeated it to myself over and over because it sounded like a long-ago kingdom: "Setcreasea."

"Setcreasea!" cried Mrs. D———, clapping her hands. "Utterly lovely! The long, purple stems and leaves, like the most beautiful twilight has gathered right beneath your windows and stays all day! And then the pink flowers, the crowning glory! Yes, setcreasea love the cramping for their roots. Don't water the boxes too much! But your grandmother knows that; she's been at it longer than most and knows what they all need, every last bloom. I think they tell her, the flowers. Do you think?" She batted my arm again, jovially. "Here we are! Thank you so much, you dear, gallant gentleman!"

I was grateful that we'd arrived at her gate. I was feeling worn out, and not from the shopping burdens.

"And what's it to be at the back?" asked Mrs. D———, taking the basket and package from me. "There in the shade, where the trees lean in? She always has the best ideas for what to put there!"

I thought for a moment. "I think she said fuchsia," I said. "For the butterflies." By habit, I said "I think" so as not to sound too forceful, but I knew that's what Grandmother had planted there.

"Fuchsia! Of course! Like lanterns in the dark—a brilliant choice. Fuchsia will outshine her trumpet vines of last year, and we all thought those were divinely inspired! Such a sharp, clever young man you are, to keep all these names straight—not that I'm surprised, considering the source. 'The apple doesn't fall far from the tree'— that has a good meaning, too, you know. Well, now, thank you again, dear sir. I suppose you'd best hurry on back to her. Good work to do!"

I thought nothing at all of the conversation then, only that I was glad to be out of it. I hardly thought of it when I told Grandmother I'd helped Mrs. D—— with her groceries, and Grandmother had asked me to repeat the conversation word for word.

"What did she say then?" Grandmother asked. "And what did you say? What did she say next? What did you say?" Unlike Mrs. D——, Grandmother waited for each of my answers with her full attention. Even then, I didn't understand her interest.

When Grandmother didn't say a word to me for the rest of the day and all through supper, I began to think back through what had happened, what Grandmother had asked me to repeat. As we finished washing the dishes in utter silence, Grandmother's movements brisk and icy, I felt a growing, hollow ache in my chest. My eyes filled with tears.

"I'm sorry," I said quietly.

Grandmother looked up at me from drying her hands. "What are you sorry for?"

I hung my head, unable to endure her gaze. My stomach hurt, and my face burned. Somehow, I had transgressed; I had let Grandmother down, and I hated that I'd done so. I still didn't understand it exactly, but it had to do with telling Mrs. D—— too much.

"Your business is yours," said Grandmother, and I thought at once of my letters, my trip to the post office. "My business is mine. We don't talk about the garden. It reveals itself in its own time."

"I'm sorry," I repeated, really crying now, my nose streaming.

"You didn't know. Now you do." Grandmother rinsed a cloth, wrung it out, and handed it to me. "Wipe your face."

*   *   *   *

Spring became summer, and Mrs. D—— learned that it was no use asking me anything else about the garden, though it did nothing to dampen her good cheer. I was greatly relieved when the garden finally revealed itself, for I felt a stab of guilt each time a villager said to Grandmother, "I hear it's to be setcreasea this year, and fuchsia in the shade!"

More than once, when Grandmother seemed to be in the best moods, I asked if we could go up into the forest. She nodded and said we would soon, but in the moment, there was always something to do in the garden or something to buy or mend or clean. Once I'd taken note of the fact that Grandmother didn't seem to share Mrs. D——'s dread of the woods, I asked her why Mrs. D—— was afraid.

Grandmother shrugged. "She can't see into the woods, so she assumes all the bad she can't see is there. She thinks the sea is friendlier, but if she were out in a little boat, or swimming in it, it would occur to her that she can't see under the water, either."

I liked the postmaster, who at first pretended I was his boss. The joke began because I was always bringing him work to do, my letters to weigh and stamp. He would snap to attention when I'd come in and tell me that he'd just swept the floor or organized the closet. Once, he said, "I washed the window, Boss. Does it pass inspection?"

"It looks good," I said.

"Too clean, though. Now V—— can see me when he goes by, and he comes in and talks both my ears off. Man should be in politics. I can only get rid of him by saying you'll fire me if you catch me standing around."

"I won't fire you," I told him.

"You're a good boss. Got more letters for me today? I won't let you down, Boss."

After a few weeks, when we both got tired of the game, he would ask me about myself, leaning on his elbows, peering at me over the tops of the eyeglasses that clung to the last half-inch of his nose but never fell off. He had thick black hair, a lean, droopy face, and huge eyes that rarely blinked. It impressed me how he could be kind without ever laughing or smiling. Although he was curious about what I found to do in the village, what I was reading, what I wanted to be, or what I thought, he never asked about the garden or Grandmother beyond whether she were well. I'd learned from the Mrs. D—— incident to be careful of what I said. Still, the postmaster was the one grown-up that I usually saw on my own, without Grandmother, so he felt like my friend.

"Your father," he asked me, "he's an officer in the Army, isn't he?"

"Yes. A captain."

"That's very fine! You should be proud of him. Are you proud of him?"

I nodded.

"Good man," he said, and I wasn't sure whether he meant my father or me. "I remember him here. Smart! Always first in the school, always doing things—involved, you know, and famous. Famous as one can be here!" He laughed softly. "He used his head, didn't he, before they got him into the Army? In the city, he was some kind of a . . ."

"Locomotive engineer," I said. "He designed a diesel engine."

"Smart," said the postmaster with admiration. "You got his smarts?"

I shrugged and looked at my shoes.

"Sure you do. You got them."

One day, the customer in line ahead of me, an old man in a brown hat, told the postmaster about some wild vegetables he'd gathered in the forest. Of course, I paid close attention when the man muttered about how dark it was up there, even in the morning.

The postmaster looked hard over his glasses. "Not up here!" The gesture he made with his head seemed to indicate the mountain slope above our end of the village.

"No, no, of course not!" said the man. "Above the old harbor, past the point."

The postmaster nodded, and the man added, "Hard telling *what* grows up there!"

When he'd left, the postmaster and I were alone.

The postmaster greeted me by name, not with "Boss" anymore. "Been writing again, huh? How much paper you got up there, anyway? Do they bring it to you in trucks?"

As I handed over my letters—one each to my parents, and one each to my friends—I asked, "Are the woods above my grandmother's house really haunted?"

He froze, staring at me with his wide, dark eyes. Then he looked at my letters for a long time, as if the addresses were new to him. Finally, he glanced back at me and opened the stamps drawer. "Yes. They're haunted."

"By ghosts?"

"I don't know what ghosts are," he said. "But there are places that belong in the past and need to be forgotten." He paused then, and for the first time I'd ever seen, he pushed his glasses higher on his nose and resettled them. "You don't want to go up there, G———. You shouldn't ask about the woods, either."

I was too respectful to ask him why not, but the question was burning in me like a coal.

He could see it. "They teach curiosity in school, don't they? It's not always a good thing." He leaned on his elbows and gave me a long, sober look. "The world's getting worse. Until it gets a lot better, it's best not to ask too many questions."

I supposed he was thinking of the war. But he was afraid of the woods, afraid like Mrs. D———. I didn't see how the war could relate to the forest, or how the forest could relate to a past that needed to be forgotten.

And so the spring passed, gardens all through the village sprouted into blazes of fragrant loveliness, and we came to the day of the shot-down airplane, when it crashed into the waves and sank into the unseeable depths, down to the gardens of the mer-people. I imagined them all in a wide circle among the coral, holding their tridents, their hair floating, their silvery tails slowly fanning to keep them upright, as the wrecked plane floated down to rest in their midst.

That very night—quite late in the night—Grandmother and I were awakened by a rapping at the door. I was jolted to full consciousness at once and sat up in my squeaky bed, my heart pounding. Of course I imagined soldiers, come to tell us to evacuate. In the faint light of the lowering moon, I located my suitcase, always packed with the things I considered most important, always ready to be snatched up in a dash out the door. But in another moment,

I realized that the urgent tapping came from the back door, where a single mossy step led down into the garden—hardly the entrance soldiers would approach. Nor was the sound very loud; nor was it accompanied by any shouting.

I swung my feet to the floor, the boards cool and smooth. In the next room, Grandmother rustled about—pulling a housecoat on over her nightgown, I supposed. After turning the cast-iron doorknob, I peered out into the darkness of the main room as Grandmother emerged from her bedroom.

Her expression was serious but not afraid, which I found reassuring. The knocking had stopped, and a silence descended that was more nerve-wracking than the knocking itself. With hardly a glance at me, Grandmother crossed to the back door, picked up the walking-stick from the umbrella stand, and demanded, "Who's there?"

I heard the murmur of a reply but could make out none of the words. Grandmother, from her position, heard enough to satisfy her; she put down the stick, lifted the latch, and drew open the door.

Though the garden farther out was bright with slanting moonlight, the back step beneath the trees lay in deep shadow. The silhouette there belonged to a thin person in a rumpled felt hat and a long coat. When the door opened, this person began to bow and speak in a soft torrent of words—a man's baritone—sonorous, like that of a singer or radio announcer.

"My dear M———, forgive the intrusion." (He called my grandmother by her first name.) "I am so sorry to disturb you at this hour, but a matter has come up . . . or down, rather . . . and it would seem swift action is called for. It is—well, you know better about these things."

Grandmother had been listening with a fist on her hip, her other arm gripping the hat rack to steady her. Now she smoothed her tangled hair and pulled her housecoat closer about herself. "Come into the garden," she said to the man. "You always think more clearly in the moonlight." With a stern look at me, she added, "You stay there."

I nodded readily.

The man in the felt hat seemed to notice me for the first time, and his frame stiffened.

"It's my grandson," said Grandmother, pushing the man ahead of her. "I told you he was here. Have you forgotten, or were you not listening again?" Her glance repeated her orders to me, and then the door closed.

I stood in the doorway of my room, bewildered. Even after three months, I knew so little about my grandmother. Apparently, this man was no stranger to her, and their conversations frequently took place by the light of the moon. Grandmother, who never went into the street by day without her headscarf and her collars buttoned, thought nothing of being outdoors in her nightclothes with this gentleman. My parents had mentioned no other relatives in the village.

The main-room windows looking out on the garden were shuttered at night. I considered opening the door just a crack—but I didn't want to disappoint Grandmother again. I hovered on my threshold for a long time, then sat on my bed. For reassurance, I glanced at our family photo, but it was too dark to see us. Still, I knew we were all there, inside the frame, and my parents were smiling, my sister newly born.

The night was warm; summer had fully arrived, and it came

with an airiness much more pleasant than the muggy nights in the city, where the heat took on garbage smells and lay heavy and still among the buildings. Grandmother's front and back gardens were overrun with blossoms and aromatic trees. She was trying to teach me the names of them, but most flowers were as new and strange to me as the village. I suspected, moreover, that the names by which Grandmother knew them were not always their names as listed in books. I left my room's shutters open at night, because I didn't like pitch blackness. My window peered out over one of the fuchsia boxes. I could look at it without guilt now. One afternoon, out of the blue, as if reading my thoughts, Grandmother had said, "I was mostly angry at H—— that day." (She meant Mrs. D——; that was her first name.) "Using you like that—bah! She knew what she was doing."

I sometimes crouched among the fuchsia, in the shaded gallery of the side yard, where the white and magenta blooms draped down from the box like a primeval jungle. Turning my head now, I could see the moon touching the treetops—only a few nights past full, and still mostly round.

After what seemed a long while, the back door opened again, and I returned to my open doorway.

"Get dressed," Grandmother said, marching past me. "It will be light soon. We may as well start today early."

"What's happening?" I asked. "Who was—"

"Get the big shears and the brush knife," she ordered. She paused in the door of her bedroom. "There's a place you should see, anyway. I've been meaning to show you, and time is getting on. Today's the day. Yes, you should come: I may need your help."

"My help?"

"Get dressed."

"But—" I was speaking now to her closed door. I could hear her bustling about on the other side. "But where are we going?"

Her words were hard to catch as she opened drawers and lifted squeaky lids. "You like your stories of the long-ago, don't you? Curious and strange things—monstrous creatures?"

I held my breath and hurried closer to her room, my heart racing again. She'd closed the back door; our visitor was either gone or waiting outside.

"Yes," I said.

"Well, we're going to the grove of monsters."

With the moon down, the night was very dark as we left by the kitchen door, let ourselves out by the back gate, and climbed through the steep field of arbors and the open meadow. From every side came the scent of living, growing things, so different from the city's smells of dust, rust, and engine exhaust. Grandmother carried an old-fashioned lantern that she'd lifted down from a shelf and lit with a match. It smelled of heat and the oil it burned, and it threw a circle of golden light around us.

There was no sign of the man who'd come to our door. "That was Mr. Girandole," Grandmother explained when I asked her again. "He's a very old friend. He's gone ahead of us."

I was overawed by this sudden turn of events—we were really going up into the forest, the place I'd wondered about for so long. It crossed my mind that I might be dreaming, but everything was too detailed and continuous to be a dream. I could feel the tag of my shirt scratching against the back of my neck; occasional birds called. I didn't want Grandmother to change her mind, so I kept all questions to myself. Somehow, talking would seem intrusive in the night. Besides, I was burdened with a bucket, a metal pan inside it, and the garden tools Grandmother had asked for. She'd tied them in a canvas bundle and put other things from the kitchen into a large carpet bag while I dressed. The bag hung from her shoulder; in her free hand, she gripped her briar walking-stick. I marveled that we were doing this, all before Grandmother had had so much as a cup of tea.

The grasses glistened with dew that soaked my pant cuffs in no time and dampened my ankles, though my old leather shoes kept my feet dry. Mist flowed along the ground under the grape trellises. Insects sang all around us. The sky was a deep blue, sparkling with stars. I'd never seen so many stars in the city. By the time we reached the forest, I'd already seen two shooting stars flash and vanish.

I suppose it would have made sense to feel some kind of dread. But Grandmother was not afraid.

We didn't follow a path. The lantern's glow fell in warm swaths on the moss and leaves, sending shadows lurching among the trunks. We switched back and forth in the steeper places, sometimes coming to outcroppings of bare stone where Grandmother would perch for a while to rest. In one narrow ravine, tree roots formed a natural staircase. The mist floated thick in places, its frosty whiteness broken by glistening black trees.

Beneath the hem of her dress, Grandmother wore thick woolen stockings, and her feet were snugged in sturdy leather high-topped shoes that I suspected had once been my grandfather's, though he had been dead for many years. Like most villagers, she was accustomed to walking. Had Grandmother lived in the city, I doubt she'd have considered taxis worth the fare.

As we progressed up the mountain, the stillness deepened. The voices of insects and night birds faded away, and even the wind ceased to stir leaves or creak the high boughs. I wondered if this solemnity always filled the last hour before sunrise, or whether it was because of the place. Were monsters watching us now, lurking beyond the lantern's shine?

Grandmother poked her stick at a moss-bearded boulder on our left, then at a dead tree on the right with two limbs like the dangling arms of a person. She was figuring out the way to go.

The brush rustled, and something ghostly and pale moved slowly between the trees, just beyond the point at which we could see any details. I kept still, watching it, and didn't dare to speak. I thought it was a four-footed animal, probably a deer, though it might have been anything.

When it had passed, Grandmother led us onward again. Even in the wildest stretches, the footing was never too difficult. We crossed carpets of leaves, stepped over logs crusted with fungus like fairy dishes and cups; we traversed aprons of moss so plush that I felt guilty to set my feet there, as if I were blundering over someone's bed. Though Grandmother never issued a specific warning, I carefully avoided treading on any mushrooms or stepping into the rings or half-rings they formed.

We came up onto a level shelf where the trees grew ancient and immense, soaring like cathedral pillars. As we rounded a shoulder of rock, I looked ahead and nearly shrieked. Dropping everything, I covered my mouth, feeling that the breath had been sucked out of me.

Grandmother raised the lantern toward a terrifying sight.

A human figure—a man—dangled limp, hanging among the branches. All around and above him was a web of countless strands, a silky whiteness draping the limbs, billowing gently with the wood's breath. I thought of the spiders in Grandmother's garden, of the webs they spun in the darkness, and of the tiny winged things caught there when the sun rose. But the spider that had spun this web must be the size of a horse.

My scalp felt pierced with cold needles. I turned in a circle, searching the gloom above and behind us.

"What's wrong with you?" Grandmother shot me a scathing look, apparently unafraid to use her voice here.

"Where's the spider?" I blurted.

She narrowed her eyes. Then her expression softened, though she didn't smile. "You silly boy. That's not a spider web. It's a parachute."

At once, my face flushed with heat. I knew I should have understood what the cords and the pleated silky cloth were. But it was a dark place, and I'd been looking for monsters.

Grandmother moved forward again, prodding her way through some bushes to circle the man and eventually to stand directly beneath him. His boots swung with the smallest rocking motion about two body lengths over her head. She poked with her stick in the leaves around her shoes.

"He's lost some blood," she said. Then she raised her voice and called up at the man, "Hey! Can you hear me?"

There was no answer, no movement. I could see that the right leg of his canvas trousers was soaked with blood. I crept closer. At first, I'd thought his head was bald and blackened, perhaps as an effect of the giant spider's venom; now I saw that he wore a close-fitting leather pilot's hat.

He hung completely limp in his harness, supported by two broad straps above his shoulders. When a draft of air bellied the chute and stirred the bundles of cord, he twirled ever so slightly.

Trudging a few steps away, Grandmother stooped and picked up something . . . a heavy twig. She clamped her stick in her lantern-hand, took aim, and flung the twig up at the man. It missed him by a wide margin. So did her second try, with another twig . . . her third bounced off his hip.

Grandmother breathed something that might have been a curse word, set the stick and lantern down, and ordered me to help her.

It wasn't as easy as it looked. A chunk of bark I threw almost hit the man's arm.

Then, with a loud *whop*, a rock of Grandmother's struck him squarely in the stomach.

Immediately, the leather-capped head flew up, and the man shouted and flailed his arms and legs, looking like a marionette . . . an angry, blood-soaked marionette. His eyes were hidden behind big goggles. The language he was shouting in was not ours.

It was then that I finally made the connection. The plane that had fallen from the sky to crash into the sea . . . Clear and bright in my memory, I saw again the emblems on the wings and fuselage. This man above us had parachuted out of it. He was an enemy fighter pilot.

I cried out as I saw him pull a handgun from a holster beneath his arm.

Spinning right and left with the frenzy of his struggles, the man yelled a stream of harsh-sounding words, trying to aim the gun at Grandmother. His arm swayed and bobbed, the gun bouncing up and down.

Grandmother said nothing. She stood as straight as her curving back would allow and watched the man. I have no doubt she came within a hair's breadth of being shot, but she didn't shout back or try to run. She only stood and breathed and studied the pilot trying to get her in his gun sight.

But I hollered enough for both of us. I ran toward her, screaming at the man not to shoot. The goggled eyes turned toward me, and the gun wavered uncertainly, swinging in my direction, then back at Grandmother.

The man looked up into the nest of straps and lines that held him. He clawed at the buckles on his chest, but his panicked shouts had now taken on the tones of complaint. He gesticulated with the gun, now waving it in the air, now pounding it against his side. At one point, he seemed to be weeping.

"That's enough!" Grandmother had picked up her walking-stick, and something in her voice got the man's attention. She pointed the stick at him and shook it. "Enough," she repeated. "Drop that gun right now and be still if you want any help from us."

"Shut up!" yelled the man. He spoke at least a little of our language. "Shut up! No drop gun, no drop gun!"

"Shoot it, then!" Grandmother called back. "Shoot it, and everyone in the village will hear you. Soldiers will come. Do you want their help or ours?"

It was hard to argue with her logic. After a few more epithets, he stuck the gun back into his holster.

"Not there," said Grandmother, pointing with her stick. "The ground."

This seemed too much for him, too tall an order, but then he lost consciousness again. He'd missed the holster, only shoving the barrel beneath his arm—and when his limbs went slack, the gun tumbled onto the carpet of leaves.

I stared and thought about how close to death we'd come. After a pause, Grandmother bent close, regarded the pistol as if it were dog manure on her front walk, and picked it up by its middle. Holding it at arm's length, she moved off behind the pilot's back and hid it among a pile of rocks.

"He's alive, then," said a voice at my back, and I jumped.

It was Mr. Girandole, peering around the bole of a tree and wringing his hands, like someone in a play.

"Too alive for his own good," said Grandmother.

Gray light was brightening the thickets. Beyond the wood, the sun was about to rise. The leaves and trunks were no longer entirely black, though the mist still floated in curtains. The air was damp and cool in a fresh, pleasant way. Birds chattered again, near and far.

I had my first good look at Mr. Girandole. He came forward with what seemed reluctance, as if he would have preferred to watch from the shadows but had no choice. His thinness made him seem taller than he was; as he drew near, I saw that he was scarcely taller than Grandmother. His face was mostly large eyes and a prominent, sharp nose, his mouth and inconsequential chin half-hidden by a short, groomed mustache and beard. I could not imagine his age: perhaps thirty, perhaps fifty.

His skin was dark, only a shade lighter than his brown whiskers. He wore a knee-length coat, the belt cinched tight, and had the hat pulled low, so that the rumpled brim covered his ears. There was an oddity to his walk, which I guessed must be a limp.

Smiling awkwardly, he offered a hand. From his manner, I couldn't help thinking of a child who has been ordered to shake the hand of a dubious stranger. His fingers were surprisingly long, and the back of his hand was hairy. I wondered if he were a foreigner, perhaps from behind the mountains—though he had no noticeable accent.

I was none too eager to shake his hand either, but as he was a friend of Grandmother's, I did so.

"Well, it's a fine mess," he said, trudging past me and returning his hands to his coat pockets. His gaze took in the dangling pilot and all the entangled folds of parachute, the skeins of cord.

Grandmother stood studying the problem too, her palms on her waist. "He'll die if he keeps hanging there," she said. "May die anyway."

Mr. Girandole nodded. "Which is why I thought it best to . . . As you can see . . ."

Grandmother paced slowly, examining the trees and limbs.

I was a passionate climber of trees now that I had a whole garden full of them to choose from. Grandmother had learned early that I was easily entertained by sitting in a fork among the boughs, reading one of the books I'd brought. Now I guessed what she'd had in mind when she'd said she might need my help.

But there was no way to climb these gigantic trees. The first limbs began high in the air, and no branch came anywhere near the ground. It would be impossible to get above the pilot in order to cut him loose.

"Let's gather leaves and dirt," Grandmother said at last. "Pile them right here." She pointed with her stick at the bloodstained forest carpet straight below the hanging man. "Should have brought the rake and spade."

"Ah!" said Mr. Girandole, as if he grasped her plan. She handed him the bucket I'd carried, and he hurried off in one direction; Grandmother untied the canvas bundle and led me in another. Finding a patch of soil where few plants grew, she sliced into the earth with the brush knife. Onto the square of canvas we piled handfuls of crumbly dead leaves and dirt. Beetles and gray rollup bugs scurried between our fingers. Grandmother hummed to herself, exactly as she did when working in the garden.

When we had a load, we dragged it back to the pilot. A drop of his blood spattered the canvas as we shook the soil loose. He groaned but did not raise his head.

Mr. Girandole worked quickly, bringing his third or fourth bucketful. He glanced up at the man and pursed his lips. "I fear this may be in vain."

"H'mm," Grandmother agreed. We headed back for another load. I looked with interest at a deep bed of plush moss, but Grandmother shook her head. "We're not tearing up the grove for him," she said, and I remembered the monsters. This was their home.

At first, we labored within the circle of the lantern's glow, placing it on the ground near the growing earth pile, but when the forest lightened, Grandmother had me blow the flame out. Birds warbled, flitting from branch to branch. From the direction of the village, far away, a late rooster crowed.

Even by daylight, this section of the wood reminded me of parlors I'd seen—dusky rooms with high ceilings and forbidding furniture, reserved for times of greater importance than the present. And yet in other ways, this place was like nothing in any human dwelling. There were age and stillness here. The furnishings were alive.

finger. I couldn't help looking him up and down, trying to decide what was so unsettling about the *way* he crouched.

Yet it was also hard to look away from his luminous brown eyes. "Young sir," he began with determination, "you have heard, I take it, the tale of Cinderella?"

Grandmother snorted with amusement—why, I wasn't precisely sure—and continued her impression of nap-taking.

I nodded.

Mr. Girandole examined his never-still fingers, as if finding his words there. His nails had soil caked beneath them now, as mine did; his hands were smudged with drying muck.

"A lost slipper," he said. "A slipper of glass—or of fur, as the tale used to be told. The details change. The truth . . . the truth behind the story . . . is that no foot would fit the shoe but hers—the foot of that one girl. Why do you suppose that was?"

I blinked, thinking of the story. "She . . . had small, dainty feet."

"Do you really think so?" Mr. Girandole leaned forward earnestly, and I flinched, unsettled.

"The prince searched the length and breadth of the land!" he said. "Maidens from far and wide tried to force their feet into that slipper. Are we truly to believe that Cinderella had the smallest feet in the kingdom? The tale always assures us, no matter who tells it, that she was beautiful . . . that the prince had to find her again, at any cost." Mr. Girandole spread his hands decisively, as if I could not fail now to see his point. "Tall people and small people can be very beautiful, of course. But could she have towered over him, or stood no taller than a child? Surely she must have been of a fairly ordinary size. If the prince had been looking for someone of extreme stature, why let all the typical maidens try on the slipper? Do you see?"

Twice as we worked, the man over our heads woke up
grumbled. I supposed he was feverish.

"Perhaps we look sinister to him," said Mr. Girandole, m
us as we emptied our loads of earth together. "Perhaps he
we're digging his grave."

"Perhaps we are," said Grandmother.

Here, where none but the rarest sunbeam reached the
floor, it was still a summer day. My shirt was sticking
back, wringing wet, and Grandmother had long since sh
scarf. Mr. Girandole, in his unseasonable coat, looked ab
expire.

He dabbed with his sleeve cuff at his forehead beneath t
brim and glanced furtively at me, not for the first time.

Grandmother announced that it was time for us all to r
perched on a rock, and I gratefully flopped down on the
nearby. "Really, Girandole," she said. "How long are you
keep this up? Whose eyes are you afraid of here?"

Mr. Girandole's mouth twitched. His gaze flicked tov
then up at the man in the tree, who hung limp again. Tw
hopped along the limbs, clearly talking to each other as they
the pilot—speculating.

Mr. Girandole sighed. "I suppose you're right, M—
scrunched his brows, took a breath, and played with th
one sleeve. Several times, he seemed about to speak but
and always his eyes darted back to me.

Grandmother propped her arms on her walking-stick
head on her wrists, and closed her eyes, lazily tapping on

"Well," said Mr. Girandole. "You see . . . That is, er . . ."
to find his focus then, he crouched beside me and held up

I had no answer. He did make an excellent point.

Above us, the pilot moaned and murmured something under his breath.

Mr. Girandole looked down at his own worn boots. "Cinderella's foot wasn't larger or smaller than that of most women. *It was of a different shape altogether.*"

Grandmother raised her head and said matter-of-factly, "That's true. As I first heard it, the stepsisters mutilated their own feet trying to make them the right shape. One cut off her toes. The other cut off her heel."

"And both attempts failed!" said Mr. Girandole. "If the shoe fit Cinderella's foot, what does that tell us about her?"

I tried to imagine her foot, and the picture in my head wasn't pretty.

"Why, she must have had neither," said Grandmother brightly. "Neither toes nor a heel."

"And what does that leave?" Mr. Girandole finished. "And who gave her the slipper? Who changed her fate?"

"F-fairy," I managed. "Fairy godmother." The sweat on my face and in my shirt had grown chill.

"And you don't just *get* one of those." Leaning still closer, he lowered his voice. "For reasons beneficent or nefarious, the tale handed down to us has been altered to obscure Cinderella's origins. The fact is that she was ill-treated by her step-family because she was *different.*" He glanced sideways, conspiratorially, then straight back at me. "Cinderella was not a daughter of the Second Folk or humans. Her people were *older.*"

Before his words had quite sunk in, Mr. Girandole plucked loose the laces of his right boot, grasped it in both hands, and pulled it off. There, in the somnolent light of morning, I saw protruding from his trouser cuff a bony ankle covered in coarse brown hair—and instead of a foot, the sharp, split hoof of a goat.

I sprang to my feet, barely containing a yelp. *"Old Mr. Clubfoot,"* Mrs. D—— had said. *"Witch-weasels and sickle-winds."* I backed away, heart pounding.

"Sit down," Grandmother told me gently but firmly. "Don't be rude."

"I suspect it was a fur slipper," Mr. Girandole said. "A hoof would shatter a shoe of glass." He looked up at me with a sad, lop-sided smile.

My mind was so numbed that my body was left to make the decisions, and it decided on flight. I turned and bolted into the forest, too deeply shaken to obey Grandmother's order that I stop. The ground descended in a slope, and the undergrowth became denser. Bushes clutched at my knees; branches lashed at my face. I skidded, landed on my arms, and got up again, dodging right and left between the trunks. As I careened down into a wide ravine, my pulse pounded in my ears.

It wasn't long before I came back to my senses. Clearly, Mr. Girandole meant me no harm. I didn't run far. But I ran just far enough, crashing through briars and low branches, to carry me headlong into the grove of monsters.

Looming above the bushes straight before me was the huge, dark head of a beast.

I stopped so abruptly, my feet shot out from beneath me, and I landed sitting, paralyzed with fear. The creature, too, seemed frozen in rapt attention, its round eyes fixed on me, its jaws gaping wide. Neither horse nor lion, it had round ears high on its head and tufts of streaming hair between them and its mouth. Overlapping plates of leathery hide armored its muzzle and neck. From its back, in the grove's half-light, rose two shadowy wings.

I was certain this was my last moment of life—that the beast would spring upon me, snapping tree limbs with its lunge, and devour my upper half at one bite. I flung up my arms to cover my head.

But after a long space, when I opened my eyes again, I saw that the beast had not moved. Still its bulging eyes watched me, and still its jaws gaped; yet I heard no rumbling breath, no ponderous movements. Birds twittered, and a breeze stirred the branches.

Eventually, it occurred to me that the monster's grayish hue was not elephantine skin but the gray of weathered stone, that the darker patches on its sides were fans of lichen, and that fallen leaves clung to its back. The beast was a statue—a craftsman's sculpture.

I sat there breathing, clutching my shirt-front, the sweat drying on my neck. As I rose to a crouch and looked around, I saw that fantastic shapes loomed everywhere, half-buried in the undergrowth. Bearded stone faces peered between vines; a muscular giant towered among the trees; a sea serpent reared above green waves of bushes; a stately king or god occupied his throne. In the distance, a tall tower was just visible past three interposing trees. As I studied it, tilting my head to one side and the other, I saw that this building leaned at an odd angle, as if stuck in the act of toppling over.

So, these were the monsters, and this was the haunted woods, the sacred woods, a garden long overgrown and abandoned, hidden in blue shadows, in shafts of early sun. How truly strange it was!

It sang to my heart in a silent voice. Every vine-obscured shape intrigued me—every secret space drew me forward. I wanted to discover every figure the garden would reveal. Yet I remembered how I'd left Grandmother and Mr. Girandole. With a last, longing glance, I hurried back toward them.

Mr. Girandole seemed to have been more worried about me than Grandmother was. He breathed a sigh when I reappeared, and he kept glancing at me as if seeking some kind of reassurance. His boots were both in place again, and I felt bad for reacting with such shock to his hoofed feet. He was Grandmother's friend.

Grandmother watched me with a serious expression, waiting.

Mr. Girandole had taken off his coat and held it folded over an arm. Beneath, he wore a gray shirt with old-fashioned, pointed collars. When he laid the coat neatly on a rock, I saw the reason for his odd gait. His legs, clothed in trousers the color of dust, bent differently from those of other people. His knees were apparently backward, sticking out behind him. Despite myself, I felt another rush of fear, but I resolved not to stare. I showed him a sheepish grin, which seemed to relieve him further.

Grandmother said, "Have you been to the grove?"

I nodded and fell in beside her as she took up the brush knife and started back to work.

"It's beautiful, isn't it?" she asked.

Again, I could only nod. The grove seemed too significant for me to wrap words around.

Grandmother scooped decaying leaves. "I first found my way there when I was younger than you. That was a long time ago. Obviously."

I noticed that Mr. Girandole's hands paused in his own labor across the clearing. Just for a moment, he was motionless, gazing at the ground—listening or remembering something.

I asked Grandmother, "Which monster did you see first?"

"The mermaid. I came upon her from behind, and I knew at once she was a mermaid, though she has two tails instead of one. I wondered why she wouldn't turn and look at me. I supposed she was angry at me, like my mother. That's how I found the place, you see: I was running away from a scolding at home."

I laughed. This was the most Grandmother had ever told me about herself at one time, and I was enjoying it.

"What had you done to get in trouble?"

She shooed a beetle off our canvas. "I don't even remember now."

Mr. Girandole spoke as he emptied his bucket. "You'd gone out to play in your new shoes and lost one under the hedge, and you tore your dress on the fence." He looked away suddenly. "At least, so you told me once, I think."

Grandmother chuckled. "If you say it was so, it was so." To me she added, "Girandole remembers everything."

We worked then in silence. My mind was busy, thinking of Mr. Girandole's goat-like legs, of his Cinderella story . . . and of the monsters in the grove's half-light. At last, I said to Grandmother, "That's all the people are afraid of—those statues?"

"That's all I know of that could have started their foolishness," she said. "Old stone shapes in a forest."

Every now and then, Mr. Girandole would bound toward the pilot and wave his arms to drive off the crows, who were hopping nearer and nearer in the branches.

"His eyes should be safe enough behind those goggles," remarked Grandmother.

"All the same," said Mr. Girandole.

After a moment, Grandmother looked at me and said, "There's a riddle to it, though—that garden of monsters. The longer you look at it, the more questions it raises. It's a big mystery, a puzzle that wants a solution, though I can't guarantee it has one."

I waited for her to say more, but typically, she didn't.

There was so much I wanted to know, but it seemed rude to ask. Did Mr. Girandole have those feet because he was born with a deformity, like a boy at my school whose right arm was withered and small? Or was he really a different sort of person entirely, like Cinderella?

"All right, then," said Grandmother, when we'd emptied a last canvas-load of earth into a pile that was over knee-high. "See if you can wake him up. If not, we're back to where we started."

Dusting her hands on her skirt, she looked at Mr. Girandole and me until we went hunting for sticks and pebbles and started aiming them once more at the man hanging above us.

"Hey!" Grandmother yelled at him. "You! Wake up!"

A few of our tosses clopped, not too hard, against his jacket. At first, I thought we'd taken too long, that he was dead; but after a minute or two of being pelted, he lifted his head again. He seemed to have trouble focusing, and he'd grown paler. At some point, he had pushed the goggles up to his forehead. His eyes, clearly visible for the first time, made him look gentler than the enemy faces on posters. He was younger than I'd thought, too.

Grandmother had been digging inside her carpet bag, and now she held a ball of twine that I remembered seeing in the kitchen—

string she saved from grocery parcels, all tied together into one much-spliced strand of unknown length. Keeping the string's loose end in her hand, she gave the ball to Mr. Girandole to throw.

"Catch this," she ordered the pilot.

Mr. Girandole's first throw was perfect, the ball hitting the man square in the chest, but the pilot seemed not even to have seen it coming. He didn't so much as raise his arms, and the ball dropped back to the ground, string unwinding.

I retrieved it, hurrying to gather up the loose coils and rewind the ball, which had become tiny. Next, I took a turn, sending the ball up to a zenith near the man's arm. He took a feeble swipe at it, but again the ball came down uncaught.

Having an inspiration, Grandmother instructed Mr. Girandole to throw the ball over the man's head, between the two straps of his parachute.

Mr. Girandole managed it nicely, and now the twine, completely unwound, ran from Grandmother's hand, over the pilot's shoulder, and halfway to the ground again, the free end floating on a draft.

Grandmother told the pilot to take a firm hold of the string, and he did so. When Grandmother tied her end to the brush knife, I finally saw her plan.

"Pull this up," she commanded him. "Cut the straps."

The pilot understood, seeming to find new strength. Mouth set in concentration, he hoisted the scythe-like instrument up to himself. Grandmother had tied it just below the crescent blade so that it hung handle-down, jiggling and swinging as it rose.

"Don't drop it," Grandmother said.

He grasped the handle and tipped back his head to examine the parachute straps.

Grandmother called, "As soon as you start to fall, throw the knife *that* way." She pointed across the glade, away from us. "Don't land on it."

"Not stupid, Grandma," the pilot said, beginning to saw at one strap.

"How am I to know that?" Grandmother said, folding her arms and watching critically.

The two crows cawed and flew away.

I didn't know if the man would have the strength to free himself, but Grandmother kept the brush knife sharp. Soon, the first strap parted. The pilot paused to grin at us. His face glistened with sweat as he set to work on the second.

With a ripping and a snap, the last strap separated, and the man finally completed his fall from the sky. He didn't throw the brush knife far, but far enough. He flopped into the dirt pile, sending dust and leaves flying.

Because of his injured leg, I supposed, he screamed through clenched teeth and passed out again, lying spread-eagled on his back.

"Well done, M——!" said Mr. Girandole with enthusiasm, patting Grandmother's shoulder.

She carried the carpet bag over to the man's side and rolled up her sleeves. "Now we see if he's savable. We'll need a fire."

"I laid the wood already." Mr. Girandole pointed toward the trees through which he'd arrived earlier. "It only needs lighting."

"See to it. Wash out that bucket in the stream and get some water boiling in the pan. We'll need all the water you can bring us, so fill the bucket again, too." Grandmother handed him two potholders. "When it's ready, bring it here."

With a nod, he hurried off at a trot, the bucket swinging from his arm. I allowed myself to stare at his retreating shape, intrigued by how nimbly his strange legs carried him over the roots.

Grandmother had me take one edge of the canvas, and we shook it hard, beating it as clean as we could. Then we spread it beside the pilot for a work-space. She took her shears and cut the pilot's pant leg open from ankle to hip.

"This will be an awful sight," she warned me, and it was. As she peeled back the soaked cloth, we could see sticky blood still welling from at least two jagged wounds in his upper leg. I thought I'd been ready for anything, but I had to look away, and for a moment I thought I would be sick.

"Sometimes, it's best not to eat breakfast," Grandmother said quietly, thumping my back.

"Did another plane's guns do that?" I asked when I could speak.

"I don't think so," she said, "because his leg's still here. Something exploded—maybe flak. He may have metal or glass in there. We can't see much till it's clean."

She snipped through the ties of a protective vest and unzipped his leather jacket beneath, pulling it open and passing her sun-browned hands over his shirt, along his sides, up to his armpits. She told me to undo his chinstrap and pull off the leather hat, which I did without much trouble. The man was no more than thirty. He was going prematurely bald, with a point of hair on his forehead and a much scarcer patch behind that.

Grandmother's fingers found blood oozing from three more places; in all, the pilot had injuries to his right leg, right side and shoulder, and his neck below the left ear, though that last one seemed little more than a graze.

39

Lifting his head, Grandmother poured something into his mouth from a dark brown bottle which bore no label. The smell of its contents made my eyes water. The pilot coughed.

"Can you hear me?" Grandmother said, in the tone she used when talking to Mrs. O———, who was hard of hearing. "What is your name?"

"R———," he said, breathing heavily, blinking up into the leaves, where his parachute hung in an undulating white ceiling, the bundles of cord swaying. The pilot smiled faintly and raised one finger to point upward. "Circus. Circus tent."

"Yes, well, R———," Grandmother said, "you must make a decision. Do you want our village doctor? He will come here if we ask him. But he is an important man with a position—he will report you to the Army."

"No!" The pilot shook his head. "No doctor."

I looked anxiously at Grandmother.

"The other choice is that I can try to stitch you up. I've delivered babies, and I sewed up my cousin once, on a farm. But I'm no doctor. We can't take you to the village. You may die."

R——— seemed to be searching for Grandmother's hand. She didn't help him find it. "Fix up me," he said. "Please. You, please. No doctor. No Army."

Grandmother sighed and pushed the bottle's neck against his lips. "Then you'd better drink a lot of this."

We waited for Mr. Girandole. The sun had climbed much higher; it was mid-morning. An engine droned in the distance. We'd heard and seen so many planes that we recognized it by the sound as a cargo plane.

What was happening scared me. If the Army or the police found out that Grandmother had helped an enemy pilot—or even failed to report him—she would be arrested. I had no doubt that any one of our neighbors in our position would have gone immediately to the police office and turned the matter over.

I saw Grandmother watching me. "Do you think this is wrong?"

Wordlessly, I shook my head no.

"I'm not fighting a war," she said. "Nor is this man now. These woods are not a battlefield."

I nodded agreement.

"Where is Girandole?" she muttered. "I hope he's not sitting there staring at the pan. They never boil when you do that."

"Why didn't he lay the fire closer?" I asked.

"I expect he was afraid this man might wake up and see him."

I gnawed my lip, and at last I came out with the question I really wanted to ask: "What *is* Mr. Girandole?" But at that moment, he came trudging into the glade, holding the steaming pan between the potholders, the full bucket dangling from his arm.

"Good." Grandmother leaned close to her patient. "R——? Are you good and drunk?" He moaned as she pried the bottle from his fingers, checked the amount of liquid inside, and re-capped it. "He ought to be," she said.

R——'s eyes were closed, and his breathing seemed more regular.

"Oh, my!" said Mr. Girandole when he saw the pilot's mangled leg. He backed a few steps away.

Grandmother drew out a metal soap box and we washed our hands as thoroughly as we could with the cold water, each taking our turns pouring dollops from the bucket over the other's hands. For good measure, we splashed and rubbed our hands with the alcohol, too, then used more soap.

Next, she produced a clean rag. I marveled at all she'd thought to bring in the carpet bag. I'd seen her make rags by cutting up threadbare clothes that were beyond repair, saving the buttons from shirts in an ornamental lidded tin. Satisfied with the pan water's temperature, she soaked the rag and wrung it out over the pilot's leg wounds, rinsing them clean. I winced at the sight.

Mr. Girandole retreated to a rock and sat down, facing toward the trees.

The injuries were bad. They looked deep, and it seemed to me that some of the flesh was missing. There was an awful whitish layer of something exposed—muscle or fat or deep tissue—that should never be seeing the light of day.

"Maybe this is too much education for you," Grandmother said, giving me the rag to hold and telling me to keep it off the ground. It was so hot, I nearly shrieked; I couldn't imagine how she'd swished it through the pan and wrung it out. I tossed it from hand to hand until it had cooled a little.

She fished in the carpet bag, came up with a pair of tongs like those I'd seen my mother use for handling canning jars, and steeped them in the hot water. "Do you want to sit over there with Girandole?" she asked.

"I'm all right," I said.

"Then put the rag in the pan and take off his jacket. We've got to do that shoulder before the water gets cold." She'd produced a needle and a spool of thread. As I wrestled the flak vest, gun holster, and jacket off R——, she threaded the needle and dropped it, thread and all, into the water, leaving the thread's end hanging out over the side as a way to retrieve it.

R—— didn't come fully awake, but he groaned as I shoved him

around, his head lolling. Blood dripped from his neck wound, and his shirt's right sleeve was drenched. By the time I had the jacket off, my hands were sticky with blood. I looked at them in dazed revulsion.

Grandmother tossed me a dry rag. "Wipe them on this, and then spread it under his shoulder so he's not lying in dirt. And cut his sleeve off."

Mutely, I nodded and set to work.

"If you can spare me," said Mr. Girandole, "I'd best put out my fire."

Grandmother was too busy to answer him. After a moment, he stood up—but he had gone no more than two steps before Grandmother called him back. "There's too much bleeding here for me to stop with a needle and thread," she said. "Take the brush knife with you. Get the blade red hot, and bring it back here quick."

"Oh, dear," said Mr. Girandole, looking queasy. He picked up the long-handled knife and hurried off.

I couldn't watch as Grandmother probed with the tongs, searching for shards of anything that might be in the pilot's wounds. But even with my head turned, the wet sounds drew icy sweat from my pores.

"Wring that rag over this," Grandmother ordered. "I can't see what I'm doing."

I tried to rinse the wounds without looking as she went in with her fingers, pulling out jagged pieces of black metal.

"If we don't bleed him to death, it'll be a miracle," she muttered. "The blood can't congeal with all this water." Finished with the leg, we worked on the shoulder, where Grandmother found more shrapnel. By the time she'd finished, she had quite a collection of metal shards.

The wound in the pilot's side wasn't deep; something sharp had gouged him as it passed. Grandmother examined the gash in his neck, and then there was nothing to do but wait. She squeezed shut the worse of the two leg wounds and held it until Mr. Girandole came charging back, the knife's curved blade glowing, its tip bright red. I saw that he'd taken off his boots, presumably so he could run faster and be less likely to trip. Sure enough, his left foot matched his right, a sharp, cloven hoof beneath a goatish ankle.

I couldn't watch the next part, either. Grandmother took the rag in one hand and the knife in the other. With my arms crossed over my stomach, I got up and moved away. Behind me, I heard the trickle of water and a sound like when my mother ironed clothes. The pilot mumbled something, and twice he emitted a scream. When a terrible, hot odor reached me, I dropped to my knees and retched. Mr. Girandole sat on the rock and watched me with a look of sympathy.

By the time Grandmother had finished her awful surgery, she had scorched R—— in some places and sewn him up in others. He was horribly pale, but his blood was no longer trickling into the earth. For the moment, at least, he was still breathing. Grandmother cut clean, dry rags into bandages with the shears and used the string to bind them around R——'s leg, shoulder, side, and neck. We cleaned our hands again. Mr. Girandole went to extinguish his fire and to wash the other rags and canvas in the stream.

As we collected our gear and waited for him to get back, I repeated my question about Mr. Girandole.

"He's a faun," Grandmother said. "And he's very old—much older than me."

I stared at her. "But he looks——"

"He's looked the same since I met him, when I was seven."

"You met him here, didn't you—in the sacred woods?"

She nodded. "He's the last of his kind. Or at least, the last around here."

"If they don't get old, how can that be?"

"The other fauns went away, as I understand it. Girandole fell in love with a human woman. He left the forest to live with her. But she grew old and died. When he came back to the grove, his people had gone."

I watched the pilot breathing, his chest rising and falling. More planes droned past—a patrol of ours, I thought, though they were far away. "So, Mr. Girandole lives alone here in the woods?"

"Yes. His home is high on the mountain, in the steep places where no one ever goes, in a cave. He's always stayed around here, because he has no place to go in the world of humankind. I think he's always hoping his people will come back, or that he can find a way to rejoin them. He's from Faery, the other world. He misses it."

The story was very sad. I got the impression Grandmother was telling me these things partly to take my mind off all the stitching and cauterizing. But now I was thinking of the statues in the grove—of dragons and giants, of the mer-people under the sea. I'd always wanted these things to exist outside of fairy tales. A part of me had always believed that they must, somewhere, even if it were in a world humans couldn't reach. But if fauns could live—here in our own country . . . "Are the others real?" I asked, so full of hope that it hurt my chest. "All the creatures from stories?"

Grandmother gazed at me, looking tired, resting her chin on the head of her walking-stick. "You've seen all the ones I've seen.

Maybe they all were here once. The stories had to come from somewhere. I think Girandole is the last."

Sadness settled on me like a weight. "They've gone back to Faery? Why?"

She shrugged. "Too many of us, I expect. The world is too noisy for them now."

I hoped she was wrong. I wanted desperately for there to be others.

"Don't be so gloomy," Grandmother said. "Think of it: yesterday, you never thought you'd meet a faun."

"Where there's one," I said, "there might be more!"

"That's an expression about snakes," she said.

Mr. Girandole returned. I watched him come, swinging along with what seemed a cheerful aspect, the boots now back on his feet. I supposed the boots must be padded with wads of cloth in the toes and heels—for if ordinary feet would not fit Cinderella's slipper, the reverse situation must also be true.

"I spread the wet things out in the sun to dry," he reported. "I'll bring them and these tools back to you after dark tonight."

I saw his reasoning: it would be best if no one saw Grandmother and me coming out of the woods with an armload of strange gear. I knew how the villagers loved to gossip. Only a narrow meadow and the belt of arbors separated Grandmother's back garden from the forest's edge.

Grandmother took his hand. "Thank you for all your help, Girandole. You are always so kind."

He bowed his head in a courtly way. There was worry in his lean face. "You should go now. Tread very carefully, M———. If anyone finds this man, alive or otherwise, it will be clear he didn't stitch himself up."

"We'll be careful," Grandmother said. She frowned into the treetops. "Can nothing be done about that parachute?"

Mr. Girandole took off his hat for the first time and ran his long, dark fingers through his hair. I felt my eyes widen at the sight of two small nubs of horn on his forehead, nearly hidden by his matted locks. "A rock tied to a rope, I suppose," he said. "If I could snag some of the cords, I could pull one way and another until it all came down."

Grandmother nodded. "I have some clothesline rope that ought to be long enough. I'll give it to you tonight. There's nothing more we can do for . . . R—— here . . . until he decides whether he's going to live another day."

Mr. Girandole agreed. "I'll bring a blanket and cover him. I don't smell any rain coming."

Leaning on her stick, Grandmother turned to go, but Mr. Girandole cleared his throat. "There's . . . also the matter of his weapon."

I looked toward the gun, hidden in the pile of rocks.

"Out of sight, out of mind!" said Grandmother, laughing at herself for forgetting it. She narrowed her eyes, thinking. "It doesn't belong here. We'll take it out of the forest."

"I could take it to my cave," Mr. Girandole offered. "Or bury it somewhere high on the mountain."

"No. If R—— dies, he won't be needing it. If he lives, he'll want it back, and you'll never hear the end of it. We'll carry it beyond any retrieving. I know a good way." So, Grandmother put the heavy black gun into her carpet bag, and we took our leave.

Glancing back, I saw Mr. Girandole, his coat folded over his arm, pacing slowly around our patient.

*   *   *   *

We arrived home just as the noon whistle sounded from the fish cannery. If you listened carefully as it ended, you could hear its echo from the cliffs. First, we pumped up water from the well in the summer kitchen and washed our hands and faces thoroughly. Then Grandmother fixed us a lunch of bread and honey, sardines, cheese, fruit, and tea. I watched her strong hands peeling a pear, and I remembered with a shudder the sight of those hands sewing skin. When we'd washed the dishes, she went to her room for a nap.

I saw that the pan under the ice box was nearly full from the melting ice block, so I carried it out and dumped it according to the rotation pattern. Today, it was the third pear tree's turn for a drink. Flowers and vegetables shouldn't be watered in the heat of the day. When I'd replaced the pan, I sat on a bench in the sun and watched butterflies flit in the germander. I felt wrung out, like one of the rags.

Until three months before, Grandmother had been only a name, a photo in a round frame on the mantel. She was my father's mother, and I don't think she and my mother liked each other much; at least, we never visited her as a family. In my childhood, I knew Grandmother wrote letters to my papa sometimes, and he wrote back. He'd asked me now and then for some of my drawings to send her. Papa used to tell me stories of growing up in the village, where time hardly seemed to pass at all, and every arbor, every garden gate, might be the doorway to a magical world. Seeing the place for myself, I thought so too. Grandfather had been alive then, when my father lived here.

I yearned for a better look at the sacred woods. For now, my eyes were heavy, too; exhaustion swept over me. Curling up on the bench, I was soon fast asleep.

I awoke to the growl of a plane.

Springing upright, I blinked into the thick, hot light of late afternoon. Golden sun slanted through the garden, and the shadows under trees and bushes were dark. My head had the sluggish feeling that comes when consciousness has been far away for a long time. My face was sore from the bench on one side and sunburned on the other.

There was not one plane but two. They were sleek, angular fighters of our side, from the airfield to the north. Very low, they roared over the village in repeated loops and buzzed up the mountain, making pass after pass.

Grandmother came out of the cottage, her hair in disarray. "They've seen the parachute," she said.

A chill passed through me. "I can run fast," I said. "I'll go and warn Mr. Girandole."

"No." She watched the planes, the sun gleaming on their wings and canopies. "They've warned him themselves, with their noise. If you go up there, you'll run into a lot of soldiers. It's the hardest thing, but what we have to do is wait and see what happens."

I couldn't stand it. "But they'll catch R———! Mr. Girandole will be too scared. He won't know what to do."

Grandmother gave a short laugh. "Don't go counting on that. He's only timid when there's someone nearby to be brave for him. Left to his own devices, he does just fine."

My heart was pounding. "We've got to do something."

"Let's see if there are any ripe tomatoes," Grandmother said.

That was the longest evening I had spent in my life. I could focus on nothing but the sounds of planes, of cars and trucks in the street, and the snatches of voices that passed. We heard two large trucks roll by, but they were gone before either of us reached a window.

About an hour before sundown, an Army truck drove slowly through the streets. Soldiers with rifles on their shoulders sat in the open bed, and their commanding officer clung to the rear of the cab, using a megaphone to repeat an announcement over and over:

"AN ENEMY SOLDIER IS SUSPECTED IN THE AREA, THE PILOT OF THE CRASHED PLANE. REPORT ANY STRANGERS TO THE POLICE IMMEDIATELY. A GENERAL CURFEW WILL BE IN EFFECT BETWEEN THE HOURS OF 8 P.M. AND 6 A.M. UNTIL FURTHER NOTICE. REMAIN INDOORS AT NIGHT WITH WINDOWS AND DOORS SECURED."

I looked bleakly at Grandmother, but the announcement seemed to have cheered her up. "You see?" she said. "They've been to the forest already and found the parachute but not the man. They're up against a faun in his own woods."

Still, it worried me when supper was over, sunset came and went, and the moon rose, but still Mr. Girandole made no appearance. I pictured him wringing his hands in the dark. R—— was probably dead, and Mr. Girandole didn't know how to break the news to us. Or might the soldiers have caught Mr. Girandole? Might they have shot him? But we'd heard no gunshots; I supposed a gunshot could be heard a long way off in the quiet woods.

After nightfall, there were no more planes, and the only traffic was a truck passing every hour or so. Grandmother worked on stitching a quilt. "He may not come tonight," she said. "The soldiers are likely watching the open field, and the moon is bright."

So, I pulled my feet up onto a high-backed chair near the same lamp and tried to read *Arabian Nights*, but I couldn't concentrate. I kept reading and re-reading the same line.

"When your mind's too restless to think," Grandmother said, "move your hands."

Getting out my sketchbook, pencil, and eraser, I drew a picture of the grove of the monsters as I remembered it, with the winged beast snarling over the bushes, and faces peering through the vines near and far.

"You'd better not draw or write anything about Girandole or R——," Grandmother said. "Not in your book there, and not in your letters."

I nodded. "I'm only drawing the monsters."

But I found myself unable to remember the details. My lines on paper did no better than words at framing the secrets of the shadowy wood. A silence passed in which I drew and erased, brushing away the eraser's gray crumbs, my fingers smudged with pencil lead.

Suddenly, as if we were still in the midst of our morning's conversation, Grandmother began to speak. The things she told me were personal, and I marveled that she was trusting me with so much and talking to me in the same tone she used with adults. As I look back on it, I think she'd been testing me that day—or perhaps for many days—and I'd finally passed.

"Girandole's my best friend." She put down her quilting and sighed. "You ought to know this, because someday you'll wonder about it, and I won't be around to tell you. First, he was like an uncle or a father to me. As I got older, he was like a brother, but even more than that . . . When I grew up, he insisted I find a man to marry—one of my own kind, who could grow old with me. He didn't want to repeat the mistakes of the past, you see. So, all the while I was with your grandfather, I didn't go to the woods, and Girandole didn't come out. I didn't see him for more than thirty years, but I knew he was watching me sometimes, hidden among the hedges near the garden. He wanted me to have a normal life, but at the same time it broke his heart—he loved me, you know, even though he tried not to. The heart is uncontrollable."

I had no idea what to say. At last I managed, "Did you love him, too?"

She smiled faintly and seemed to fix her gaze far beyond the cottage walls. "Yes. I did, and I do." Her eyes found me again. "But I'm an old woman, and he's a faun. What that means for us is friendship. And the knowledge that there's more to the larger story of things . . . much more, beyond the borders of this world—beyond the walls of time."

I wasn't sure exactly what she meant. But since she seemed to be in an answer-giving mood, I asked, "Did the fauns carve the statues?"

"No. The monsters in the grove were commissioned by a nobleman—a duke—nearly four hundred years ago. It took many years as the garden grew, piece by piece—his life-long project. He employed the finest sculptors in the land, the ones whose work is still to be seen in the cathedrals."

"Why did he make them?"

The kettle boiled, and Grandmother laid aside her quilting to brew a pot of tea. "No one knows for sure, though there is more than one version of the story. Some say the garden was a tribute to the duke's beloved wife, a woman named G———. But some say she took one look at it and fell down dead with fright. Not very long after she died, the duke simply vanished. No one knows what became of him. The garden was left abandoned, and in time, it was overgrown by the woods. Even the duke's castle up on the mountain is gone now; not so much as a foundation remains. I read what I could about it all years ago in the national library, on a trip to the capital. You won't hear many facts around here."

I wasn't happy with my drawing: the winged creature's mouth wasn't right. Erasing it, I tried yet again.

"People talk as if the monsters were real," I said. "Do they know they're only statues?"

"A few of the brave ones have been up there to see them—enough to keep people reminded that there *are* monsters. There's always been superstition about the place—the duke wasn't around to defend himself after he vanished, and there were all the ugly rumors of what might have gone on in the garden." Grandmother sighed and listened as a truck motored past.

"And now this—" She tipped her head vaguely toward the truck sound. "These times, and the world all upside down. The current regime forbids any celebration of our glorious past in art or music or books. We're not supposed to have spirits; we're supposed to be good children and obey. For most people, it's easier to be afraid of monsters that are safely off in the woods." She smirked. "The haunted woods."

"They call it haunted; you call it sacred."

Grandmother chuckled, placing a cup of tea on a saucer beside me. "When your father took you to the Great Cathedral, how did you feel? Frightened, or full of holy awe?"

I thought of the gargoyles, the soaring stained glass and colored light . . . the vast space and dim heights . . . the joyous and fiendish and suffering faces, carved in high places and in low, in brightness and shadow. "Both," I answered.

"There you are, then. Haunted and sacred. Maybe they *want* to mean the same thing, but neither word is big enough."

I darkened my monster's eyes and began adding the teeth. "Did Papa go to the grove?"

"Of course he did, though he learned not to speak of it in front of your grandfather. The forest was forbidden, even then. Funny . . . I always felt as if the place were *calling* me."

I nodded, tapping my pencil against my lips, planning how I would ask my father about his time in the garden—what he thought of it, and what he did there. Setting aside my sketchbook, I got out letter paper, but Grandmother frowned.

"You should wait a few days, until things settle down," she said. "Unless you want your letter opened and read by the Army right there in the post office."

I didn't want that, so I put the paper back in its box.

When the hour grew late, Grandmother announced that she intended to sleep on the couch, in case Mr. Girandole rapped on the door too lightly to be heard from the bedroom. I joined her in the vigil, dragging my mattress and bedding out of my room and arranging them on the floor before the wood stove.

"Don't worry," Grandmother told me when she blew out the oil lamp. "We've done what we can for now." She seemed to take her own advice; in minutes, she was softly snoring.

I lay awake for a long time in the glow of the embers behind the stove's grill, listening to the frogs and crickets, and to the rustle of leaves when the wind picked up.

At last I slept, but my dreams were a repeat of the day: rags soaked in blood, planes flying low, trucks full of soldiers . . . and the grove of monsters. In my dream, the monsters blinked and shifted when I wasn't looking directly at them, and I could hear them whispering together in the far parts of the garden, the parts I couldn't see behind the leaves.

In the morning, Grandmother bustled and clattered, going to and from the summer kitchen by the side door, complaining about how the couch had given her a stiff back.

"It's a fine morning," she said. "Let's have breakfast at the garden table. Then we'll go on a spy mission to the market and hear what we can hear."

The ideas of breakfast and market made me think. "What if R—— wakes up and is hungry?" I asked. "He'll need food and water."

"Girandole will take care of him, *if* R—— is alive. You mustn't get your hopes up about that. But even if he's alive, I doubt he'll be in any condition to eat yet."

Grandmother had made it a point to tell me the names of everyone she knew—and she seemed to know the whole village. She was forever introducing me to people, and we could rarely walk down the street without running into someone who wanted to stand and talk.

Today, the village buzzed with nervous tension and a wild excitement that no one would have admitted to. A single enemy lurking somewhere, possibly injured, and most likely trying to stay hidden, was just dangerous enough to be thrilling without presenting a cause for real alarm. In the bakery, Mrs. P—— said that she'd discovered her garden gate inexplicably unlatched, and the large footprint of a man's shoe in her onion patch. Mrs. C—— had heard someone trudge past her bedroom window at half past three this morning, but as the nearest telephone was at the corner grocer's, she'd had no way of notifying the police. Mrs. D—— could afford me no more than a beaming glance, and none of the usual exclamations. She was eager to show us all the stamped-out end of a cigarette she'd found in her lane—a slender, exotic sort of cigarette that had most definitely not come from anywhere around here. She had folded it in paper and was on her way to deliver it to the police.

"What about you, M——?" she asked my grandmother. "The woods practically touch your back fence. Did you see or hear anything?"

Several pairs of wide eyes turned toward Grandmother, who held the silvery baker's tongs and had just put a fig-loaf into the shopping basket. "Now that you mention it, there was something," she said, "though I dismissed it as my imagination at the time."

I peered at her with as much interest as everyone else.

"Around midnight I woke up," Grandmother said, her voice just above a whisper. "I'm not sure why, since I usually sleep like the Lord in the back of the boat. I think it was too quiet. There was a small sound which I thought was the cottage settling—old houses do that, you know. But as I remember it now, it could only have been the sound of someone *trying the front door.*"

There was a chorus of gasps and exclamations.

Grandmother accepted Mrs. C——'s praise for keeping her door locked and Mrs. P——'s adjuration to be extremely careful, and she smiled amiably at what looked like a glance of envy from Mrs. D——.

When Grandmother had swept out of the bakery and I'd made sure no one could hear us, I said, "Isn't lying a sin?"

"Yes," she answered soberly. "But that wasn't a lie. That was camouflage."

An Army truck was parked outside the police office, and a group of four soldiers stood in front of the building, chatting and smoking. My chest fluttered whenever I saw the uniforms—every single time, for the first instant, I expected to see my father among the soldiers. But he wasn't here. These were men I didn't know. Two of them tipped their cloth hats to Grandmother as we passed.

We completed our grocery shopping, then paid the electric bill. Grandmother wasn't fond of electricity, since it didn't come in tanks like the lamp fuel or in blocks like the ice, and no one delivered it in a truck; she thought it was a mighty suspicious thing to be paying for. She'd allowed the workmen to hook it up, she said, only so that she could listen to the radio.

Our morning's investigation confirmed, from snatches of conversation here and there, what we already knew: that patrols of soldiers had been combing the forest but had apparently found nothing except the parachute—if they'd found the pilot, they wouldn't still be searching.

As we came out of the public works building, Mrs. D—— passed us on the sidewalk, on her way into the grocery store. I saw that she still held the folded paper containing the dubious cigarette from her lane. She'd come right past the police office but had apparently not stopped in there yet.

Grandmother looked sidelong at me. "Ignorance multiplies itself better than yeast. If we could make bread out of rumors, no one in the world would go hungry."

For the rest of the way home, we talked little but kept our eyes open. In front of the barber shop, one soldier was speaking into the handset of a portable radio strapped to another soldier's back. There was so much code in what he said that we couldn't make sense of it, but his tone sounded weary and annoyed. A military launch chugged through the harbor, and an Army staff car was parked outside the three-story inn. Grandmother deliberately crossed the street so that we could walk past the wide glass windows of the inn's dining room and peer inside. I glimpsed only a blur of reflections, dark spaces, and lamplight, but Grandmother murmured, when we'd turned the corner to climb Bridge Street, "That was the major, all right."

"At the inn?"

"Mm. From the garrison."

"Do you know him?" I asked.

"Not personally, but I know his face." Grandmother turned a critical eye on a poorly weeded herb garden to our left. "He is not the sort of man your grandfather would have liked."

I expected her to say more and was puzzling over why she'd brought Grandfather into it, but she stood still, her attention now on a group of five soldiers tramping down out of the arbors.

They'd clearly come from the woods, their shirts dark with sweat, their trousers covered with burrs and prickle-seeds. In no particular hurry, they had nearly made it to the road when they seemed to think better of it, and all flopped down in the shade.

"Nothing to report," said Grandmother under her breath, walking again.

I watched a moment longer as the men leaned rifles on a fence, pulled off hats, and poured water over their heads. One had a receding hairline, and aside from his hair's color, he looked rather like our patient, R———. Yet this man and R——— were enemies. Another man, who perhaps looked like them both, had shot down R———'s plane. There were trucks full of men, ships carrying them on the seas, squadrons of planes with more men inside, and all together they made up the war. And my father was somewhere among them.

This was Papa's second war: he'd had to fight in one when he was young, and now he had to fight in this one. He'd been summoned back into service nearly four years ago, and had been home only twice in that time; already I had trouble recalling the exact sound of his voice. I would stare at his photo and re-read his letters, striving to recapture a clear echo of his laugh. I wondered if he was patrolling today, joking with his fellow soldiers, pulling burrs out of his trousers, and drinking warm water from his canteen. I prayed he would never be wounded like R———. *Please, God, keep him safe.* I wished a letter from him would come.

Grandmother's next-door neighbor on the side toward the village center was a fearsome old woman named Mrs. F———. That's what Grandmother called her, never her first name. Mrs. F——— was white-haired, as tall and hard as a dead tree bleached by the sun. Her garden was a dark cavern, overrun by juniper and laurel and myrtle, covered in vines, and she seemed not to care for flowers. When Grandmother had first introduced us, Mrs. F——— glared at me from her wrinkled face, and she had not spoken a word to me since. Every time I passed in front of her house alone, I hurried; when I was in our back garden, I was glad for the stone wall between the properties and Mrs. F——'s high hedge immediately on the wall's other side. Once, though, late in the afternoon, I'd been reading in my sanctuary beneath the fuchsia, and feeling an uneasy prickle in my scalp, I'd looked up. Mrs. F—— had been standing at a side window beneath her gable, staring down at me. I'd given a timid wave to be polite, but she had not returned it. She'd continued to watch me, motionless. I'd closed my book and gone indoors.

As Grandmother and I crossed in front of Mrs. F——'s gate, nearly home, I saw Mrs. F—— crouching beneath a cypress tree, clipping the vines. Grandmother said a bright hello.

"What's the news?" asked Mrs. F——, not looking at me.

"Everyone's got a story," said Grandmother. "No one knows anything."

Mrs. F—— gave a bark that might have been a laugh and went on with her trimming.

When we were inside with the door shut, I asked, "Why doesn't she like me?"

"She doesn't dislike you," Grandmother said. "Her own boys were hellions, and I suppose she suspects any child of being the same."

The ice man had been by on his twice-weekly rounds: a fresh chunk sat in the top compartment of the ice box, which was a boon to the milk and cheese. Grandmother had me take down the diamond-shaped ice card from its hook in the front window—a device that fascinated me, since it looked like something a magician would use in a trick. It had a number at each point; the number you turned upright told the ice man how heavy a chunk of ice to bring. I spun it in my hands, watching the numbers go around, always one right-side up.

We had a light, early lunch. Then Grandmother said, "After I stretch out for a bit, I think we'd better have a look for ourselves up in the forest."

I sprang up straight in my chair. "Can we do that?"

"There's no curfew in the afternoon, and I've heard of no restrictions on where one can go—well," she added after a moment's thought, "there's some foolish new law about trespassing among ruins, I think. But ruins are as much a part of our land as the trees and the rocks. May as well order us not to walk around on our feet!"

"What if the soldiers see us?"

"We'll be gathering wood for the stove. We'll take along the hatchet."

So, we did precisely that: Grandmother took a nap, and I dozed again on the garden bench—the one beneath the camphor tree, protected from Mrs. F——'s windows. It was still early in the afternoon when I lifted down the hand-axe from its pegs and Grandmother picked up the binding cords from the wood bin. She poured some milk into a jug with a stopper and packed it, along with a tin of crackers, some fruit, and a wedge of cheese into her carpet bag.

I glanced at the bag. "Did you take out his gun?"

Grandmother nodded. "It's hidden in my room. Getting rid of it may be our mission tomorrow, if the weather's good."

We paused at the edge of the sloping meadow to look around.

The grasses waved in a slight, wandering breeze. Like a green cliff, the forest eaves rolled away in both directions, the hollows between limbs full of purple shadows, windows of twilight at midday. I loved this boundary, where the bright world met one full of secrets.

"You live in the best place on Earth," I told Grandmother.

She laughed, not in a scornful way, and leaned on her stick, slowly studying the distance. A woodpecker knocked somewhere. Off to our right, a vine-tender whistled a tune.

"If there are soldiers here," said Grandmother quietly, "they're under one of the arbors, watching with binoculars." She rested on a bench, examining the grapes on the lattice over our heads. The crop was still tiny, hard, and green, but Grandmother said they would ripen well this year.

"I can carry the bag," I said.

Grandmother peered at me with one of her appraising looks that ended in the hint of a smile. "You're a good boy," she said, and handed the bag over.

I smiled then, knowing that praise from Grandmother didn't come lightly. "Was Papa like me when he was my age?"

"Eerily so."

We left the arbors and crossed the meadow then. If any soldiers saw us, they issued no challenge. To give credibility to our wood-gathering ruse, we picked up a few sticks where the trees began. When the forest's emerald shadows had closed over us, I asked Grandmother about something else I'd heard earlier in the summer, from two elderly men inside the smoky open window of the pipe lounge while I waited for Grandmother outside the apothecary's—about dancing fires on the mountainside at night, music among the trees, and something called a "procession of souls."

"There's an old belief," she said, "that the souls of those who die throughout the year don't go to Heaven one by one; on Midsummer's Eve, they all go together, in a procession."

"Is Heaven that way—on the mountain, or beyond it?"

"That's the direction I'd head if I were looking."

I didn't ask any further questions, because we both wanted to watch and listen. Birds sang, insects hummed, and we met no patrolling soldiers. Wildflowers shone like droplets of cream and butter and honey in patches of sunlight; some clustered in deep places where the shade was blue and cool. The village sounds grew distant: a carpenter's hammer, a few motors, the wallop of someone beating a rug. Then once more, we passed into the heart of silence, where the trees stood huge and dark. Shadowed by the thick canopy, the glens became caverns of leaf, trunk, stone, and mossy earth.

Grandmother pointed with her stave at places where boots had trampled the moss and smashed some of the white toadstools. She shook her head gravely.

We came at last to the parachute. R—— was gone, and we were alone in the glade. The soldiers had not bothered to drag the chute down; it still hung in tangles, the soft earth beneath it crisscrossed with boot tracks. The mound we'd made for R—— to fall into had been flattened out; I supposed Mr. Girandole had scattered it to make our assistance less obvious. I saw no traces of blood. But if one looked, our excavations among the leaf-beds were plain to see.

I picked up the mashed remains of two cigarettes, and Grandmother snickered. "You want to take them to Mrs. D——?" I didn't, choosing to bury them instead under a handful of soil.

We found nothing of interest. After a few moments, Grandmother led the way toward the grove of monsters. Without asking, I knew we would go there. We descended the long slope where sunlight fell in occasional golden shafts.

As my gaze settled on one such circle of light, I halted and stared. The sun illuminated the base of a tree with a riot of twisting, overlapping roots. For a moment, I thought I saw a village there, all in miniature among the ferns in the blaze of light: houses of stacked pebbles with mossy roofs; bridges of bark; towers and tiers and petal banners; and galleries stretching into the dim caves beneath the roots. But when I looked closer, I saw that all was merely the forest floor. Its myriad colors and textures had fooled my eyes. A dragonfly like a long green needle whirred lazily across the sun-patch.

Blinking, I hurried to catch up with Grandmother.

"I found the grove from its other side when I was a girl," she said quietly, "so this has always seemed like the back door to me. But the real front gate is in those bushes down there"—she pointed south, toward the village—"at the bottom of the hollow that holds it all."

As we threaded through the bushes, I stretched to my full height, trying to catch sight again of the gray dragon. Soon enough, I saw it, still rearing and snarling, its mouth open wide. My heart raced with the same thrill as when my parents would take me to the carnival or a picture show.

I could see the top of a broad arch to the south, which must be the main entrance Grandmother had meant. Trees stood here and there like colossal pillars, roofing the garden over with their impenetrable crowns. Grandmother stopped and put both hands on the head of her stick, listening. I kept still, giving her the chance to hear anything the grove might tell her. But I couldn't help easing closer to see the dragon.

Dense bushes had grown around him as high as his shoulders. This green tangle extended to both sides, a mass of thorny branches that choked much of the ravine. Peering through thorns and a spider web, I examined the dragon's clawed feet and the pedestal they gripped. Then I noticed why the beast was roaring and unfurling his wings: buried in the undergrowth around him, at least three dogs were attacking him. Carved with the same skill, they bared their fangs, surrounding the monster, one preparing to lunge. It was hard to contain my excitement and curiosity for what might lie hidden just beyond sight in the bushes.

To our left stood a second, smaller arch, about the size through which a tall man could walk without stooping. Vines had cloaked it, but faces were visible all up and down its span, some bearded, some beautiful, some monstrous. They peered out from among leaves and blossoms like spirits of the forest.

This arch had escaped the encroaching bushes. Grandmother led me beneath it, and we passed into a clearing like a vast cavern of viridian light. Randomly columned by trees, the clearing spread from one steep wall of the ravine to the other. To the right I saw again the sea serpent, its long neck rising from the same brake of bushes that engulfed the dragon. On the left, near at hand, sat a crowned, bearded man on a throne. He held a gigantic fork, both weapon and scepter. "That's Neptune," said Grandmother. "God of the sea. And I think that's Heracles." She pointed at the figure towering over the bushes beyond the sea serpent, near the hollow's eastern wall—a muscular man with short, curling hair and a mighty club. "I know I'm mixing my Greek and Roman mythology," she added. "But this looks more like a Neptune than a Poseidon, doesn't it? And 'Hercules' just doesn't seem to fit that one."

"Was Heracles that big?" I asked, trying to remember what I'd heard of Heracles—some hero or warrior of long ago.

"Probably not," Grandmother said. "Maybe it's just some giant. But he looks like Heracles to me. If he were holding up the *sky*, I'd say Atlas . . ."

In the half-light of the hidden garden, moss lay thick, and more strange figures loomed near and far. The lack of breeze combined with the age of the statues to give me the sense that time did not pass here.

Before us and a little to the right, across a mostly unobstructed expanse of forest floor, rose the tower that leaned at a disturbing angle. Nearer to us was the sculpture of a wild boar with real vines growing over his back. A large, square basin had once contained a pool or fountain but now held only a brackish accumulation of rain-water, leaves, and fallen branches. Four identical stone women stood delicately poised, one on each corner of the basin's rim. Each woman bore a water-jar on her hip, a slender arm curled around it. None wore a stitch of clothing, and I looked quickly away. When Grandmother moved ahead of me, I took a second, longer glance.

"That's really awful," she said, and I jumped, feeling my face begin to burn.

But Grandmother was talking about the tower. "For the life of me, I can't fathom why anyone would build it that way. It makes me dizzy just to look at it, and if I go inside, I feel ill."

"A mystery," said a voice, and I barely held back a yelp.

It was Mr. Girandole, his face in a narrow window on the tower's upper story. Grinning, he leaned out with his elbows on the sill.

He still wore the floppy brown hat, but now his shirt was a dusky blue. "Whatever mischief the old duke was up to when he built it," Mr. Girandole said, "it's come in handy."

"So, there you are." Grandmother looked up with her typical restrained smile—a smile that seemed to look beyond the reason for smiling to the next ache or nuisance or grief, and still farther beyond that—a long telescope of foresight. "Are you all right?" she asked.

"Very well, thank you, though there have been some anxieties."

"And that one?" Grandmother lowered her voice further.

"Alive." Mr. Girandole looked over his shoulder once, into the tower's interior. "But not awake yet. He's had water and tea, and a sip or two of broth, but he's burning with fever. I think he dreams dreams."

Grandmother laughed. "Of course he does, in that catastrophe of a house. It would drive anyone mad. If he lives, he's likely to come out of there crawling on all fours and eating straw."

For all her brusqueness, I thought Grandmother sounded happy. I studied the building and decided it wasn't a tower at all, though its height gave that impression. It seemed to have only two stories, if the windows were any indication, though its flat roof had a crenellated parapet, like a castle. The rooms—of which there could conceivably be only two—must be about the size of my own bedroom in Grandmother's cottage, but they must have very high ceilings.

"He's in here," said Mr. Girandole, though we'd gathered that. "Do you want to come up and see him?"

"No, you come out here," Grandmother answered. "I know what a delirious man looks like."

Mr. Girandole disappeared from the window, and Grandmother started up a flight of weathered stone steps that led to a terrace at the foot of the leaning house. The terrace itself was level, not leaning. There was a matching stairway at its other end, and in the spirit of adventure, I took that one. I paused before climbing to peer across the glade at the statue of a mighty elephant who held an armored warrior in his trunk, frozen in the act of dashing the man to the ground—the violence of the scene gave me a chill. Beyond the elephant a stone tortoise, broad as a table, appeared to creep from the bushes.

I hurried up to the terrace, where weeds grew in the cracks between flagstones. Grandmother mounted from the other side, grunting as she labored up the stairs. Stone benches lined the platform along every side. She chose one against the building, where she could lean back against its wall and face outward. The terrace had a mossy railing with ornamental pilasters and seven planting urns, spaced at regular intervals. Each urn now held a thicket of natural growth, leaves and vines spilling from its rim and along the railing—like pots of forest that had boiled over.

Mr. Girandole emerged from a doorway in the tower's side and joined us. He wore no shoes, and his hoofs clicked on the stones. When he settled himself on the western bench, above the stairway Grandmother had ascended, I saw beyond his shoulder the desolate fountain of the four unclothed women.

I perched beside Grandmother. Between our feet and Mr. Girandole's, a tiny brown lizard skittered for cover. I sprang up and followed it to see where it would go. Reaching the platform's back edge, past the corner of the house where the open doorway yawned, the lizard raced over the brink and straight down the block wall to the ground, not caring that the stone beneath its twiggy feet was vertical. I lost sight of it then.

Raising my eyes, I found myself facing another great stand of matted bushes and close-set trees, which blocked another large swath of the garden behind the leaning house. But another archway led onward in a gap, as strangely clear of undergrowth as the one through which we'd come.

Then I saw, in a patch of such deep shade that I'd missed it at first, a statue stained black with moisture or mold. It was the image of an angel, but not the sort I'd ever seen in a church. This angel's long hair and robes blew back in what seemed a fierce wind. The face made me draw a frightened breath, for its mouth was a line of unyielding purpose, and its eyes seemed colder and darker than the stone of which they were carved. In one hand the angel held a ring of keys, and in the other a chain, which looped down to cross and re-cross the square base on which the angel stood—as if the chains held that base bound against the earth.

I backed away and returned quickly to the bench.

"So, you heard those planes," Grandmother said, "and knew they'd seen the parachute."

Mr. Girandole nodded. "It was too far to take the man to my cave—too hard on him, even if I could have managed it; so I brought him here. Had to drag him most of the way on my coat, then sweep up the worst of the drag-marks."

"Resourceful," said Grandmother. "And clever thinking, I'm sure; though I doubt it did him much good to be dragged up all these steps."

Mr. Girandole nodded ruefully. "I was as gentle as possible."

"But didn't the soldiers come here, too?" I asked.

"Yes, they came," he said. "They gawked at the monsters, prodded the bushes, and inspected this listing house. But what I'd hoped came to pass."

Grandmother had a knowing gleam in her eye.

"What came to pass?" I asked, looking up at the colorless wall. Two windows gaped without glass or shutter, one above the other.

Mr. Girandole bent close and spoke behind his hand. "They didn't find the secret space, where the man and I were hiding."

I know my eyes brightened at the mention of a secret space. "Can I see it?"

"Yes," said Grandmother, pulling me back into my seat, "he'll show you presently." She waited for Mr. Girandole to continue his story.

"Then I collected the tools and washed the canvas in the stream, as I promised. I knew it would take the soldiers time to get here, so I worked deliberately. I smoothed out the mound we made, brought water here in the bucket, and washed the blood from these steps."

"He was still bleeding?" asked Grandmother.

"No, not really. I think it was from his clothes, and my poor coat, too. I fear it may be time for a new one."

"I expect so," said Grandmother, "when the excitement dies down."

"Yes, yes, there's no hurry."

It occurred to me then that Mr. Girandole must depend on my grandmother for things such as clothes; he couldn't walk into the village on those back-bending legs of his and shop for his own. But Grandmother, I supposed, could buy second-hand men's clothing "for the buttons" or "for quilting."

How lonely Mr. Girandole's life must be, I thought. He had no person to talk to but Grandmother; and for the more than thirty years of her marriage, he'd had no one at all. But maybe time passed differently for ageless fauns. Or maybe here in the sacred woods where time itself seemed an unproven fancy, the waiting had not been so bad.

I thought of my own two friends from home and imagined the fun we might have exploring this garden. Our letters had tapered off. I'd tried to describe the village to them, but they'd never seen such a place, and now our lives were entirely different—theirs so full of chores and anxiety, and everything rationed. They had no time for letters. And now there was so much I couldn't write about. I felt like the statues here, grown deep into a world of shade and silence, isolated and concealed. I hoped the letters from my parents wouldn't stop coming.

There was a long, comfortable quietness then, during which we sat on our benches and gazed out at images the world had forgotten. Without getting up, I could see the pool, Neptune on his throne, our first archway, the boar, the dragon's head, the sea serpent, the elephant, and of course Heracles, wading in the bushes like a man at the green sea's edge.

"Not much has changed," Grandmother said. At first, I didn't know what she meant. "The bushes are wilder now. More paths are overgrown, and more is hidden."

Mr. Girandole nodded, looking around thoughtfully, and I figured out they were remembering the garden as it had looked years and years ago, when Grandmother was my age.

"More is broken down and rounded off," Mr. Girandole said. "The mermaid is the worse for wear, and the vine roots are not kind.

It's hard to hold back a forest that's so eager and full of life, but I've done what I can to keep the main pathways open."

Now I understood why the archways were free of vegetation. Mr. Girandole cared for the garden, trimming back the bushes when it became necessary. But he'd been discreet; he'd let the woods grow wild enough that no casual visitor would suspect the intervention of a caretaker. Branches were left to decay where they fell. The forest made its choices.

"Mermaid?" I asked, remembering that Grandmother had spoken of seeing a mermaid first of all the monsters.

"There's another half to the garden," Mr. Girandole said. "Behind you, through the second set of arches. That's the upper part, and this is the lower."

Grandmother was still thinking of the past. "This is where we met, isn't it, Girandole? On this very terrace. You were reading a book."

He chuckled. "One of those books I brought back with me from my foray into the world of the mortal folk. I still remember which one it was, and the page and the place I was reading when I looked up and there you were. I nearly jumped over the rail—no one else has ever sneaked up on me—no one else before or since. I wondered who this could be, to walk so silently!"

"Could never do it now," Grandmother said. "You'd hear me huffing on the bottom step, and my joints creaking."

"You were very small, but you gave me quite a fright."

Grandmother blinked languidly. "I wasn't afraid of you, and you had goat feet."

"You've never been afraid, M———. Not of your world, and not of the other."

"What good does it do to be afraid?"

They had forgotten all about me, but I didn't mind. It was good to hear them talking this way, their voices warm and soft and worn as old leather. I wandered to the rail and peered out across the bottom of the garden. In my head I tried to picture Grandmother as a young girl, gliding soundless across the carpets of leaves.

The deep glade was not in absolute shadow. The most delicate beams of sunlight pierced intermittently, making brilliant flecks no bigger than coins on the moss.

After another long silence, Grandmother suggested I go with Mr. Girandole to see how R—— was doing. "And we'd better take the brush knife home, at least. It will need sharpening."

No mention was made of Mr. Girandole's not having come to our house the previous night. We understood that for him to visit us would only risk danger for us all. And he had his hands full caring for the patient.

"Don't forget to leave the provisions we brought," Grandmother said, pointing to the carpet bag. "If R—— can't eat them, then you can, Girandole."

Mr. Girandole thanked her and stood, and I followed him to the doorway. It had no door and was forever open.

The coolness of ancient stone washed over us. Beyond the threshold lay exactly the sort of chamber I had expected: absolutely bare, its floor strewn with dead leaves. As Grandmother had said, the building's tilt was much more disturbing inside. At once I felt a weariness in my ankles, since they had to bend to keep me upright. Dampness streaked the walls. Immediately to our left, a short stairway descended into a low annex like Grandmother's summer kitchen. Ahead of us, an enclosed corner of the room housed a dim, winding stairway. Mr. Girandole led me upward. Enough light filtered in from above and below that I could make out the footing.

There seemed too few steps for the space they had to climb. To compensate, each step leaped high above the preceding one; this fact and the stairwell's tilt made the going difficult. "Be careful not to fall," Mr. Girandole said gently. "It's rather more like a ladder than a stair."

"A ladder on a sinking ship," I answered.

I also noticed at once that the risers between steps all bore numbers, one number on each vertical plane. But the numbers were all out of order and made no sense that I could see. Four and nine gave way to two and eleven and fourteen: moreover, some of the numbers were carved upside down. "What do these mean?" I whispered.

Crawling up the stairs above me, Mr. Girandole shook his head. "Another mystery of the garden."

Grandmother had said there was a riddle to this place, a puzzle. I began to understand that she meant more than just the gathering of fantastical statues and architecture.

The room at the top of the stairs was of the oddest construction I'd yet seen. Though the ceiling and walls closely resembled those of the chamber below, the floor had two levels. Its front half, on the side of the house above the terrace, was even with the threshold where we now stood. But between us and that farther section of floor lay a sunken half, into which a short stairway descended. It reminded me of a swimming pool with all the water drained. A narrow ledge, just wide enough to walk upon, ran from our feet in both directions to join the upper half of the floor. There across from us was the window through which Mr. Girandole had been looking out. I also noticed a stone ladder built right into the wall in the rear corner straight opposite our doorway; presumably, the closed hatchway at its top led to the roof.

Down in the sunken well was the pilot, R———. Flat on his back, he occupied a pallet made from Grandmother's canvas and a bed of grasses and leafy branches; I saw ends of these sticking out from beneath him. A stoneware cup, a tea kettle, and some rags were arrayed around him, along with our bucket and pan, the brush knife, and the unlit lantern. There was also a pile of rumpled blankets that must have come from Mr. Girandole's house, and in a corner lay the long coat, now badly stained and tattered.

R———'s face looked terrible—deathly pale with a slight bluish cast, and shiny with sweat. His breath came out in hisses and moans.

"You see, he's quite bad off," said Mr. Girandole, trotting down the steps into the well. With the equipment and blankets, there was scarcely room for him to crouch beside the man. "I don't know whether to keep him covered or not. He kicks the blankets off." He looked up at me with bleak eyes. "This anguish, this inevitable approach of Death," he said, "it's such a distressing part of the human world."

I nodded, understanding enough of his big words to agree with him.

"But what's secret about this room?" I asked. "Why didn't the soldiers find you?"

"Ah. Watch this." Mr. Girandole seemed glad for the distraction. He stooped and spread his hands on the wall of that lower space, the wall beneath the higher half of the floor.

I noticed now that the surface was pitted with hundreds of tiny, regular holes in rows, each hole about the size of a fingertip and connected to those surrounding it by faint grooves.

Finding the precise place he was seeking, Mr. Girandole stuck his thumb into one hole and his longest finger into another. I heard a loud, mechanical click, and the upper floor jerked, sliding by a fraction. Half of the floor was a moving slab!

Mr. Girandole grinned, reached up, and pulled it toward him, over his head. It rumbled, crossing the chamber, shutting Mr. Girandole and R—— into a hidden compartment, now completely gone from sight. Where the moving floor had been at first was a second well, a twin to the first, with another stairway leading down into it. To look out the window over the terrace now, a person would have to stand on the ribbon of ledge that remained there.

Mr. Girandole's voice rose, muffled, through the stone. "You can walk across above us. This is still the solid floor."

I did so, marveling at how well it fit in its new position, having perfectly concealed the first well to reveal the second. The stone ladder to the roof seemed more naturally placed now, rising above this floor rather than above a pit.

"It must be pitch-black for you down there," I said.

"Yes. But I can find the latch again by feel."

I couldn't help smiling. It was such a nonsensical and delightful thing to build, like the entire leaning house. Was this whole house, then, meant to be nothing more than a magic trick-box? The sunken wells partly explained the odd height of the structure: it needed some extra space between the first and second stories.

On the floor of the newly opened well I saw an engraving that startled me. It was a giant face drawn by lines carved into the smooth stone. Roughly human, the face had round eyes and a gaping mouth, as if it were screaming. In a long arc above it was an inscription. I recognized our language but in a style so old I had trouble making out the words.

"What does this say?" I asked, loud enough for Mr. Girandole to hear.

"'Reason departs,'" came his muted reply.

I repeated this to myself, puzzling over the meaning. "Is there a face like this in your half?" I asked.

"Yes. Here under R——'s bed—exactly the same."

I returned to the doorway. Mr. Girandole asked if I was clear, and then he rolled back the floor.

"How did you ever find the secret space?" I asked.

"It was long ago," he said. "I knew there must be a compartment there—why else build the floor so strangely? And I guessed the holes meant something. It was just a matter of feeling inside them one by one. The fact that the trigger has two separate catches took me a while."

Just then I heard the tap of Grandmother's stick and her voice as she climbed the stairs behind me. She'd decided to come in after all.

"This place makes my head spin," she complained. I got out of her way so she could clamber down into the well and see R—— for herself.

She changed nearly everything that Mr. Girandole had done, first moving every item on the floor to a different place, then poking and rearranging the pallet. She opened the patient's shirt and washed him with a wet rag, muttering over the state of the water in the bucket but rejecting Mr. Girandole's offer to go to the stream and get another bucketful.

I knew it was the house's tilt that she truly disliked. It was making me queasy, too. Droplets seemed to fall at an angle from the squeezed cloth; the water rose nearly to the bucket's rim on one side only.

Untying all the bandages, Grandmother dabbed carefully at the wounds and smeared them with something dark and oily from a bottle in her pocket. Then she made new bandages from more of the rags, bound them in place, and poured liquid from another bottle into R——'s mouth.

He spluttered, gagged, and said something in his language but did not regain consciousness. I thought he looked marginally better after the bathing, but Grandmother wasn't happy.

"He should be in the hospital," she said.

"Unquestionably," said Mr. Girandole.

"But we did what he wanted," I reminded her. "He didn't want a doctor."

She sighed, wringing out the rag. "What will be will be." Leaving one of the bottles with Mr. Girandole, she lined up the food and milk we'd brought and gave him more instructions than I could follow, let alone remember. But Mr. Girandole listened with solemn intensity and nodded when she'd finished.

"We'll go home now," she said to me. To Mr. Girandole, she added that we'd bring cloth soon to make some better bandages, and that if he needed help or advice, he should come to the cottage anyway. She also looked with concern at Mr. Girandole and asked if he was remembering to eat and sleep.

"As much as ever," he told her.

"That's not very reassuring. You don't do enough of either." Grandmother pressed his hand between hers, as I'd seen her do before. "This is good of you, Girandole. You have the hardest work."

"What else have I got to do, M——? Leave it to me." The corners of his eyes crinkled, and a look of great fondness passed between him and my grandmother.

She left the lantern and some matches, and we took the brush knife to bundle with our hatchet and firewood.

It was quite a chore for Grandmother to descend the stairway, but at last we safely reached the level ground and sat again on the terrace until our heads cleared. "If that poor fevered man lives to see another day," she said, "it will only be because this house makes Death too sick to collect him."

We retraced our steps out of the grove of monsters, leaving the upper glade for me to see the next time. My gaze lingered again on the statues we passed—even the slender women with their water jars.

"You like them?" Grandmother asked, hooking a thumb at the women.

My face burned again. I attempted a casual shrug and said, "Yes," in an offhand way.

"Boys!" she said, chuckling.

To change the subject, I asked her what Mr. Girandole ate.

"He's quite a gardener and a hunter. The forest keeps his larder full."

"Does he *need* to eat?"

"Perhaps not to live, but he feels better when he does. He becomes morose when he's tired or hungry."

We picked up enough sticks to make a proper load, but we encountered no one. When we'd tottered at last through the back gate, Grandmother went straight to her room for a nap, and I sank onto the garden bench in the hot, drowsy, westering light.

I found myself imagining what the hour of dusk would look like back in the grove, with shadows deepening, the last light red through the leaves, fireflies winking like fairy lamps, and curtains of soft night falling everywhere. I remembered my dream of the monsters beginning to move when I turned away from them. If ever they came to life, it would be in the twilight. I thought of Mr. Girandole keeping his vigil there, watching alone over a man who hovered between life and death.

It had been only two days since R—— had fallen from the sky—two days, but I'd seen so much since then. The world for me had grown bigger and older and wilder; like the sacred grove, it held secrets buried within its tangles.

Grandmother woke me early the next morning and announced that we were going to Wool Island. Of course, there were good reasons: Grandmother had run low on yarn for knitting, a trip to the island made a pleasant day's outing, and I hadn't been there yet. But Grandmother also had it in her head that this was the best way to dispose of R——'s gun once and for all. I didn't quite follow her reasoning: it seemed to me Mr. Girandole's idea had been better— to take the gun somewhere into the mountain forests and bury it. But I also knew that, in her thinking, Grandmother was usually at least ten steps ahead of me.

After breakfast, she set the gun carefully onto the kitchen table, kept the barrel turned away from us, stayed well clear of the trigger, and worked with it until she found out how to remove the magazine. She put this clip and the gun separately into a cloth bag with a drawstring, closed the neck, wrapped it in a large rag, and nestled this bundle in the bottom of her carpet bag. Then we loaded the bag with crackers, sardines, a dented silvery water bottle with the cap screwed on tightly, and eight or nine bright-skinned tangerines. Grandmother remembered little cups for the water. Finally, we each tucked in the books we were reading: hers was a novel and mine was *Arabian Nights*. Just as we were leaving, I thought I might need my sketching kit and tossed it in, too. There was still plenty of room for the wool yarn Grandmother would buy, but the bag was heavy, so I carried it again.

We passed along the main street, Grandmother stopping at her favorite resting places. These were usually beside particularly well-tended gardens she could admire. She would sit for a few minutes on an iron bench or a low wall and study the fruit trees, the rows of sprouts, or the rose bushes. To me, none of the gardens seemed quite as complete or as satisfying as Grandmother's, with its balances of color and shady depth, splendor and secrecy.

Soldiers still made patrols, and the town continued to buzz with speculation about the enemy fugitive. Mrs. O——, who was out watering her tomatoes, delivered her opinion (quite loudly, because she didn't hear well) that the missing pilot had gone over the mountain and was headed inland. But another lady with thick eyebrows theorized that he'd stowed away in a cannery truck and was even now traveling down the coast behind tins of tuna and salmon. Mrs. D——, not one to let the tension dissipate, suggested that the pilot might be hiding in a cellar or in one of the sea-caves, and that he prowled through the village at night, ransacking the garbage for food.

"It wouldn't be easy to elude the patrols," Grandmother said.

"Easy enough for *him!*" Mrs. D—— insisted. "In that country, they live by trapping and shooting wild animals. They're like wolves!"

I didn't think wolves either trapped or shot their prey, but Mrs. D—— seemed fond of the idea of an enemy who could see in the dark and evade our soldiers like a puff of night mist.

As soon as she could, Grandmother hurried us onward.

The Army launch was gone from the harbor. Through the window of the lunch kitchen, we saw three soldiers sitting at the counter, drinking coffee. None of them was my father, of course—I couldn't move on until I was sure, though I knew he wasn't in our country.

"Give them another day or two," Grandmother said, "and they'll decide they have better things to do elsewhere."

The early ferry had left for Wool Island at six a.m. We were taking the second one, scheduled for ten. Though we'd left the house in plenty of time, after so much resting and visiting along the way, we were only just in time. We hurried up the gravel walk to the ticket office, a white building with a row of decorative cabbages along its foundation and a flag dancing above it.

Grandmother was intent on reaching the entrance—already the ferry's engine chugged, and its horn blasted a long, coppery note. But something caught my gaze, and I turned in the doorway. On a second narrow street that joined the first at a sharp angle, an Army truck stood parked against the curb, its canvas sides flapping in the breeze; and just behind it was the staff car we'd seen outside the hotel. I wondered which of the shops or tall boathouses the soldiers might be in. Dashing into the ticket office behind

Grandmother, I opened my mouth to tell her about the vehicles—but stopped short when I saw that the waiting room was full of soldiers.

Chattering, puffing on cigarettes, they slung their rifles over their shoulders and filed out the boarding door. They were all going to Wool Island, too.

I'm sure my face turned a shade paler. My instinct was to back out the door. All I could think of was the carpet bag on my arm and of the gun hidden inside it. When I turned in horror to find Grandmother, I saw an Army officer smiling at her, tipping his hat.

I disliked this portly man immediately. His smile was wide and toothy, his slick hair as shiny as his boots. Ornamental pins glinted on his chest and collar. "Take your time, Madam," he said to Grandmother. "I'll see that we don't leave without you."

Calling a polite thank-you, Grandmother found my shoulder with a reassuring pat that became something of a death grip, and steered me to the ticket window.

I started to express my disbelief that we were still going to buy tickets, but she obliterated my words with a bright "Come along, now."

With a steady cheerfulness, she picked the exact change from her coin purse and slid it across to the gray-haired man at the window, who tore two tickets from a roll and handed them over. "Comes back at one and five," he told her through his prodigious mustache, his scowl and tone saying that he thought we were the sort who typically missed ferry departures.

I looked at Grandmother in panic. Her eyes glittered, but she said, "Calm down. Good behavior," and guided me ahead of her out the door after the last soldier.

We turned left, climbed down three steps, and moved along a wooden pier that clunked beneath the soldiers' boots. A few of the men out at the dock's end were singing as they jostled each other. One of the song's lines made me raise my head in disbelief and try to hear more—but another soldier jabbed those men and yelled at them to shut up, gesturing toward us. Grandmother was concentrating on her footing. The smells of sea-brine and engine exhaust washed over us. I eased past a coiled rope as big around as my arm, thinking it looked like a giant snake. Another man took our tickets and helped Grandmother down a short metal stairway into the ferry.

As I clambered over the boat's side, a soldier offered a sun-browned, callused hand. "That bag's as big as you," he said. I grinned back, wishing I were anywhere but there.

The ferry's horn blared again, right over my head, and I winced. Looking up, I saw a plane whine past, flying low—one of ours.

"Flyboys," said one of the soldiers scornfully, and his friend laughed.

The ferry had two levels, its interior much like that of a bus or train, with a central aisle and bench seats along both sides, all facing forward. Its pilot occupied an enclosed cabin at the front of the lower level. We were taking the smaller passenger ferry; Grandmother had told me of a larger one that could carry cars and trucks, but it made only one trip per day.

At least ten soldiers spread themselves around, wandering the aisle and finding places they liked, some sitting sideways with their legs up and arms on the seat backs, shouting to one another over the revving engine. Some clattered up the stairs to the top deck. All the windows were open, letting in the fresh salt breeze. Perhaps half a dozen people from the village were scattered throughout the cabin.

The soldier nearest me, with pale eyes and a shaved head, twirled his cap on a finger and stared at me without grinning. I froze, terrified of taking another step. I glanced toward Grandmother, who was peering up the front stairwell, shading her eyes. The soldier tipped his head sideways, still intent on me. I imagined it was how he would look at an enemy prisoner.

He leaned toward me, his face no more than a foot from mine. I could see a fresh shaving cut on his chin and an old scar that interrupted his right eyebrow. Still I could not move.

His companion gave him a shove.

Both soldiers laughed then, and the one with the pale eyes clapped my arm. "It's all right, C——!" He called me by the name of the cinema star.

Grandmother shuffled back to me. "Want to go upstairs? You can see more from up there."

I wanted to be wherever the soldiers weren't. I couldn't tell yet where most of them would settle, so I nodded. Telling me to go ahead of her, Grandmother took her time, gripping the handrail and her stick. Outside, the ticket-taker undid two more of the fat snake-ropes from huge cleats and threw them aboard. Again, the horn blasted.

The engine changed pitch, and we churned away from the dock. There were only three soldiers on the top level—so far—and another handful of civilians. I didn't see any that I knew to be Grandmother's friends. I watched the harbor slipping by, the boats and the wharves, the rocks and the houses. Sunlight sparkled on the water. Two fishermen waved from a boat's deck; most of the people and soldiers waved back. A seagull landed right on the ferry's rail and balanced there looking about, enjoying the ride.

We'd no more than gotten settled on a bench near the front, to the right of the aisle, when a gaggle of soldiers tromped up the stairs. The first one "crawled" with his hands clutching the seat backs, right and left. The men all looked at us, some wishing us a good day, some tipping hats to Grandmother, a few serious. Grandmother nodded back, austere and dignified. The one with the pale, staring eyes didn't come up, and I was glad.

I couldn't help turning in my seat to look at the men. Did any of them know my father? Had some perhaps trained with him or marched with him? Had they fought the enemy together? Most of these looked young, even to me then, more like my friends' older brothers than like our fathers. They might have been a boatload of schoolboys horsing around, noisy and carefree. One groomed his slick hair with a comb, two others messed it up, and a fake fight ensued. My gaze drifted to the rifles leaning beside each man, the metal parts dark and gleaming in the bright light.

One soldier sat on a bench by himself, reading a soft-covered book small enough to fit in his pocket. Studying his large, beakish nose, the red blotchiness of his teenaged complexion, I wondered what the book was.

My heart sank as the shiny-haired commanding officer appeared and stopped in front of us. "You made it aboard, Madam," he said. Behind us, the tomfoolery died quickly down.

"With your help, Major," answered Grandmother.

I made the connection: this was the major Grandmother had seen through the hotel window, the one whom Grandfather wouldn't have liked. I was sure my father wouldn't like him, either.

Removing his flat-topped hat, the man raised his eyebrows in surprise. "And how do you know that I'm a major?"

"Well, even if you weren't wearing a major's bars, we in the village all know our Major P——."

He laughed in obvious delight. Grandmother didn't talk like most of the villagers. She tended to stand out wherever she went.

"May I?" he asked, indicating the seat across the aisle from us.

"Of course," Grandmother said to my dismay. But what else could she have said?

"You're no stranger to the Army," the major said. His aide, who carried a bulky black case on a shoulder strap, took the seat in front of him.

"No," Grandmother said. She explained that her son—my papa—was currently serving as an Army captain, and she cited his name and that of his regiment. Moreover, she went on, her husband in his youth had put in six years of voluntary service before the First War.

"Well, then!" exclaimed Major P——. "You're quite a patriot! Mrs. T——, is it?" (He'd gotten her name from her mention of my father.)

Grandmother introduced herself properly and added that I was her grandson, that I was staying for the summer.

I didn't like being under the major's gaze. "And are you going to be a soldier, like your father and grandfather?" He leaned toward me with his elbows on his knees.

"I don't know," I said in a small voice. I meant that I hoped not, that I didn't want to be a soldier any more than my papa did. But that hardly seemed the wise thing to say.

"You have a tradition to uphold!" he said. "Don't you want to make your family proud?"

"Yes, sir."

He laughed, showing his teeth, and batted my shoulder. "Well, you have a long while to decide yet, and there are many ways to serve the motherland."

He returned his attention to Grandmother, which made me feel marginally better. I still had the carpet bag over my shoulder, pinned beneath my elbow on the side toward the wall. I imagined R——'s gun making a gun-shaped bulge in the bag's fabric—though that, of course, was ridiculous.

The major repeated Grandmother's family name. Then a light seemed to go on behind his eyes. "In fact, I've heard of you, Madam. Your name has come up more than once in the last couple days. I'd made a note to come and see you—and fate brings us together here!"

"Really?" asked Grandmother, looking amused. "In what connection has my name come up?"

"Nothing but good is attributed to you, I assure you. Particularly . . ." A curious expression crossed his face, and he gestured absently with his hat. Its bill was as black and shiny as his boots. "Particularly, I've heard that you are the local authority on those unusual old statues up in the forest."

I felt as if someone had touched cold metal to the back of my neck.

Grandmother smiled. "The grove of monsters? I'm hardly an authority."

"Yet you are clearly a woman of education."

Perhaps to change the subject, Grandmother explained how she'd gone away to school, and how her husband, after his time in the Army, had been a finish carpenter of some renown. She'd traveled with him to sell his bookshelves and cabinets even in the neighboring countries. Together they'd attended many concerts and known the friendship of poets, musicians, and artists; they had vacationed at the beach cottage of the writer T—— L——, for whom Grandfather had crafted a bed. On trips to the grand and ancient cities, Grandmother had entertained herself in museums and libraries while Grandfather installed his exquisite mantel-pieces in many a fine home. (Which explained, I thought in later years, how it was that Grandmother had never needed to work at the cannery or take in washing and mending like so many of her friends did; she spent her long widowhood in modest comfort.)

The major looked at her in apparent wonder. "Am I to under-stand, Mrs. T——, that you might have lived anywhere, and you chose this village?"

"I was born here," Grandmother said. "I've lived all my life in the cottage my father built. I love the people. I love my garden and the sea and the mountains and the sky. The sky is different, you know, depending on which part of it you live under."

Major P—— tossed his hat onto the bench beside him and tapped his aide on the shoulder. "A meeting with such a remark-able woman calls for a toast."

Grandmother protested, but the major would hear none of it. The aide pulled from the black clasp case a corked bottle of wine and a set of ceramic cups. Popping the cork with a flourish, the major began filling them. "Please forgive the barbarity of the tableware," he said. "Tulip-stemmed glasses do not travel well."

He placed one cup in Grandmother's hands and one in mine, giving me a fatherly wink. Then he filled one for the aide and one for himself. I glanced over my shoulder to see some of the soldiers watching us with curiosity and the villagers looking on impassively. We were near the front of the upper cabin, so we couldn't help providing a show for everyone behind us.

"To victory," the major said, "and to our country, with its noble history of struggle and perseverance."

"To our country," Grandmother agreed.

The wine was a full-bodied type, a little more bitter than I was used to. I held the cup with both hands, afraid of dropping it.

"But these fantastic monsters in the wood," the major resumed suddenly. "Giants and dragons and such. You're not afraid of them, are you?"

"Why should I be?" asked Grandmother. "Of all that humans can design, art is fairly innocuous."

The major chuckled. "Some would debate that."

"No doubt. But no, I think our monsters, asleep up there on the mountainside, are more in the nature of guardians. They represent a time when we celebrated beauty. Myth and story and dreams."

"When we had the leisure to do so," said the major. He swirled the wine in his cup, savoring the bouquet. "That time will come again, when we can return to the finer things. For now, we must be practical, though pragmatism is a bland feast. I understand that there is actually a law in effect which prohibits trespassing into any ruins of this type, of which our land has many."

Grandmother chose to address only his last few words: "We were an artistic people."

"And always shall be!" The major sipped his wine, and I noticed how rarely he blinked as he studied Grandmother's face. "Those statues are marvelous pieces. They should be preserved."

"I suspect they will be," said Grandmother. "When . . . we can return to the finer things."

"Perhaps the day will come sooner rather than later. I was speaking the other day with a friend of mine, an artist . . ."

I saw Grandmother glance at him through narrowed eyes.

"But I've nearly said too much." The major smirked and lowered his voice. "He's an artist of considerable fame, you see, and doesn't wish it to be widely known that he's traveling in this part of the country. He's hoping for peace and quietness."

"As are we all," said Grandmother quite pointedly. "*Praying* for it. But with your artist friend, Major, what were you speaking about?"

"The statues. That enchanting garden above the village. He had heard of it; I expect he'll pay it a visit soon. With the proper permissions, of course."

I refrained from looking at Grandmother in alarm, but I didn't like the thought of a stranger prying into our sacred woods. The fear of R——'s being discovered only accounted for part of my reason. I had already begun to regard the grove as our own private space. I didn't want Major P—— to think of it or to speak of it.

The major drained his cup. "I envy my artist friend. He can spend his days in the imaginary landscape of his mind, while I must be more concerned with the mundane. When the war is behind us, men such as I will at last have leave to indulge our spirits again. In the meantime, we do what we can." He held up the bottle to demonstrate his devotion to fine culture. As he poured more wine, he asked Grandmother to tell him what she knew of the monsters' history, and she did so, relating what she'd told me: the duke, his obsession with adding to the garden, and his tragic romance; but she left out his strange disappearance.

As she finished, Grandmother deftly returned our empty cups to the aide before the major could refill them.

"So, we're bound for ———," said the major, using the name that was printed on maps.

"Wool Island, yes," answered Grandmother. "We're going to buy yarn. But I'm surprised that you're going there—and so many of you, at that. Is it possible that the enemy soldier has gotten over there?"

"I doubt that, unless he's part fish. No, our visit is an inspection . . . by which I mean mostly a diversion. My men are tired of tramping through the woods, and the beaches over there are lovely."

"That they are," said Grandmother. "But the man you're looking for . . ."

Major P—— shook his head. "I suspect he's dead of his wounds in some ravine, and five years from now, a woodcutter will happen upon his bones. Or else in a few days, he'll wander down starving into some village and give himself up. At any rate, I think we've done what we can. Try not to worry, Madam. I'm sure he presents no threat."

Grandmother pursed her lips and gave a nod with her brow furrowed.

The major corked the wine bottle and handed it back to his aide. "I'm afraid I offended the good sisters at the abbey. We made a rather extensive search of their premises." Smirking again, he brushed at something on his sleeve. "The Church shows compassion to the wounded and the homeless—which is virtuous enough in times of peace."

Grandmother sighed. "And when have we ever been at peace?"

"Alas, not in my memory."

"Nor in mine." Grandmother reached across me and opened the carpet bag. I had a vision of her pulling out the gun and handing it to Major P——. But instead, she came up with tangerines and gave them to the major and his aide, two each. "Thank you very much for your kindness," she said. "If you don't mind, my old legs need stretching. All this sitting and vibration is bad for the circulation."

"The pleasure has been mine," said the major. His glance fell upon the carpet bag. "What a charming piece of work! Surely that didn't come from a local market?"

"No," said Grandmother. "I made it myself, actually, out of some good remaining parts of the carpet we had when I was a little girl."

The major held out his hands to see it, and to my shock, Grandmother tugged it off my arm and gave it to him.

He made a dramatic show of straining under its weight. "Are you carrying bricks? It's a good thing you have this young soldier to tote it for you."

As he ran his hands over the plush side, tracing the swirling patterns with his fingers, Grandmother explained. "This was the part of the carpet that lay under the bookcase for years. It didn't fade or get worn out like the rest."

"And you found its use," said the major.

"Like your artist friend, I often prefer the 'landscape of my mind.' That's where I find the uses of things."

Balancing the bag on his knee, he shook his head with a bemused grin. "Mrs. T——, you are an extraordinary person."

"Major P——, you are too kind." Grandmother bowed humbly.

After what seemed an eternity, he handed back the carpet bag.

Grandmother passed it to me, and I lifted it to my shoulder. We each thanked the major again as we got up, and he waved.

"I wish your husband were still doing his carpentry," he called after us. "I've acquired a set of antique chairs and would like a table that matches."

Grandmother paused to glance back at him. "He could have helped you, sir."

We passed between the benches. Once when the boat rocked, a curly-haired soldier lent Grandmother a steadying hand and cheerfully advised her to watch her step, calling her "Grandma" as R—— had done.

An open door at the rear led out onto a tiny aft deck, shaded by a roof but open on the sides and back. To our left, a steep metal stairway descended to the lower level. From the deck's rail, I looked down onto the edge of a similar deck below, which stuck out a little farther than ours. Beyond this, the churning white wake of the ferry's engine stretched in a long swath. The land was far away now, green mountains shimmering. All around us was blue air and the dazzling sea.

Seagulls swooped along beside us, coming up from behind, overtaking the ferry, then circling back to overtake it again. They screeched and crossed one another's paths, now dipping low, now soaring high.

Grandmother placed her walking-stick in a corner of the railing where it wouldn't fall over. She dug in the bag again and brought out the tin of crackers. Breaking one cracker up, she showed me how to feed the birds: first letting them see what she held, then flinging the morsels into the air, one bit at a time. Gulls veered and snatched the pieces before they hit the water. Other people must have been feeding the seabirds through open windows on the lower deck; some of the gulls dove that way, and sometimes I saw bits of bread in the waves until the birds snapped them up, hardly leaving a ripple.

By the time we'd gone through four or five crackers, I was enjoying myself so much that Grandmother's next words caught me completely by surprise.

"Now look behind us," she said quietly. "Is anyone watching?"

At once I knew what she intended, and it was as if my blood had been replaced with ice water. Mouth going dry, I turned and peered in through the doorway. I saw mostly the backs of heads. The soldiers who were sitting sideways seemed engaged in conversation. A few were dozing. None were looking our way.

"No one's looking," I murmured back to her. "But some might see us out of the corners of their eyes."

"This is about as far from land as we get," Grandmother said, tossing another piece of cracker. "I'll block the view. You'd better throw it. You can get it farther out there." She took the bag from my shoulder. "It's supposed to be unloaded, but a bullet could be in the chamber or whatever they call it. Don't touch the trigger, and point the barrel away."

Trying to swallow, I nodded.

Fishing in the bag, she came up with the gun's magazine, the metal clip loaded with bullets. With a quick motion, she tossed it overboard. A seagull winged close but didn't like its looks, and the magazine spun into the sea.

Grandmother nodded in satisfaction. Handing me another chunk of cracker, she said, "Check one more time."

I wandered into the doorway again. Just as I did so, one of the sideways soldiers looked right at me. He touched two fingers to his forehead in salute, then made his hand into the shape of a gun and pretended to shoot me. I gave him what I hoped was a grin, but I probably looked like I was about to throw up.

Going back out to Grandmother, I flung the cracker piece to a gull.

"Are they looking?"

"Yes. One was."

"But no one's coming?"

"No."

"All right. Then stand right in front of me."

I did so, facing her.

She'd taken the gun out of the little cloth bag. With our stomachs almost touching, she laid the weapon into my hands. This was the first time I'd touched it. Though I'd held a handgun of my father's before, I was startled anew at how heavy such things were.

"Quickly," she said. "Straight out."

I turned toward the sea and stooped, putting my hands down between my knees, bunching myself for the throw.

Just then, bootsteps clanged on the metal stairs beside us.

"Now," Grandmother whispered.

Whoever was on the stairs would be facing forward until he got to the landing halfway up; then he'd be looking out over the stern. I had maybe two seconds to throw.

I hurled the gun outward into the sunlight. It flew with agonizing slowness, black and unmistakable. I imagined it getting stuck in the sky, as if the world were a drawing, showing me with my arms raised toward the enormous gun that had replaced the sun. A gull darted toward it and careened away. A second bird collided with it—I was sure I heard the thump over the engine's growl—but the gull stayed airborne, and the gun was falling again. For a long time after that, I half-believed the gull had gotten the pistol unstuck from the sky, that a shining bird had saved us.

Grandmother patted my back. We gazed down the ferry's wake as if down a road to another world, a magical land across the water, and our village and our mountain far away became that green world beyond time. The sun was burning the sea, turning everything to molten gold and silver. Birds came streaking and crying out of the blue and the fire.

With the sun in my eyes, I barely saw the splash when the gun finally met the sea, somewhere out in the wake.

Then two soldiers topped the stairs, rifles on their backs, and the first looked down at me. It was the one with the shaved head, the wide eyes.

I shrank against Grandmother, trying to get enough air into my lungs.

Leaning down as he passed me, the soldier touched the center of my chest with his pointer finger. He lingered again, staring at me. In a husky whisper, he said, "It all ends in fire."

Then he ducked through the cabin door behind the other man.

"What did he say?" asked Grandmother.

I shook my head, too afraid to answer. The words reminded me vaguely of something, some old fear or dream. I didn't understand what he meant, but it felt as if I'd heard a voice from a burning bush. To repeat it might bring knowledge too terrible. I watched the soldiers go, hand-crawling between the benches, to join their comrades. No one was looking at us.

Grandmother wore a mild expression, but I noticed she had a

firm grip on both her walking-stick and the rail. Glancing around to see who might be within earshot, she let out a long breath. "I should have told you not to throw it *quite* that far. But anyway, well done. We've taken an enemy gun out of the fighting permanently. If that's not doing some good for the war effort, then I don't know what is."

We could easily have spent the entire day on Wool Island. Beaches of clean white sand wandered away in both directions from where the ferry docked. Shops along the boardwalk sold fruit and hats, pans and dishes, figurines, paintings, wood-carvings, stoneware, pinwheels and noisemakers, noodles and fried breads and an array of other foods with enticing smells—and most of all, wool: yarn dyed in every color imaginable, and yarn knitted into caps, shawls, sweaters, socks, and blankets. People bought these warm things, even in the summer.

Sheep covered the green mountainsides so thickly that they seemed to be growing there, a ubiquitous woolly shrub.

To make the best use of our time, Grandmother sent me to wade in the surf while she browsed among the stalls, choosing her yarn. I played tag with the waves, following the ones that retreated, then reversing my course and scrambling to safety as reinforcements arrived. Though I'd left my shoes and socks high up the beach, my pants were soon drenched past the knees.

The smooth, wet sand ground deliciously under my feet. I picked up shells of amazing shapes and colors, washing them in the swells, turning them in the light. Several of the best I dropped into my pockets.

Farther along the coast, I saw a group of the soldiers at the water's edge, their boots and rifles abandoned. They laughed and shouted and pushed each other, splashing. Seagulls glided as they fished.

I ran back now and then to check on Grandmother. When she had the carpet bag stuffed with yarn and two full shopping bags besides, we bought noodles and sat at a boardwalk table under a fringed umbrella. To lighten the load, we ate as many tangerines as we could and drank the crock of milk. After we sat for a while, Grandmother waded, too. Her feet were like things grown in her garden under the soil, bulbous with shiny bunions.

I had calmed down enough to repeat what the soldier had whispered to me.

Grandmother didn't seem alarmed by the words at all, which relieved me.

"What do you think he was talking about?" I asked.

She shrugged, stooping to let a wave crash over her arms. "The end of the world, maybe. Soldiers think about such things."

"Does the world end in fire?"

"Yes, next time. Water the first time, fire the next."

I watched the foam sluice landward around my feet, then retreat, trailing silt—in and out, the sea always roaring. Out beyond the breakwater, the water was deep blue, and the scattered white caps on waves were like shreds of the clouds.

Neither of us wanted to leave, but we thought it best to take the one o'clock ferry back. For one thing, the soldiers and Major P—— would likely stay until the five o'clock departure; and for another, I think Grandmother felt as guilty as I did for playing on the beach when R—— lay in his condition in the leaning house, and Mr. Girandole had the whole job of watching over him. We wanted to be back home where Mr. Girandole could find us, at least.

There wasn't a single soldier in the ticket office or on board, which relieved us. The ferry itself was a different boat but designed the same: this must be the one that had left the mainland in the early morning. The only drawback was that Mrs. C—— waved to us from the middle of the cabin, and there was no escape. She talked without stopping, showing us everything she'd bought and then explaining how she'd come over on the six a.m. ferry, which strictly speaking was a violation of the curfew, but she lived near enough to the ferry dock that she'd decided to brave the short walk through the streets in the gray light. And a tense journey it had been: she'd heard footsteps crunching behind the garden hedge where Mr. and Mrs. A—— lived, moving along in parallel to her as she hurried down the street. Since she knew neither of the A——s were early risers, the sounds alarmed her greatly, especially when—looking back from the corner—she saw the dark figure of a man watching her from between the rose bushes. She'd run the last few steps to the ferry and counted herself lucky to have made it with her life. Then her talk ranged on through a radio show she'd heard and a visit she'd had with Mrs. D——.

In time, Grandmother's polite replies became mere grunts, and she closed her eyes for longer and longer intervals as she listened. Even I abandoned her, taking a turn through the upper deck and out onto the back platform, where I watched the gulls and the waves. I wondered if the mer-folk down in the quiet emerald depths had found R——'s gun, and what they might do with it. I imagined their king feeding it to the greatest of the giant clams, and that someday, the gun would lie at the center of a huge pearl.

Back in the village at a little past three o'clock, we noticed a pair of soldiers trudging up the main street and a couple more patrolling a field. I thought it was unfair that not all of them had gotten to go to Wool Island.

At home, I put the seashells into the drawer of the table beside my bed, then picked up the photo in its frame and studied my parents' faces. Grandmother had said that soldiers thought about the end of the world; I wondered if my papa did as he sat in his tent or watched the waves or the night sky. I touched the four of us with my fingertips, wishing we were all together.

Grandmother went straight to her room, exhausted. But she suggested that if I had the energy, I might want to hike up to the sacred woods and see how things were going there. The idea thrilled me—Grandmother was asking me to do something important in her stead. "Do you remember the way?" she asked.

I nodded.

"Well, you can't get really lost," she said. "*Up* leads to the mountain, and *down* will bring you back to the village." She determined I should take nothing with me. "If anyone asks, you're just exploring the woods. See if Girandole needs anything. Get back before dark." Having an afterthought, she asked, "You're not afraid to go up there alone, are you?"

"No." But I agreed with the notion of leaving the garden well before dark.

She nodded. "You don't have to go, you know. If you don't, I expect Girandole will come here tonight."

I told her I wanted to visit the grove again.

"Be careful," she added.

*   *   *   *

As we'd done the day before, I looked carefully around from the shelter of the arbors, but again I saw no one patrolling or watching. It was the hottest part of the day. The sun pounded the steaming grasses in that delightful, unrestrained way it has at the height of summer. Everything in the meadow was still, save for a few buzzing insects, a sprinkling of white-winged butterflies. A pale puff of smoke from the cannery's chimney hung stationary like the splash from a bucket of white paint, rinse-water swirled in the bucket and flung against the sky.

I moved quickly up into the green light of the woods. The shade felt good. Even so, my shirt was sticking to me by the time I'd reached the parachute. I had no trouble finding my way. There was a weary, trampled look to the underbrush; it had seen a lot of traffic. In another few minutes I faced the dragon again, forever roaring at the harassing dogs.

I hurried beneath the archway, passed Neptune and the boar, then crossed the open sward between the pool of the four women and the elephant. I moved cautiously now, listening, as I approached the leaning house.

As I set foot on the left-hand stairway that climbed to the terrace, Mr. Girandole appeared above me. His expression was so distressed that I froze, staring up at him, unable to voice the terrible question.

Mr. Girandole must have seen my shock. At once, he forced a smile and said, "Oh, no. Forgive me. He is alive, but—where is M——? Is she all right?"

I started breathing again and nodded. Trotting up the steps to the platform, I explained about our trip to Wool Island, but that we'd hurried home, and that Grandmother was taking a nap. When I was close enough to him to whisper, I added, "We threw the gun overboard into the sea. That's why we went."

He nodded distractedly, as if he weren't quite sure what I meant—or as if he had greater concerns on his mind. "I'm glad you've come. We'll all have to speak together as soon as possible."

"What is it?" I asked. "What's the matter?"

Mr. Girandole wasn't wearing his hat, and his hair was in disarray. As he ushered me ahead of him up the steep stairs in the stone house, he said, "The man wakes up sometimes . . . and then he dreams again. He *dreams*. They. . . . We must all speak together."

I understood then that he had something important to tell us, but it was Grandmother he most wanted to tell. I was curious but not offended; whatever the problem was, I'd be in no place to give advice.

R——— lay on his pallet, but now his head moved from side to side with the throes of delirium. He looked wretched in the bandages and tattered clothing, one sleeve and one pant leg cut off—like someone adrift in a lifeboat or chained in a dungeon. His face twitched expressively, reminding me of virtuoso musicians when they performed. Now and then he uttered a phrase between breaths—something in his own language.

"What's he saying?" I asked.

"'Red star,'" said Mr. Girandole. "'The red star.'"

I frowned and looked from the feverish man to the faun.

"I don't know what it means," said Mr. Girandole, brushing stray hair back from his face. "R——— had a notebook in one back pocket, and a pencil stub. I helped him get them out when he asked me to, and he wrote something strange."

From the cluttered floor of the sunken compartment, Mr. Girandole picked up a very small notebook with a worn leather cover. An elastic band, anchored in the spine, stretched around it to hold the book closed. Mr. Girandole opened it now and flipped through the pages until he came to a place near the middle, which he showed to me.

I recognized the language of R——'s country. The short, ordered lines seemed to make up a poem. But almost at once I noticed an unusual symmetry to the writing, to the shape it made on the page. Though I didn't understand a word of it, I saw that each line was written first forward and then backward—perfectly backward, as if it were being reflected in a mirror. How a man trembling with fever had done such a neat job was quite beyond me—as was the reason for it.

Again I looked wonderingly at Mr. Girandole.

"I translated it on the next page," he said, and turned one leaf.

Mr. Girandole's writing sent out loops and dots and cross-slashes in all directions, as if his letters had grown in a wild garden and were still blossoming. But in painstaking detail, he had imitated the mirroring of each line as well. The forward parts read:

> A duke the secret knew
> And locked the riddle here
> Find twice the number Taurus follows with his eye
> Sisters dancing in the water and the sky
> Heed the words among the trees in stone
> Though not all words are true
> And they will lead you home

After reading it through several times, I handed the book back to Mr. Girandole. "I'm not sure Grandmother can make any sense of it, either," I said.

"Perhaps not." He let out a long breath, fixing a troubled gaze on R——.

"How many languages do you know?" I asked, guessing that a person who never aged would have time to learn plenty.

He smiled. "All there are—and none, I suppose, when it comes down to it. We Elder Folk—fauns, fairies, all the people of the deep woods, sea, and earth—we're not children of Babel, like you. Language is not something we learn. Meaning in words is another thing we see and hear, like bark or moss or birdsong."

"But . . . what you wrote—" I pointed at the notebook. "That was our language, and that was R——'s. You translated his to ours. You said 'translated' yourself."

He shrugged and nodded. "Just as I know that when your grand-mother says 'We'll see' she typically means 'Yes, eventually.' That's translating, isn't it?"

I couldn't help laughing. "So . . . there are others?" I asked carefully, watching him. I didn't want to make him sad if all the Elder Folk had gone from the world, as Grandmother suspected.

"Others of the Old Kind?" He wore again the expression that was both sorrowful and happy. "Oh, yes, there are many others— Folk of so many kinds they can't all be counted."

I was relieved. "Grandmother said there weren't so many left anymore."

Mr. Girandole nodded slowly, looking far off. "That's true enough. Great numbers of them have gone back to where we came from. But they won't all go, as long as there are seasons here—as long as there are dawn and dusk, forests and caverns and flowers and mountains, stars and the moon and the sea—old, deep places and new places and edges to things. Some remain."

"Are all those things like where you came from?"

"Those things *are* where we came from. It's not really a different place—not *there* and *here*." He looked apologetic. "I suppose it doesn't make sense, the way I say it."

I shrugged. "It makes sense to me." It was one of those things I grasped on a deep level, with my heart rather than my mind. It has rung truer to me with every passing year: that the essence of Faery is all around us, written in every leaf.

He regarded me strangely then and looked happier.

But remembering the other part of my errand, I asked if there was anything Mr. Girandole needed.

He appeared to force his thoughts back to the situation. "I've already fetched clean water, so for the present, no. I believe M—— mentioned clean bandages. If you can, come back with her early tomorrow. I would risk coming to your cottage tonight, but I'd have to shut R—— inside the secret space. If he woke up, he'd think he was inside his own grave, buried alive."

"We'll come early." I wanted to commend Mr. Girandole for the tremendous job he was doing of caring for R——. But I only managed a shy smile and a murmured "Thanks."

Mr. Girandole reminded me of my papa in his kindness, in the warm, gentle approval he exuded—approval for those closest to him. I wondered suddenly if he and my father had been friends— surely they'd met when my papa was a boy, exploring the woods. I wished my father could come to the village again, with my mother and sister. I dreamed of what it could be like when the war was over, when we might all visit Grandmother and sit here among the statues in the quiet green light.

Since I still had ample daylight, I decided to explore the part of the garden I hadn't seen yet: the upper reaches, beyond the dense thicket at the tower's back. When I announced my intention, Mr. Girandole asked if I wanted him to come along.

I shrugged. "Only if you'd like to," I said, not wishing to seem either scared or rude.

He smiled, folding his arms across his chest. "Perhaps the garden is best experienced alone. I'm here within shouting distance if you need me." Settling on his haunches to lean against the wall, he added, "You realize, I suppose, what a rare gift is yours today?"

I wondered what he meant.

"The gift of seeing the other half of the garden for the very first time. These next few moments will come to you but once in your life. Use the gift well."

I nodded slowly. Truth be told, I often had similar thoughts about other things. Sitting in the top of a certain tree, or watching fireflies in the dusk of a particular summer day, I'd grow sad at the realization that the precise moment would never come again: even if I climbed the tree again or stood in the dusk the next day, I'd be older; the world would be different.

"Don't go with a heavy heart," Mr. Girandole called after me. "There are always other moments coming."

I grinned back. Without the belief in more moments to come, we could never enjoy anything.

I descended the bizarre stairs, stood with relief on the terrace, and made my way down to the floor of the glade. The earth was green and springy underfoot, and the richness of late afternoon light, though indirect, filled the garden. Birds twittered—sometimes the sacred silence of the woods was not silence at all, yet it was soothing.

Again, somewhere a plane droned, so far away I could not discern if it was friendly or otherwise. Of course, as Grandmother said, such distinctions lost their meanings here. I was hearing in the far-off engine the merest rumor of some other world, no more present than the other world of which seashells tell us when we press them to our ears.

First I passed, on my right, the fearsome angel I'd seen from the terrace. Still he stood in deep shade, his stone blacker than that of the other statues, his hair and robes still blown wild by an unfelt wind. Still he held the ring of keys and the mighty chain.

I wondered then at the presence of angel statues here. In the churches, there were angels and saints. This garden held angels, monsters, gods, mermaids . . . all the folk of the old stories. I knew angels to be real; they were in the Bible. And now I knew fauns were real, for one was our friend. The only logical, obvious conclusion excited me. Monsters and fairies were a part of the same world as angels. All these things were real.

Immediately behind the angel's spreading wings the grove began, a stand of huge, ancient trees rising from an impenetrable nest of bushes. More trees and brush stretched to my left, climbing the wall of the ravine and away to where, in the upper forest, the parachute hung. The single opening in this green wall lay straight ahead, framed by a vine-draped arch.

Holding my breath, I hurried quietly past the angel and through the portal. The ground rose, crossed by exposed roots that formed a natural stairway.

I came into a second clearing, this one, too, roofed over by the limbs and leaves—the other grand gallery. On the west was a gentle slope by which I might have gone back up into the forest. Forward, the ravine ended in steep walls, thickly wooded and over-grown. Eastward, the open glade followed the upper edge of the dense central grove that I'd climbed past.

Just beside me, on the left at the root-stair's top, was what seemed at first to be a stone coffin: a rectangular slab, and lying flat upon it, the sculpted image of a woman sleeping or dead. She wore a long dress that left only her face, hands, and feet exposed. Her hair flowed down to her waist, and her arms were folded over her heart.

I walked all around her, deciding I preferred the idea that she was asleep, not dead. She was larger than life, about the height of a tall man. I found on one corner of the slab a cigarette-end that one of the soldiers must have left where he mashed it out. I remembered the major talking about the statues, and that he'd spoken of them to others beyond the village. This was how *others* treated the woods. I stuck the acrid-smelling end into my pocket, determined to throw it away somewhere far from the grove.

As I stooped, studying the slab, I discovered carved letters on the vertical edge. The language was that of our country but in a very old style, so that I had trouble reading it. Part of it, I thought, said *like the rain.* Now I wished I'd asked Mr. Girandole to accompany me. But with an inward smile, I reminded myself there would be plenty of time to ask about it later: it was a sentence carved in stone and wasn't going anywhere.

North of the sleeping woman, a magnificent centaur stood beneath a tree, looking just like the best pictures of centaurs. He appeared wise and dextrous, playing an instrument like a harp. Now that I was searching for inscriptions, sure enough, I saw one on his pedestal. I could make it out a little better than the other: *Hurry now to find me,* then something obscured by moss, and then: *but not inside.*

I backed away, pondering, and turned in a complete circle. So, the garden was full of words as well as creatures—dreams and riddles. . . . Though I wanted to race ahead, I forced myself to go slowly, to look in all directions, to notice how the light fell. These moments would come but once.

Not far from the centaur, a second angel waited near the ravine's end. This Heavenly messenger didn't frighten me in the least. He held his hands up, palms forward, before his shoulders, like Gabriel making his announcement to Mary. But his inscription, cryptically, said, *I am it is very true.*

I probed all around his base, wondering if I'd missed something. Surely there was more to the sentence. I am *what?* But there was no more, only smooth stone. I passed my fingers over his sleeve. Even in its weathered state, the craftsmanship was evident; when new, the stone must have seemed as soft and rippling as cloth. *I am,* the angel asserted; *it is very true.* I found this angel comforting, as were the words to my imagination. "You *all* are," I whispered to the entire garden. "It is very true."

Turning then, I crossed back to the thicket, drawn toward the space where another statue should fit, though at first I made out only rampant foliage. As I drew very near to the wall of trees, I stopped short, my scalp prickling. A huge beast was hidden there as if about to pounce on me—yes, only another statue; but it was the image of a monstrous bear—now I saw it clearly, buried under the thorns, the base beneath its paws completely obscured. Its stone eyes peered out from the shadows of leaves, its broad head higher than mine.

Mr. Girandole had kept the main gates and pathways clear of vegetation, and I suspected he'd pulled vines off some of the statues, too. Had he let this bear be covered over because it frightened him?

As I stood quivering before the bear, a memory filled my mind, dark and chilly as an unwelcome cloud shadow.

The bear prowled in my dreams. The bear could come into any dream, always when least expected. It didn't need a forest; it didn't need the dark to hide in. I could be in a sunny room, playing with my soldiers or building a block tower, and I could hear the bear breathing. I could hear the scratch of its claws outside the window, where the curtains fluttered. I could hear the ponderous thudding of its paws in the hallway, creaking the boards. Behind the murmur of traffic or voices, I could hear it grunt. No one else in the dream heard it. Only me.

I screamed, springing up in terror, the bedcovers bunched at my throat.

The bear waited, somewhere nearby.

My mother would turn on the light. She would rock me and sit beside me and stroke my hair. She would sing softly. The bear padded away, but it was only biding its time.

My father said there were good policemen in dreams—so silent and watchful that I would never see or hear them, but they had rifles and would shoot any bear who came near me. I liked the idea, but I knew he was only saying it to make me feel better. The bear came close all the time, and no unseen policemen ever shot it.

One day when I was five, I found that the bear was not confined to dreams. I was wide awake, looking out of the back window on a dim, blustery day, and somehow—by the strange light, by the gusting, twisty wind—I knew the bear had come. It was out there, behind the fence of our narrow city yard, behind the pickets with their rusty nails, behind the stack of bricks. It was beyond the edge of the window's frame with its globby white paint. It was hidden by the curtains my mother had sewn, printed with clusters of grapes, apples, and pears. I couldn't move, couldn't look away from the window or call to my mother, because if I did, the bear would be in the house, just beyond the kitchen arch by the tall mirror. Its enormous body would fill the hallway. I could smell the bear. With that musk filling my senses, my eyesight shimmered as if everything were electric and sparking. I remember the fruit on the curtains fading to gray.

I woke up in my bed, my mother wiping my forehead and cheeks with a cold, wet cloth. My head ached; my stomach roiled. I had influenza and was in bed for two endless days and nights, unable to keep even water down. Whenever I tried to sip the water I wanted so desperately, I would have relief for a few minutes, then vomit into a pan while my mother rubbed my back, my nose searing, my body racked with sobs. She read me fairy tales, as many as I wanted to hear. I wept, so grateful that she was beside me. When he was home from work, my papa sat with me too.

I dreamed of the bear only once or twice after that. The last time, there was fire, a blaze like the heart of a furnace that was destroying everything around me. The bear stood in the midst of the fire, its fur smoking and reeking, its flesh burning. It snarled at me, its face oozing blood from many slashes, as if someone had attacked it with a knife. Maybe one of my father's policemen had tried to protect me.

In the sacred woods, my heart raced at the memory. With an effort, I shook it away and moved on, aware that the sun was lowering. I had not dreamed of the bear or felt its presence for a long time, and I did not want to think about it now. I did not want it ever to come back.

Past the angel, in a narrow gap among the trees on the steep north wall, a stairway appeared to climb up and out of the garden. I saw a hill high above, toward which the stairs ascended—a grassy rise in full sunlight.

Leaving the stairs for another day, I pushed on eastward.

Slowly, in the deepening shadows of late afternoon, a dark cliff took shape ahead. After a few cautious steps, I halted and stared.

An enormous face glowered from the rock wall. Beneath a wrinkled, furious brow, its eyes were empty pits. Nostrils flared in a broad nose, and its screaming mouth was a cave, a portal into blackness—the top lined with teeth.

The face seemed more monstrous than human, with protrusions atop that might have been ears or horns and a twisting fringe that suggested a beard or a lion's mane. A young birch had grown up beside the jaw, passing close to one eye like a wayward strand of hair. The whole terrifying visage was mottled black and gray from centuries of weather.

I crept nearer, fascinated. Never had I seen anything at once so horrible and so delightful. Hardly daring to breathe, I tiptoed up the weed-choked steps to the yawning mouth—and nearly yelled when a bird emerged from one of the eyes in a burst of wing beats.

The mouth was indeed the doorway into a single room. Rough-hewn, dank, and littered with leaves, the chamber held a stone table and benches—a picnic table, it seemed, housed inside a shrieking head. I glimpsed on the back wall a carving of angels, but I didn't look closely. It was time to head homeward.

I retreated from the cave, all the way to the bottom of the steps, and checked my surroundings to be sure I was alone. The great central thicket filled the entire view southwestward. For a moment, I thought I saw another stone object there among the giant trees—a soaring pillar wrapped in vines. But it was only a dead tree trunk, the bleached wood resembling stone.

Past the cave, the glade continued to curve, leading around the end of the central thicket and down a slope toward another arch like the one I'd come through. Far beyond it I saw Heracles towering over the bushes, so I knew the path would take me down to the lower garden once more.

As I went, a wall of rounded stones ran beside me on the left, reaching up to about the height of my elbows. Looking over its top, to where another gradual rise left the ravine, I saw her at last: the mermaid. Years ago, Grandmother had come upon her from behind, wandering down the slope I now faced, its branch-strewn ground dappled with golden patches of sun. But I was face to face with her. She wore a tranquil expression beneath plaits of curly hair. Down to the waist she was a woman, but from there, two scaly fish's tails stretched off along the ground in opposite directions, almost like impossibly long legs ending in graceful crescents.

Hurrying now, I passed beneath the arch into the lower garden, found myself back at the tortoise and the elephant, and turned west again to the leaning house.

On the way there, I discovered one more pedestal in the gloom of the thicket's edge. It was just a base; the statue that had stood there was gone, broken in some former time. Only feet remained— exquisitely carved feet in sandals. I wondered if the fallen statue might lie among the trees and bushes behind the pedestal; a cursory glance showed me nothing, but there wasn't time for a proper search. The pedestal's engraving said, *Behold in me.*

I sighed in frustration, thinking that without the statue that had stood here, some vital piece of the garden's puzzle might be lost.

I'd intended to call up to Mr. Girandole that I was going, but he was already looking out from the upper window. I had so many questions for him and Grandmother, but they would have to wait.

"You've seen it all now?" asked Mr. Girandole.

"Not all," I said, standing below the terrace. "I didn't go up the stairway to the hilltop."

"Ah. Then you have something more yet to see."

"I have to go now," I said. "Are you sure you don't need anything?"

He grinned, resting his arms on the sill. "Only the things M——is bound to think of."

On the walk back to Grandmother's cottage, I decided that I would keep a notebook about the sacred woods. As Grandmother advised, I would include nothing about Mr. Girandole or R——, but I'd write down every inscription from every statue, getting Grandmother and Mr. Girandole to help me read all the words. Maybe I would try sketching more of the statues. If there was sense to be made of it all, I wanted to try.

I also remembered the urgency in Mr. Girandole's face, and the fact that he had something to tell us.

I burst into the back garden, eager to tell Grandmother my news, but fortunately I looked before I blurted anything: Mrs. F——,

Grandmother's stern next-door neighbor, had dropped by. She and Grandmother sat on the bench under the trellis, framed by myrtle and fuchsia, like ladies in a painting. The teapot, cups, and crackers were arranged on a little folding table.

Mrs. F——, whose hair was straight, white, and cropped like a helmet, looked me up and down and asked if I'd been playing in the woods. I was sure Grandmother had already told her so, but apparently Mrs. F—— wanted to hear it from my own lips.

"Yes, ma'am," I answered.

Mrs. F—— twisted her mouth and looked reproachfully from me to Grandmother, as if I'd confessed to a crime.

"He knows not to go far," Grandmother offered.

"It's not a question of *far*," said Mrs. F——. "You don't have to go far into the ocean to drown."

Apparently, Mrs. F—— didn't like either the forest *or* the sea.

"It's no good being afraid of everything," said Grandmother mildly, with a smile in her voice.

"Fish get into nets whether they're afraid of swimming or not," said Mrs. F——. I wondered if it was a proverb, like one of Mrs. D——'s. In the village, people didn't need much more than proverbs to talk.

Grandmother said nothing but poured Mrs. F—— another cup of tea.

Mrs. F—— abandoned the subject; she'd lived next to Grandmother for a long time and evidently knew she was wasting her breath. "Well, we have different ideas about raising them, but yours is safely grown and out of the nest, and so are mine. We've been blessed."

Grandmother smiled and agreed.

*　　*　　*　　*

When Mrs. F—— had finally gone, I asked Grandmother why she'd come over.

"Being neighborly," she said. "You have to pay a visit when someone's garden is in full bloom. She was impressed with the window-boxes especially."

"Will we have to pay her a visit?"

"Not immediately, because she was just here. But we'll have others dropping by soon, and I'll have to do a bit of visiting myself. Which reminds me—we should go to the bakery." I knew she meant that we'd need ample cookies and crackers to accompany the tea we served.

She looked expectantly at me, and I made my report. Grandmother was relieved that our patient was alive, and that Mr. Girandole was managing so admirably. As I helped her get supper ready, I asked her if she knew about the words carved into the pedestals.

"Yes," she said, stirring the soup. "I told you the grove was a riddle in stone. I've read all those words, at one time or another— or most of them, anyway."

"Do they make any sense?"

She shook her head, curling her lower lip. "The more you puzzle over them, the more frustrating they seem. It's quite possible they don't have meanings at all."

"No meanings?" I stopped rinsing lettuce to cock my head. "Then why put them there?"

Grandmother carried the steaming pot to the table. "The old duke was quite a trickster. Why build a house that leans like that? Why put a picnic table inside a screaming mouth? I think he may have simply laughed himself sore over people wandering through that garden, scratching their heads."

I considered the idea. The words inside the leaning house said, *Reason departs.* I had to allow that everything might be nonsense, but that didn't ring true to me. I suppose I wanted to believe there were meanings . . . or rather, one meaning to the garden as a whole—a puzzle with a solution. If I'd built such a grove of monsters, I'd have put a meaning there and given a reward to anyone who could discover it.

"It's full of mischief," Grandmother went on. "Take the mermaid—did you notice that she's a perfect mirror of herself? If you imagine a line dividing her in half, you'll see that everything on the left is also on the right, exactly reversed—every ringlet of hair, the positions of her arms, every scale on her tails."

I told Grandmother that I wanted to make a notebook on the garden. She nodded. "I have a blank one you can use. Just don't put in anything incriminating. Protect the guilty, you know." Then, in a matter-of-fact tone, she added something that nearly made me drop a handful of silverware: "It's too bad we don't have the one your father kept when he was a boy. I wonder if he still has it . . ."

"He wrote down things about the garden too?"

"Oh, yes. I remember how excited he'd be to show me new things he'd found and copied. Sometimes, he'd need me to help him read them. He had some grand theories for what it all meant—buried treasures, magic swords . . ." She laughed softly, turned to the window, and looked out of it for a very long time.

I frowned, watching her stiff back.

When she spoke again, her voice seemed on the edge of tears—a sound I'd never heard from her before, and it surprised me.

"He so much wanted me to come with him so that he could show me the monsters. I told him I'd seen them, that it was his time to be seeing them now, and that the garden was his special place—a place only for children. Quite the opposite of what Mrs. F—— says about the woods, isn't it?"

I nodded, though Grandmother couldn't see me nodding. When Papa was a boy, she couldn't go with him to the garden; the sacred woods were Mr. Girandole's home, and Grandmother had left it and gotten married. For Mr. Girandole's sake and for her own, she could never set foot there.

There was something else I'd wondered about, and the truth surprised me. "So, Papa never met Mr. Girandole—not even in the garden?"

"No. And that's how I learned just how strong and noble Girandole is. If Girandole had befriended my son, he could have kept a part of me. He could have had constant news—could have even sent me messages. But that wouldn't have been the proper thing. It would have brought more hurt than comfort, and undone all that he wanted for me. He chose only to watch."

A small part of me was excited and proud that I knew Mr. Girandole when my father did not—when my father did not even have proof that fauns existed. But mostly, it made me sorry. All the more, I wanted Papa to come here; I wanted to introduce the two.

Grandmother crossed her arms, and I thought I saw her wipe her eyes. "I never worried about your father when he played in the woods. With Girandole watching, I knew he was safer there than anywhere else in the world."

In another instant she turned, her strong self again, and declared that the soup was getting cold.

"I wish we could live all our lives in the garden," I said, wandering over to my chair. I was thinking that there was no school in the woods, no Mondays, no alarm clocks, and certainly no war—only the green, ancient light and stories in wood and stone.

"Well, we can't," said Grandmother. "But remember this"—she pointed a spoon at me and shook it for emphasis—"there's pain, and there's misery. We can't avoid pain, but misery is always a choice."

After we'd eaten supper and washed the dishes, Grandmother found me the blank notebook she'd had tucked away in her desk. It had a beautiful cover of dusky blue cloth and a long ribbon for a place-marker, attached to the binding. The cream-colored pages were of the perfect size: big enough that I could fit a lot onto them but small enough that the book was easy to carry.

"My name and address are written inside the cover," Grandmother said. "I hope you don't mind."

"I don't mind. It's wonderful—are you sure I can have it?"

She nodded. "It's begging to be yours. I heard it begging at night and wondered what the noise was. That will be a happy notebook now; they're meant to be used, you know. I think I bought it once when I got it in my head to start a diary, but—" She waved a hand in dismissal. "I'd rather do the living than write about it."

"Thank you," I said.

"You're welcome. I can even help you start it properly." She unfolded a paper and spread it out for me on the tabletop. It was old and yellowed, and I assumed she'd dug it out of her desk, too.

The sky was dark enough now that we needed the lamp. I saw that the paper had just a single sentence written on it in Grandmother's writing, near the top. It was in the language of four centuries ago—the language of the garden. I could decipher a lot of it, but not everything.

"It's from the grove," said Grandmother. "Remember we told you about the main entrance arch, south of the dragon and buried now in bushes and vines? I wouldn't care to try getting there any more, but these words are carved into the arch, under all those leaves and roots. It says, *You who enter this place, observe it piece by piece and tell me afterward whether so many marvels were created for deception or purely for art.*"

With the shadows playing over her face, Grandmother looked like an imp. Narrowing her eyes, she said, "Tell me. Deception or art?"

I propped my chin on my palms. "He doesn't even give us the choice that there's a meaning."

"No? That could be hidden in the 'deception,' couldn't it? All the nonsensical clues could be placed to trick us and lead us away from the meaning that's there if we don't give up. Or else . . . the duke might just be snickering up his sleeve. But I'll tell you a secret: this word 'deception' used to have another meaning besides the one we're left with today. It once also meant something like 'magic'—the power to perform wonders."

Hurrying to get my pencil, I asked if Grandmother had any of the other inscriptions written down.

"No," she said. "I don't even remember why I copied this one."

To keep myself busy that evening, I wrote a long letter to my parents, telling them all about the garden. Grandmother agreed that it would be safe enough now to go to the post office without much unwanted attention. I addressed the envelope to my mother and asked her in the letter to mail it on to my father when she'd read it. Of course, I said nothing about Mr. Girandole or our patient, R——. Before I finished, I read over the most recent letter from my mother, which I'd been answering in mine. As always, she'd asked some earnest questions: "Are you eating well? Are you getting along with Grandmother? What are you finding to do?" She also said that the people in my wooden castle were holding a jousting tournament, but that some of the knights were still away on their quests, and they were greatly missed.

I tapped my pencil on my chin, wondering how to answer. Mama wanted me to be well and comfortable, but I knew she'd be sad if I sounded like I was happier here than at home. I wrote, "Grandmother is very nice. I hope we can all visit her soon. I miss you and Papa. I'm eating very well, but I miss your tomato soup and the yellow sauce. Everything is clean, but the way we do the washing here, it all comes out stiffer." I reviewed the lines, nodding with satisfaction. I added, "And a little scratchy." Perfect.

Morning came, bright and clear, with a soft wind blowing off the sea. We started earlier than usual, loaded up the carpet bag, and took along the hatchet and ropes for more "gathering of firewood" if the situation demanded such. We saw no soldiers, though we didn't patrol the village.

Mr. Girandole met us at the first archway with the news that R—— was awake but of course still very weak. So, his wounds and our surgery hadn't killed him, but Grandmother said it came down now to his battle with infection. He really ought to be in a hospital, she said.

Instead of the stone house, Mr. Girandole led us to the pool of the four women with their water pitchers. He motioned us to sit on the lichen-covered edge. The stagnant water reflected the green canopy of leaves and branches above it. Insects skimmed over the water, leaving rings where they touched the surface.

It was awkward to sit with Grandmother between two life-size, unclothed women, two more looming behind us. My head kept wanting to turn. The glade was especially cool at this hour, before the day's heat warmed it. Traces of mist lingered, and the shadows were in blues and purples. We could easily see the leaning house, the elephant, sea serpent, boar, Neptune, and Heracles rising gigantic near the ravine's east wall. And away to our left, near the second arch, stood the terrible angel with the keys and chain.

"What is that?" I asked quietly, nodding toward the angel as Mr. Girandole propped one booted hoof on the pool's rim.

He looked over his shoulder to follow my gaze. "Apollyon," he said. "The Angel of the Bottomless Pit."

I shivered, only partly because of the morning's chill. Whatever the name meant, it was fitting.

"We're talking here so the man in the house won't hear us," Mr. Girandole explained. I saw that he'd brought R——'s notebook, which he opened and handed to Grandmother. As she read the translation of the poem R—— had written in his delirium, I opened my own notebook on my knees and copied it—the forward version for now: I could add the mirror-script later.

> A duke the secret knew
> And locked the riddle here
> Find twice the number Taurus follows with his eye
> Sisters dancing in the water and the sky

> Heed the words among the trees in stone
> Though not all words are true
> And they will lead you home

"Taurus. . . ." Grandmother said at last, rubbing her chin. "Taurus is the bull."

"There aren't any bull statues here," I said. "Are there?"

Mr. Girandole shook his head.

"'They will lead you home,'" Grandmother said, and looked at Mr. Girandole with a curious light in her eyes.

"The 'words among the trees in stone' can only refer to the inscriptions on the statues," Mr. Girandole said. "And the whole thing is clearly written about this garden—mention of the duke and all."

Grandmother nodded. "It would seem so . . . but how? How could a feverish man write a poem like this about a place he's never heard of?"

Mr. Girandole pushed his hat farther back and glanced at the leaning house. "That's what I wanted to tell you. He's been dreaming as he hung between life and death. And he speaks . . . Often, he speaks." Lowering his voice, Mr. Girandole hunched closer. "He has said names—names he could not possibly know, for they are written in no book, and no mortal ear has heard them."

"Names?" Grandmother whispered back.

"Names of fairies and fauns. People I know. Names of rivers and mountains in the land from which I came."

Grandmother watched him.

"Don't you see?" he asked. "Where departed souls go . . . Heaven, Hell, and Faery, my home—it's all one when you're through the Gates of Dawn—it all connects. R—— was there, on the edge of death—he was wandering in the mists—but he didn't go on. He came back."

"What do you mean?" Grandmother asked.

"For whatever the reason, he wasn't allowed to stay. It wasn't time for him to be there yet; I guess it means he has something yet to do here, in this world. This poem came back with him. It was *sent* with him."

"A message?"

Mr. Girandole nodded. "It's not easy anymore to find doors between here and Faery, although once they were everywhere. Even when I still lived there, the two worlds were growing farther apart. Doors were vanishing."

"I think you've told me that," Grandmother said. "It's why you can't go home to your people."

"But you see, sometimes doors can still be discovered." Mr. Girandole turned his hat between his hands, thinking. "Now and then, a mortal on this side stumbles upon a fragment of the ancient wisdom in very old writings or through a knowledge of the stars. We know that our duke was intrigued by alchemy—you've told me so, M——. He may have found a secret in some musty book or scroll."

Alchemy. Magic . . . "deception" . . . the power to perform wonders.

Grandmother spoke in a hush. "A doorway into your world?"

"A doorway that can still open, though it would be hidden well and probably locked."

"But not the doorway you and the other fauns used before?" she asked. "You would remember that."

"No," he said. "We didn't use a doorway as such—we came to

these woods in a dawn mist that made this world one with ours, when such things used to happen. If there's a door here in the garden, we never knew it. When the fauns left, I'm sure they were following the Piper; the music of the pipes was their way home."

"Won't the Piper call you someday?" I asked in a shaky voice.

Mr. Girandole touched the notebook, still open in Grandmother's lap. "In this, I think perhaps he is. Do you see? *My people might know there's a door here.* They might have sent this message to help me find it."

"But I don't understand," I said, thinking of R———'s poem. "If the fauns know about the door, why do they send hints? Why don't they just come through it and lead you home?"

Mr. Girandole smiled vaguely. "The poem didn't come from the fauns. This is quite beyond them, sending words and dreams from one world to another. It must be the work of the Green Lord and the Lady of the Stars, who rule over Faery."

"Well, whoever sent it," I said, "if they really want to help, why don't they just tell us straight?"

Before Mr. Girandole could answer, Grandmother laughed and said, "Nature abhors a straight line."

The faun smiled. "And a gardener abhors a straight path. It may be a test for me. I am in exile by my own choice. The Lord and Lady may have determined that if I want to come back, I must solve the duke's puzzle. A mortal's game, since I cast my lot with mortals."

Grandmother swallowed. "Then we must solve this garden's puzzle. We must get you home."

"But—" Mr. Girandole said. Despite the darkness of his skin, he looked pale.

"No buts. Girandole, I'm an old woman. Do you love this place so much that you want to stay here forever, waiting for other kindred souls to find the garden after you've buried me?"

"Most definitely not," he said.

"Then if what you say is true, this is a gift to us both—the way we can be together." Glancing at me, she added, "All of us. For *more* than a handful of years." She turned back to Mr. Girandole and took his arm. "We humans don't need magical doorways; we go there anyway, when it's time. You're the one who isn't built to die, poor thing."

Mr. Girandole seemed at a loss for words. The turn this conversation had taken scared me—Grandmother dying of old age . . . Mr. Girandole going away through a magic door. The appeal of answering the grove's riddle was swiftly dissolving.

Grandmother patted my back. "There's nothing to be sad about," she said. "If that door really leads to what's beyond this life, then the paths will join up on the other side."

I was baffled. "Heaven, Hell, and Faery are all the *same?*" How could so many disparate things be one?

Mr. Girandole gripped my shoulder, his expression rueful and kind. "You can't begin to understand it from this side. The way there looks the same, but there are choices among the paths— paths that we're walking on even now, paths that your great-great-grandparents walked. And they go on beyond. You have farther to travel, even after you leave here. It truly is a garden, all of this. Hell is where truly dead things go. But your grandmother is right. We can all be together where things live and bloom."

I could see something in his eyes that made me feel light inside—a wondering hope, as if he'd just awoken after a long sleep, as if he'd gazed at a marvelous, glowing eastern sky.

"The journey *does* end," said Grandmother, nudging him. "We do get there, don't we, in a little while?"

Eyes brimming, he nodded.

Grandmother eyed the leaning house with a growl of disdain. Then, heaving a sigh, she ordered Mr. Girandole and me to stay close behind her on the stairs and catch her if she toppled backward. "And don't fall yourselves," she added. "A sorry state that would be, if we all ended up in a broken heap."

We kept ourselves well braced. I carried the carpet bag, and on the second step, Grandmother thrust her walking-stick into my hands and said, "Here's your stick." She went on hands and knees, with Mr. Girandole pushing, and eventually we reached the house's upper chamber.

In the sunken compartment, R—— had his head raised, as if he'd been alarmed at what sort of grunting, puffing beast might be pawing its way up the stairs.

"Good morning," said Grandmother briskly, snatching her stick back.

"Good morning," the pilot answered hoarsely, letting his head fall onto the pallet again. He looked haggard, but the slick pallor was gone from his skin. "I . . . memory you," he said. "I hear what you do . . . thank you. You save me. Thank you."

"You aren't saved yet," said Grandmother, crouching on the well's edge to study him. "How do you feel?"

"Hurt all. Sick like dog."

Grandmother motioned that we should climb into the well and lift her down, which we did. It wasn't hard with one of us on either side.

We crowded around R—— and looked him over. Dried blood

caked the bandages. Grandmother set about clipping them with her shears and gingerly peeling them loose. The pallet was stained and smelled of sweat.

"You've kept him clean, anyway," Grandmother noted. "Is the water in this bucket fresh?"

"I brought it at dawn," said Mr. Girandole.

Lifting his good arm, R—— ran a hand through his matted, thinning hair. His neck and jaw sprouted golden beard stubble, like my father got when he was on holidays. The pilot grinned at me. "You name?"

I told him my name, and he introduced himself, apparently not remembering that he'd done so before.

"You old how many?"

I told him I was nine, and he nodded.

"You no goat people?"

Grandmother glanced at Mr. Girandole, who had been R——'s only nursemaid since he woke up. "No," she said. "We're *people* people."

"Good you here. Mr. Satyr no like me."

"I'd like you better if you'd stop calling me a satyr," said Mr. Girandole. "I've told you I'm a faun. Satyrs are a vulgar folk. You won't see me guzzling wine by the skinful."

Grandmother cocked an eyebrow at him.

"Not by the skinful," he said.

"And woman?" R—— grinned waggishly. "You run catch woman?"

"Mind your own business," said Mr. Girandole. "And mind the company."

"What about you, R——?" Grandmother asked, dampening a rag to clean the wounds. "Do you run and catch women? Do you have a family?"

"Father have. Mother die. Two sister. Brother die. Wife go other man. Take child."

"I'm sorry about that," Grandmother said.

I didn't quite follow who was alive and who was dead, but it sounded as if R—— didn't have much of a family left.

Grandmother had brought along a clean, raggedy sheet. She cut strips from it to make new bandages.

"I already die?" asked R——, looking at the ceiling.

"Well, you're clearly not in Heaven," said Grandmother, "or you wouldn't be in pain. And if you were in Hell, we wouldn't be help-ing you. So, I'm afraid you're stuck in the same old world."

R—— blinked a few times. "But this house . . . funny."

"Yes, it most certainly is funny. That's not part of your fever. You're in the forest near the village of ——, which means you're well behind enemy lines."

R——'s gaze focused on her. "But . . . you help me."

"I'm not sure if what we're doing is helping you at all. I'll say again: you should have a doctor and medicine if you want to live."

"Madam Grandma." R——'s hand found Grandmother's wrist. "No doctor. Live, die—no distance."

"No *difference*?" Grandmother asked.

"Yes." R—— seemed to be looking beyond the stone walls. "The flute. They dance and sing. Better there, not back. Not go back." His hand dropped to his side, as if he'd exhausted himself.

"This is the way he talks," said Mr. Girandole. "He's been to the edge of Faery, and he'd rather be there than back in his own country, or fighting a war."

"H'm," said Grandmother.

I helped hold the sheet so she could cut it more easily.

"You wrote this," said Mr. Girandole, showing R—— the poem he'd written in the notebook.

R——'s eyes widened, and he brushed his fingers over the page.

Mr. Girandole held the book steady for him. "What does it mean to you?"

"Many man with goat foots . . . like you. Many man, woman, faces like sun, stars."

Mr. Girandole exchanged a look with Grandmother. "Why did you write the lines backward?" he asked R——.

"I write? Not remember."

It was difficult to imagine what a doctor could have provided that Grandmother did not. She made R—— swallow pills and tonics. She bathed his wounds in disinfectant, re-bandaged them, and had us help her pull the dirty canvas out from under him and replace it with what was left of the clean sheet. When all the boughs and leaves were stuffed into the pallet again, she announced that she had to get out of this leaning place. Before we helped her down the stairs, she told me to unpack the food we'd brought.

"We're out of milk," she said. "We'll have to buy more."

R—— asked for his notebook, and Mr. Girandole returned it with apparent reluctance. He also helped R—— relocate the stubby pencil. Grandmother said that was a good idea, that maybe the fairies would send another message.

"You have gun?"

Grandmother shook her head. "No one has it. It's at the bottom of the sea."

Someday it will be inside a giant pearl, I added silently, remembering the mer-folk.

The pilot blinked and squinted. "How get there?!"

"I put it there," she said.

R—— looked regretful. "Good gun, was."

I spent the rest of the morning in the grove, running from statue to statue, hunting for the inscriptions and copying them into my notebook. When moss covered parts of the words, I scraped it carefully away.

Grandmother took a nap on one of the benches outside the stone house, using the carpet bag as a pillow. While we were there to keep an eye on the patient, Mr. Girandole made a trip to his own home high on the mountain. He brought back some herbs and roots and cooking ware, and he delivered to R—— a drab green shirt and a brown pair of trousers. Going a ways off into the woods, he built a campfire and made a pot of stew with a rabbit he'd caught. He also burned up the dirty bandages and R——'s original shirt, pants, and gun holster.

We regrouped for a late lunch on the terrace. Mr. Girandole took stew and tea up to R—— and helped him eat. Then he and Grandmother explained difficult words for me, and we all read through the lines I'd found. In two cases, Grandmother and Mr. Girandole remembered a phrase differently from the way I'd written it, and I went back to the statue to check; once they were right, and once I was. It perplexed me that some of the inscriptions were not even complete thoughts. One gave me the impression that the engraver had grown bored and walked away, leaving the job unfinished; in other instances, he seemed to have begun carving in the middle of an idea. Grandmother wondered if they might be phrases copied or paraphrased from literature.

"It would be like the duke to paraphrase the classics for his own purposes," Mr. Girandole said, "which would make it harder to identify the originals."

I barely knew what "the classics" were; Papa used the word to refer collectively to some dusty books with dark brown covers on our shelves. I admired their stately row and their scent, like a solid old wall back in the dimness, holding up a part of our house. I'd never tried to read them, but it didn't surprise me that Mr. Girandole seemed familiar with the great stories of our world.

I'd found ten different inscriptions:

My steps fall softly like the rain (from the sleeping woman)

Or a thousand cheeses times a thousand if you give me days enough (I found this concealed by bushes on the bear's pedestal; it had taken some courage to approach the bear again, but in the brightness of midday, I managed it. An inscription about cheeses certainly seemed to be nonsense.)

Hurry now to find me draw near but not inside (from the centaur)

I am it is very true (the comforting words from the announcing angel)

Round and round the dancers go and my answer is in three and seven (from the chamber inside the screaming mouth, where the letters stood above embossed angels on a dull metal plating)

The Mermaid (engraved on a slab before the mermaid)

There was no writing I could see anywhere around the tortoise.

> *Or walls or ivied garden porch or doorstep have we none*
> (written along the elephant's base)
> *Behold in me* (from the pedestal of the missing statue,
> of which only the sandaled feet were left) I searched
> in the bushes behind but found no fallen statue.

The wild boar had no letters. Perhaps non-mythical animals received no inscriptions, I thought at first—but no, the bear had his . . . as did the elephant.

> *You have we have all have though perhaps home* (from
> the pool of the four women)
> *Narrow* (This single word was carved on the high-
> arching back of Neptune's throne.) Intriguingly,
> this "Narrow" arced along the top edge of an
> accompanying illustration: in an elliptical frame
> on the chair's tall back, above Neptune's head, a
> weathered relief sculpture depicted a ship sailing
> between two cliffs. Atop one cliff was a monster with
> several dog-like heads and one head that seemed to
> be that of a human woman, but it was hard to see—
> the carving had lost much detail to the passing years.
> Grandmother, who'd joined me when she finished
> her nap, pointed out a whirlpool on the ship's other
> side. She explained that it was a picture of Odysseus
> and his crew sailing the narrow strait between the
> dangers of Scylla and Charybdis.

"That's a good morning's work," said Mr. Girandole, running a dusky finger down my page one final time.

"But I don't think they're all here," said Grandmother. "I seem to remember more."

I suddenly recalled the *Reason departs* from the leaning house and wrote it down.

"Yes," Mr. Girandole agreed, "there are probably a few more. For one thing, you haven't climbed that last stairway."

So I did that.

Grandmother returned to the cottage ahead of me; there was garden work that needed doing. I promised to come and help her as soon as I'd seen what was on the hilltop.

I followed the mossy steps upward at the north end of the ravine. Over the centuries, the elements had rounded their edges. Tendrils from the bushes crawled across the path, and I pushed through branches. I wondered if the stairway would make it all the way to the top, or if a wall of foliage would block my way. Insects whirred in the brush. A spray of blue wildflowers had blanketed the stairs in one place; I threaded cautiously through the patch so as not to damage them.

First, the stair climbed far to the right, and at its bend, I looked down the steep bank to the screaming mouth. Then the track switched back left. At the next turn, I was high above the announcing angel. Wandering back to the center, the steps emerged from the bushes and brought me to a grassy meadow on the brow of the hill in brilliant, warm sunlight.

The trees held their distance all around, their crowns still higher than the hill's summit. Bright butterflies floated over the green carpet, the grasses tasseled in gold and sprinkled with more wild blossoms, an artist's palette of colors. Straight before me, grand and gray, rose a many-pillared stone temple.

It reminded me of pictures of the Parthenon I'd seen in my mythology book, although this building was smaller and in better repair, with its walls and roof intact. People in airplanes would be able to see it if they looked carefully, I supposed, but the stone was so rimed by lichen and age, it would probably appear to them as no more than some decrepit and long-forgotten shed.

On the pediment above the columns, I found the words *I am a gate*. More accustomed to the antique mode of writing now, I was sure of the meaning. With excitement I copied the sentence and noted where in the garden it was from.

Was the doorway to the other world here, just beyond the columns? Surely, it couldn't be so simple. I waded through the grass, which reached to my knees, and climbed carefully up onto the slab. Deep coolness radiated from the interior. I tipped back my head, studying the relief carvings on the triangular pediment: men and women in flowing garments . . . and fauns! I counted at least a dozen fauns, some dancing, some playing harps or pipes.

I turned, wondering if any part of the garden was visible from this high place, but I saw only the rolling tops of the trees. Even giant Heracles was lost beneath them. Trees screened the entire village from my view, though I could see the ocean in the distance, dotted by tiny boats.

The temple had only a single chamber. Two more stone tables stood among the shadows, flanked by their benches. The cross of Christ was molded onto the back wall: a plain cross of cylindrical poles, though only the forward halves of these emerged from the wall. No figure of the Lord hung there. On the floor at its base were a prayer rail and a shelf for kneeling.

I crossed myself, as I'd been taught to do when entering a church, and then padded slowly from wall to wall, from front to back, examining every pillar and corner. I pushed on the walls, tapped on the floor, and searched for anything that might indicate a hidden doorway. The cross was perfectly solid, a three-dimensional extension of the wall. I found no other inscriptions, no images.

I shook my head. *I am a gate.* How? What gate? Where?

I walked out into the sunlight and sat on the edge of the porch. In the steamy weeds, two bees hummed around the tops of my shoes. This place felt good to me, with all its brightness and air, its cross, and its lack of anything fanciful or grotesque. Much as I loved the gardens below, it was fitting that the path through the grove ended here.

The hilltop temple was the only part of the garden that was not on a circular course. Everything below could be approached from a clockwise or counter-clockwise direction; but to get here, one had to depart from the circles and move along a line. The stairway, though it meandered, led only here; nor could I discover any other path descending into the forest.

I hurried down the steps, my mind racing ahead. I wanted to ask Mr. Girandole if he thought that the temple might conceal the magic doorway. I dashed out from between the bushes, jumped off the bottom step into the upper garden—and found myself face to face with two soldiers. I felt the blood drain from my face.

"Hold it, there!" one ordered me.

I froze in panic, realizing that I'd left the carpet bag, hatchet, and firewood bundle on the terrace of the leaning house, to pick up on my way home. None of these things were in the soldiers' hands, so perhaps they hadn't been there yet. The men held their rifles—not aimed at me but ready. They must have heard me trotting down the steps, stirring the bushes.

I tried not to look terrified. I held my pencil in my hand, the notebook under my arm.

The soldiers moved closer, looking stern. Both were young. The one speaking had sharp, angry-looking features. "What are you doing?" he demanded.

"Playing," I said. "I went up there."

"What have you got there? Show it to me."

Having no choice, I handed over the notebook. Like a fool, I showed them the pencil, too, but they weren't interested in that.

They slung their rifles onto their shoulders, but the quiet one kept a close eye on me while the other opened the notebook.

I'd copied out R——'s poem, but I hadn't labeled it.

"What is this?" asked the soldier, turning a page and frowning at what he saw.

"The g-garden. I wrote down the words from the statues."

"Why?" he asked, looking at me.

"I . . . I like the monsters."

"'A duke the secret knew'—what's this poem?"

I took a breath. "My grandmother and I wrote it. We like to write things about the woods."

"Is this your grandmother, M—— T——?" He was looking at the name and address inside the cover.

I told him yes and explained how I was staying with her. He passed the notebook to the other man.

The second soldier flipped through the pages and looked up. "Is this for school?"

"No, sir," I said. "School's out for the summer." It might be out for longer than that, the way things were going in the city.

My stomach squirmed as I thought of the carpet bag. It was full of empty tins and dirty dishes to be taken home and washed. That wasn't bad—I could say we'd had a picnic. It held the kitchen shears. But far worse, I couldn't remember what Grandmother had done with the bottles of medicine. Had she left them in the leaning house, or . . . ?

"Are you out here by yourself?"

I nodded. "My grandmother was here earlier, but she went home first."

"All right. Now, listen: you can't be up here. It's dangerous. You tell your grandmother that."

"Yes, sir."

"We're putting you on report," the soldier said. "You tell your grandmother that, too. Do you understand?"

I said that I did.

The second man looked at the first and held up my notebook. "Are we taking this?"

The first soldier considered. "No. He can keep it." To me, he added, "Go home now. And I mean it. Don't come up here again."

I accepted my notebook, skittered past the two men, and ran for the archway. If I could get far enough ahead of them, I hoped to scoop up my things from the terrace before the soldiers had a chance to find them. I kept listening as I went, though, and I just barely heard the first man say, "Let's take a look up there."

Good. They were going up to the temple. That bought me some

time. I raced past the bear and the sleeping woman, through the arch, and past the Angel of the Bottomless Pit. This time, I had the presence of mind to look around. Seeing no one in the lower glade, I galloped up the steps to the foot of the leaning house.

I skidded to a halt, my eyes widening. My bundle, hatchet, and the carpet bag were gone. I looked under the benches—nothing.

Panic rising again in my chest, I glanced over the rail at the green shadows all around. There must have been more soldiers. I imagined them fanning out, doing a sweep of the grove, and two had found me. The carpet bag was likely on its way to the major right now.

Thinking I'd better warn Mr. Girandole, I was just about to duck into the house when something small and hard tapped me on the head.

An acorn—I saw it roll across the stones at my feet.

Looking up, I saw Mr. Girandole: not in the window, but on the roof. The sight of him brought some relief. "Are you all right?" he whispered.

I nodded.

"Your bag is inside, hidden," he breathed. "Soldiers in the upper garden." He waved me away. "You'd better go."

With a wave, I was off at a run, overwhelmed with thankfulness for Mr. Girandole's acute hearing. When he'd first heard the patrol coming, he'd popped down to the terrace, retrieved what I'd carelessly left there, and locked it all away with R—— in the secret compartment.

My knees felt like water. I'd have to be a lot more careful from now on.

* * * *

I had to sit through the second half of a neighborly visit from Mrs. D——, and it became clear to me that Mrs. D—— had harbored no intention of leaving until she'd seen me return alive from the woods. She didn't approve of my forays there any more than Mrs. F—— did, but Mrs. D—— also seemed to be a little in awe and kept comparing me to Papa regarding my bravery and my handsome looks. At last, she went on her way, and if Grandmother might never truly forgive her for finding out about the setcreasea and fuchsia through legerdemain, at least she praised the garden so highly that Grandmother later said, "I wonder what enthusiasm she has left for the gardens of Paradise."

I told Grandmother about the soldiers as we weeded, with millipedes and grasshoppers darting away from our fingers.

"You had a close call," she said. "Thank Heaven for Girandole. No harm was done. And this is the best kind of work to calm you down."

"We're on report," I reminded her.

"I think we'll survive that," she said, pulling up a long root. She looked sidelong at me. "You told them we wrote that poem?"

"Camouflage," I said sheepishly, and focused on weeding.

Before the post office closed, I trotted there with the letter I'd written to my parents and mailed it. I didn't see any soldiers along the route. At first, I was afraid the building was closed, because the front window was covered by plywood. The postmaster looked tired, but he was glad to see me and inquired after Grandmother.

"Have you been well?" I asked, thinking he actually looked haggard.

"Spry as salt, Boss," he said, reverting to his old nickname for me. Oddly, I felt somehow as if I'd lost ground, as if we were no longer as close. I couldn't explain it, and we only exchanged a few words.

Still, I remarked to Grandmother about how strangely he'd acted.

"I'm sure this hasn't been a good time for Mr. V——," she said, chopping an onion. That was the postmaster's name. "The Army all over the village."

"Why bad for him?"

She sighed. "He was the mayor before. The other party. He was lucky to keep his job at the post office when things changed—lucky not to have gone to prison. We all stood up for him. Mrs. F——'s husband in particular, God rest him. I wrote some letters myself . . . well, we're all fortunate, I guess, that things are no worse. I expect the major has made the last several days very unpleasant for him."

I felt sorry for Mr. V—— and disliked the major all the more.

Just before sunset, several trucks rolled down the street. Grandmother and I were finishing supper at the garden table, and she sent me around the house to see what I could see. I reached the corner just in time to glimpse the Army staff car passing. I supposed Major P—— was inside it. The trucks, I could see, were full of soldiers, and they were heading out of the village; I noticed which way they turned at the big road.

"That many of them leaving. I think they've called off the search," Grandmother said. "We're left to fend for ourselves against the enemy."

"Do you really think so? They might just have something to do." I remembered my father telling us how he'd helped turn a school into a hospital.

"They have lots of things to do," said Grandmother. "Major P—— can't spare the men here, chasing butterflies."

"Does that mean we can go back to the woods tomorrow?" I asked.

"I think we'd better," she said. "You're running out of summer."

With a pang of sadness, I went indoors to consult a calendar. When I'd arrived here, the spring and summer had seemed an endless time to spend away from home with this formidable old woman I didn't know. I missed my parents terribly and my friends quite a bit; I wouldn't mind seeing my sister—I supposed she'd grown a lot. But the thought of leaving Grandmother brought an ache to my chest.

I had just over two weeks remaining.

In the peaceful hours before bed, Grandmother sat in her easy chair beside the radio, listening to the symphony. I bent over my note-book at the table, trying to add in the mirror-script, the reversed versions of each line in R———'s poem. It wasn't easy, and I needed to keep erasing.

Grandmother had her chin against her chest, and I thought she was asleep. But suddenly, she sprang up and hurried to the book-case. At her request, I brought the lamp closer.

Running her fingers over the spines of books on the bottom shelf, she pulled out a volume of medium size with a dark blue cover. Then she straightened, seized her well-worn dictionary, and carried both books back to her chair. Unceremoniously, she turned the dial and clicked off the radio just in the middle of a crescendo.

"What is it?" I asked in mounting excitement.

"Give me a minute." As she began flipping through the blue book, she said, "Read me that poem aloud."

I did so—and then a second time, when she asked me to. With

the first book open in her lap, she turned pages in the dictionary.

I rushed to the arm of her chair.

"Aldebaran," she announced, and stared at me as if thinking.

I thought I'd heard that word before, but I had no idea what it meant. It sounded like a name from *Arabian Nights.*

"It's a star," she said. "A giant red star."

I drew a breath. "He said that! R——— kept saying 'the red star' over and over!"

"It's from an Arabic name, *Al Dabaran.*" She showed me the dictionary. "It means 'The Follower.' Aldebaran is in the constellation Taurus—the Bull!"

Now she laid the other book on top, and I saw the starry outline of a bull, with lines drawn to assist the viewer's imagination. Grandmother pointed at the bull's red eye. "There it is," she said. "People say the red star is the eye of the bull. It 'follows' these other stars in the constellation as they all move across the sky. The others are the Pleiades—also known as the Seven Sisters."

I looked back to my notebook.

> Find twice the number Taurus follows with his eye
> Sisters dancing in the water and the sky

I gazed at Grandmother in amazed admiration. She had to be right. It fit perfectly.

Now she pushed past me, set the books on the table, and went back to hunting in the bookcase.

"But 'dancing in the water and the sky'?" I asked. "What—?"

"The whole poem is a mirror! It's all about mirrors. That's why every line is written forward, then backward. The Pleiades are in the heavens—the sky—but their reflections 'dance' on the water below—the sea or a pool."

Dropping a third book on the table, she peered over my shoulder at the poem. "Five, six, seven!" she said. *"Aha!"*

"What are you doing?"

"Counting the lines. Seven lines in the poem. Seven Pleiades. Seven Sisters." The new, very thick tome she'd brought out was a dictionary of classical mythology. I glimpsed entries for "Nestor" and "Polyphemus" as she riffled the pages forward and backward, homing in on "Pleiades."

We read about them, daughters of Atlas and Pleione, set in the sky as stars. "Atlas held up the sky in his hands," Grandmother said. "Pleione was the daughter of Oceanus and Tethys, who was the queen of the sea and mother of three thousand Oceanids—so the girls in one sense are children of sky and water. It's the mirroring again. Quite a poem, that one!"

I remembered how our mermaid's two sides and two tails were mirrors of each other.

Grandmother gnawed her lip. "Lots of mirrors—lots of division into two. There's an upper garden and a lower—two halves. There are four smaller arches, two on the left and two on the right. Those angels inside the screaming mouth point at each other, one with the left hand and one with the right, like when you point at yourself in a mirror. There are two equal but opposite compartments in the leaning house."

I paced around the room, unable to sit still, yearning to run to the sacred woods by lamplight and search for more clues. I tried to remember numbers and things I'd counted in the garden. Of course, there were the numbers on the risers of the stairway in the leaning house. I'd have to copy them into my notebook tomorrow.

Grandmother heated milk for me at bedtime, seeing that I was far too keyed up to sleep. I drank it, cleaned my teeth, and crawled into bed—but I lay awake for what seemed hours. It was hot in my room, another part of summer that I loved—hot nights, when the bedclothes clung until you kicked them off, and you lay there sizzling in the blackness like bacon in a skillet. My mother said I was "moon-touched" to relish heat the way I did, but that's simply the way I've always been. But that night, with my head too full of ideas, the damp stickiness of my pajamas began to bother even me.

The poem rolled endlessly through my mind, chased by the inscriptions and the statues themselves—the women with their pitchers, winking their sly stone eyes at me . . . the sleeping woman, who seemed to dream fitfully, nearing a moment of wakefulness when she would sit up on the stone slab, frightening the birds . . . the mermaid, raising her face to breathe the salt breeze off the sea in which she could never swim. And did the tortoise slowly crawl in the moonlight, once around the entire garden and back into place by the first pink glimmer of dawn? And did the dragon gnash its teeth, and did the dogs snap and lunge? Did the sea serpent swim through the bushes? Did the terrible angel shake his keys and chain? And under the light of Aldebaran and the Pleiades, did the vanished statue return, perhaps as a ghost, and stand again on her pedestal? By daylight, only those beautiful feet in sandals remained. The garden's secret might be lost forever with her, into whatever far place she'd been carried by thieves.

Listening to the night chorus in our own back garden, I tried to sleep, sizzling in my fry-pan of a bed. At some point, I did.

*　　*　　*　　*

To my intense frustration, Grandmother had changed her mind about the urgency of returning at once to the woods; instead, she insisted that we go shopping after breakfast. "We can't just disappear every day," she said. "Not unless you want search parties up there looking for us. Besides, we need supplies, and we should catch up on the news."

There was no news to speak of in the village, and the resounding lack thereof was music to our ears. The soldiers had indeed gone back to the barracks. Depending on which shop we entered and who was speaking and listening, Major P——'s men had either been a rude, noisy, disrespectful lot, or they had been bright and cheerful gentlemen, and if they were representative of the young generation, there was hope for our country's future. All in all, life was returning to its drowsy summer pace. There was still talk of the enemy fugitive, but he had to share time now with digressions into fishing and the weather and the ripening grapes.

We saw Mr. L——, a retired sea captain, standing on the flat roof of the police office and looking through binoculars. But he was looking up toward the orchards and the mountains, not out to sea. The baker told us that Mr. L—— had taken it upon himself to keep watch for the fugitive since we couldn't depend on the Army. He spent mornings up on the cliffs and afternoons on the roofs of the dockhouse or the police station.

Grandmother had some letters of her own to mail—one was to my papa, and she'd let me write a greeting in a margin—so we stopped in at the post office. To my relief, Mr. V—— looked much better, and he called me by name again. He asked Grandmother all about her garden and said he'd been hearing wonderful things from those who'd seen it. Grandmother said he ought to come by for tea.

The postmaster thanked her. "But I've also heard," he added, "that it's difficult to catch you at home these days."

"Have you heard that?" Grandmother exchanged a longish glance with him. "Well, we're making the most of summer. I'll have plenty of time to warm my old bones by the stove when the young one's gone."

Mr. V—— with his long, droopy face, gave me a mournful look. "I'll go out of business!"

"No," I told him. "I'll write Grandmother a lot."

"I'm counting on you," he said.

When Grandmother had received her change and put it away, she gazed meaningfully at the boarded-up window. "You should have let the major's men replace that glass for you."

The postmaster laughed, several explosive barks.

Grandmother smiled back, and we left. I didn't understand what was funny or why no mention was made of how the window had gotten broken. But I'd reached the age at which I realized grown-ups didn't talk about everything they might, and I wanted to be grown up.

Because of the war, some things such as coffee, salt, sugar, and flour were rationed, and Grandmother had to surrender little gray tickets for them. But produce from local gardens and orchards was plentiful, as were eggs and chicken and anything from the sea.

Grandmother clearly wanted to make our presence felt in as many places as possible. Instead of buying most items at B——'s Grocery as we might have done, we shopped all up and down the street, purchasing a fish here, a bag of beans there. It was quite infuriating for me, with my theories and questions about the sacred grove burning holes in my mind. I couldn't help thinking

Grandmother was being a bit obstinate in chatting to the very last word with Mrs. Z——— and Mrs. K——— and Mr. B———. Precious hours slipped by. It was past mid-morning when we made our last stop—at the grinder's dim little shed, where Grandmother got her kitchen knives and her scissors sharpened. We had stopped in at her house to get them and the brush knife. The shed smelled of oil, and a spider had built a web in one corner of the cloudy window.

"Rain coming," said the grinder, repeating a prediction we'd heard at least five times since leaving the house. "Won't have to water that garden for a while, Mrs. T———." He looked like a huge insect in his goggles, hunched in the half-dark over the spinning white wheel. It had a pedal like Mama's sewing machine, and I admired how the bright sparks flew from the knives' blades.

Grandmother inquired after the grinder's son, who was also away in the war.

He shook his bald head wearily and tested the cleaver's edge. "He don't write; he don't come home. He's not like your boy."

"Yours is a good boy too," Grandmother said. "I remember him on that bicycle. Always polite, and a hard worker."

"Long time ago," said the grinder. He put Grandmother's money into a cash register with a missing handle and a broken glass pane, its drawer always open.

We came out into the sunlight and the sound of the flapping flag on the post office, and we stopped in our tracks. With a sinking in my stomach, I held my breath and stared.

Major P———'s staff car cruised toward us down the main street, the sun on its windshield making a blinding glare. Behind it, I counted three Army trucks with canvas sides—troop carriers.

"Why are they back?" I asked.

Grandmother said nothing but slowly lowered her shopping basket to the ground and straightened again, watching with a grim face.

Bicycles braked; people hurried out of the trucks' way; shoppers poured from stores to line the sidewalks. I saw the barber gazing out of his window, and beside him a man with a lathered face, half-shaved. Three policemen emerged from the police office as the staff car stopped there against the curb. On the roof above them, Mr. L—— put down his binoculars and stared.

The driver opened the car's back door and Major P—— climbed out and gazed around with an enormously self-important air. Taking a deep breath of the morning breeze, he placed his hat over his shiny hair, adjusted its angle, and turned to the policemen, who saluted him.

I heard them say "Good morning, sir," and then I was sure the major said, "Now we'll get somewhere, just when I'd called it off. They took their time, but my request went through after all."

I felt Grandmother's hand on my shoulder. Her gaze was fixed on the troop carriers.

From the two rear trucks, men and dogs jumped to the ground. Barking, whining, the dogs strained at their leashes and stuck their noses in all directions, taking in the thousand scents of our village's main street.

I looked at Grandmother in horror. I knew that hunters used dogs, that guards used them to track down escaped prisoners. When a man walked or ran across the earth, he left an invisible trail that the nose of a dog could follow days afterward, a trail as clear to it as the beam of a lighthouse. The scent of R—— would lead from the parachute straight to the grove of monsters and up the stairs of the leaning house. Mr. Girandole's scent would be everywhere, too—as would ours, in an often-traveled line between the cottage and the woods.

Major P—— called out, "Good morning, Mrs. T——!" Across the street, he waved a hand and tipped his hat to Grandmother.

Forcing a smile, she waved back and gave him a nod.

"What do we do?" I whispered.

For a long time she said nothing but only watched the men lining up and an officer giving them orders. To our further dismay, the major finished his words with the policemen and sauntered in our direction. I could see it in his face: he had time to be at leisure while his men went to work. I envisioned another toast coming, another excruciating chat with this man my grandfather would not have liked. And all the while, the soldiers and dogs would be climbing the mountain. The world was spinning. My heart pounded in my ears.

Grandmother whispered, "You'll have to do this. It's up to you now. Trust Girandole and help him however you can."

It was the last thing she had a chance to say before the major was within earshot. As her words sank in, I heard her exchanging pleasantries with him. I thought I might be sick on the major's gleaming boots.

"And how is the young soldier?" asked Major P——, shaking my hand. His grip was hard, warm, and slightly damp, and he smelled of cologne. "Is he following orders well?"

"Commendably so," said Grandmother. For the life of me, I didn't know how she could sound so calm. "He has his orders right now, in fact." She opened her pocketbook. "While he's here, I'm taking full advantage of an extra pair of hands. This is our marketing day, Major." She handed me two folded bills and counted out some coins.

"Oh, but I was hoping," said the major, "that since fate has once more granted us a fortuitous meeting, I might thank you for the pleasant time the other day."

"Well," said Grandmother, glancing down at the shopping baskets.

"Please," said the major. "I will be wounded if you do not accept. We can drive to your house, and you can put these things away. Then join me for lunch in the hotel restaurant. I recall that they serve a particularly good mackerel."

No famous actress could have bested Grandmother. She actually appeared to blush as she averted her eyes, hesitating. It also struck me that she had an effect on people, as if she were a lantern in a dark room. People noticed her; what few strangers we met that summer in the village would take a step or two closer, perhaps without realizing it, to get a better look at her. The major might have focused his attentions on some woman thirty or forty years younger—there were many in the street around us. Probably, I thought, he would do just that before the day was over; but for now, he seemed to want Grandmother as a lunch companion.

"Very well, then," said Grandmother. "I certainly can't *wound* a defender of our country."

"Splendid!"

"But I think," Grandmother said, "we should let the 'young soldier' do his errands as planned. He is so often subjected to the gossip of old busybodies—I speak of my friends, Major, not you!"

The major laughed, displaying his teeth. "How about it, my good man? Aren't you tempted by a ride in an Army car?"

Camouflage, I told myself. "Yes, sir. But I . . . I'm writing a book."

I don't know why I blurted that, or what sort of excuse it was supposed to provide, but that's what came out of my mouth.

"A book?" said the major. He pointed at me suddenly, remembering what I'd told him on the ferry. "You like to draw pictures! The artist is writing a book?"

"Well, and illustrating it," I said weakly.

"I would love to see this opus!"

"Thank you, sir. I'm . . . getting my ideas together."

"And what is this book about?"

Behind the major, the men and dogs were moving out, following the street in different directions, working in teams. I guessed they would leave the village by separate paths and converge on the parachute. I had no time to waste.

"The sea voyage," I answered, grasping after words.

"Eh?"

"Sea voyages—and battles," I added, expecting the major would like that.

"Ah. Well, then. I suppose we must leave the artist to his contemplation. The coast, they say, is inspiring to the creative mind. The painters and poets all want to move here, to villages just like this."

"And you wonder, Major, why I've never moved away." To me, Grandmother said, "Off with you!"

I needed no further prompting. Leaving the basket where it lay, I stuffed the money into my pocket and dashed along the street, away from our house. I would have to take an indirect route, but once I was outside the village, I could make straight for the grove; the dogs would not, so I should still arrive ahead of them. But it was risky: I'd never followed any path but the usual one to the garden. I hoped I could find it.

And once I got there—what then? The secret compartment would do us no good. The dogs would smell us inside, and we'd be trapped.

Trust Girandole, Grandmother had said. I could only hope he would know what to do.

I raced along the street, weaving among people, sidewalk displays, vegetable carts, and parked bicycles. At the corner with Harbor Street, I turned away from the waterfront and headed up the steep hill. Already I was painfully aware of the day's heat. My drenched shirt stuck to me, and light glared off the white houses, where bedding and laundry hung on steamy balconies. Flowers in window garden-boxes made dizzying splashes of color and filled the air with a lushness of scent. Old people eyed me with the general disapproval shown toward all things disruptive. No one should be running on such a day.

Pausing at another corner to wipe sweat from my eyes, I could hear dogs baying in the distance. A cramp knifed in my side, but I had no time to rest. The streets were not at right angles. *Don't get lost,* I ordered myself, trying to decide which lane would take me up to the woods. Some internal bell rang at the cannery, much nearer at hand than I was used to. In a yard trimmed with yellow and orange flowers, a woman shaking out a rug cautioned me to slow down or I'd get the prickly heat. When the street forked, I followed the lane on the right between two-story houses and hedged gardens. It became a stairway, which I dashed up, taking two steps at a time, afraid that it might dead-end in a walled park or loop back down. But finally, at the cobbled pavement's end, I could see a meadow, and beyond it, the forest.

I broke from the village into the belt of arbors and orchards. A fat-bellied cargo plane droned across the sky, escorted by three of our country's fighters—aircraft that looked decrepit and old-fashioned compared to the warplanes of our stronger allies. Far off to my left, two soldiers with dogs also crossed the meadow—so far away they were mere specks in the shimmering green. Whether anyone saw me or not, I had no choice but to keep going.

Before passing into the wood, I tried to gauge the terrain above me. If I misjudged the direction and got lost even for a matter of minutes, I would arrive too late. I leaned against an umbrella pine to catch my breath, then ran on.

The shade brought relief from the sun, washing over me with the aroma of bark and ferns. Birds sang. I looked around, realizing that I didn't even think about the way any more when I went by our usual path. Here, the moss was undisturbed, crisscrossed by fallen logs. Boulders reared up like grazing creatures whose heads were buried in the brush. Groves of saplings clustered in the shadow of their giant elders. At first, I wondered if the forest would let me in at all. Following the natural courses of ravines and ridges, I labored up the mountain, pausing often, listening for familiar sounds in the village to check my bearings: the bell at the harbor mouth, the huffing machines at the cannery. I wasn't certain if I actually heard dogs barking behind the wind or if those sounds were phantom echoes in my head.

When I thought I should be getting close to the grove, I found a tall tree on a rise and hoisted myself into it, scrambling up from limb to limb. High enough at last to peer out over the crowns of the other trees, I searched the forest to the northwest. I saw only treetops whispering and rolling, a boundless sea of leaves beneath the sky. My heart sank. Somewhere, the dogs were drawing ever closer to the garden, their noses to the ground, but I had no path to follow, nothing to guide me. I'd been foolish to think I could get there quickly by a way I'd never used before. From this vantage, I realized how hopeless that was.

Here, but for the occasional murmur from the village, it was easy to believe I was alone in the world, the only human being. This was the kingdom of trees, a place of shifting light and rustling music old almost as the mountains themselves. I had the sensation that I'd passed beyond time itself, that I'd been running up the slopes for years upon years, like a character in a fairy tale—a half hour for me, perhaps, but the village I heard behind me was no longer the same village, and everyone I'd known—Grandmother, my parents, my sister, my friends—was long dead.

I took gasping breaths, overwhelmed with frustration. Burrs clung to my pant legs, and my wet shirt made me shiver. My hands smarted from the rough bark. The major's men would catch R——. They'd probably shoot Mr. Girandole, with his goatish legs and hoofs; they'd think him a monster or the devil. And what would become of Grandmother? They'd find her things in the leaning house—carpet bag, lantern, medicines, bucket, and pan; the men would force R—— to tell them who'd helped him. And the major knew the carpet bag well; he'd held it in his hands on the ferry.

Feeling worse by the moment, I prayed to God for help.

I'd never before had a prayer instantly answered, but how could I suppose what happened next to be anything but an answer to prayer? Turning to gaze south, wondering if I could make out anything of the village or the sea, I glimpsed—half-hidden by interposing trees—what seemed to be an open hilltop. And on the bare knoll between trunks was a straight, vertical line. I stared at it, wondering what it could be. A phrase of Grandmother's played in my mind: *Nature abhors a straight line.*

All at once, I recognized the corner of the many-pillared temple! I was looking at the hill above the garden's ravine—the structure to which the stairway led, where the inscription proclaimed, *I am a gate.*

Breathing my incredulous thanks, I fixed the direction in my mind and returned swiftly to the ground, then dashed off at an angle that would have seemed entirely wrong to me. I'd overshot the grove; if I'd gone just another twenty paces before climbing a tree, the glimpse of the temple would have been lost among the foliage.

The last obstacle was a deep crevice in the ground, a crack with rock walls, its bottom a depository of broken stones and dead leaves. This trench lay across my path, too wide to jump over. But not far away, a fallen tree bridged it.

Clambering through thorns and vines, I reached the trunk. It was hardened and bleached, a great bone of the forest. Having tested it for strength, I eased across on hands and knees, gripping the stubs of shattered limbs. Then I was on the far side and running again, downhill and uphill.

I slid from a bank into a glade where the trees and brush thinned . . . and no more than a good stone's throw to my right was the back of the mermaid. Tears of relief stung my eyes. Blinking them away, I hurried forward, moving quietly, remembering to stay alert for soldiers.

I passed through the archway into the lower garden and moved back westward, toward the stone house. But once again, Mr. Girandole surprised me by springing from behind the pedestal of the missing statue. He seemed to spend most of his time outdoors, where he could listen to the forest and breathe its scents. And I was sure he didn't fancy sitting beside R—— for hours on end.

Mr. Girandole trotted toward me, his gaze dark with worry.

"They've got dogs!" I blurted. "The major's men are all back with dogs, and they're headed this way!"

His eyes flashed, and slowly he nodded. "Come on," he said, motioning me toward the leaning house. "I knew by the wood's voices that something was afoot."

"What can we do?" At his heels I pelted up the stairs, my legs rubbery from my long run.

"We have some advantages. One, I expected dogs from the first day."

So, he knew about dogs and what they could do. His voice echoed around me as I mounted the dangerous steps inside, their jumbled numbers staring me in the face.

"Two, they don't know what R—— smells like. They'll have to start at the parachute, and there have been men tramping all over the ground there and here and everywhere else. Soldiers . . . and the three of us."

"Us—that's not good, is it?"

"It's not that bad. You and M—— don't have to hide the fact that *you've* been in the garden." He reached the chamber and jumped down into the well, drawing a cry of surprise from R——. When I got to the edge, I saw Mr. Girandole stepping back and forth over the patient to rummage through the paraphernalia on the floor. He emptied out the carpet bag and tossed it up to me.

"What is happen?" demanded R——, who looked improved enough to be alarmed.

"And three," said Mr. Girandole, "I know from bitter experience how dogs react to me. They'll go mad when they catch a whiff of faun."

"Dogs?" asked R——, his eyes widening.

"Yes." Mr. Girandole held a finger sharply before the pilot's face. "We'll shut you in here, and you will be absolutely quiet if you want to live. You've got food, clean water, and the pan. The space isn't airtight. I'll take the lantern—someone might recognize it. You'll be in the dark, so take a good look now at where everything is."

R——'s lips twitched. He asked a question in his own language.

"I don't know how long," Mr. Girandole said. "I'll have to lead the dogs quite a ways, and they probably won't all follow me—some will come here."

I touched the compartment's rim. "They'll smell him through the floor, won't they?"

"Yes, they normally would." Mr. Girandole held up a large yellow gourd on a shoulder strap—a dried gourd shaped like a bottle. "But we have this. Here; don't drop it—it's heavy." He handed the gourd up to me. From the way it sloshed, I realized it was full of liquid. Two wooden stoppers blocked holes near the top.

"What's in here?" I asked.

"Don't open it yet." Mr. Girandole was not above the annoying adult tendency to answer a question with an order, but I didn't care. He had a plan, and I was relieved. He stuffed the lantern, the medicine bottles, his own cookware, and Grandmother's stray dishes into a knapsack of his own. Finally, he used the shears to clip a long strip off the edge of the sheet from R——'s pallet. He looped it through an arm hole of the flak vest and laid the vest across R——. "Hug this," Mr. Girandole told him. "Wipe your face on it. Rub it against yourself."

R—— did his best.

"Good," said Mr. Girandole. He dropped his own shoes into his pack and hung it on his shoulder. "We'll do all we can to keep them from finding you, R——. But if they do, you'll say no word about the kind woman or her grandson. I am the only one who helped you."

R—— nodded. "Thank you," he said.

Hesitantly, Mr. Girandole offered his hand, and the pilot shook it.

Having floundered up out of the compartment beneath his load, Mr. Girandole slid the stone lid closed. R—— watched bleakly as the slab crossed between us and him and locked shut with a *boom*.

Mr. Girandole hurried to the window, where he stuck his head out. Then he pulled a stopper from the gourd he'd given me. I gasped and covered my nose and mouth. My eyes watered.

"Mixed it up myself," Mr. Girandole said. "I was beginning to think we wouldn't need it. None of the ingredients individually is as bad as you imagine. But put them together and let them ferment. . . ." He clapped my shoulder. "It smells twenty times worse to a dog." He turned to the stairway. "A little goes a long way. Sprinkle it around this room and on the stairs as you come down. And all across the terrace, and the ground nearby. Then do the whole garden until you run out—here and there, you know, spread it out. The dogs will tie their leashes in knots and hang the major's men from trees before they'll come near this place."

I nodded. "But won't it be too obvious? An awful smell in the one place we don't want them to look?"

Mr. Girandole narrowed his eyes. "They'll know *something* happened. They'll look around here again, but I'm hoping they won't suppose there's anywhere to hide. If I can give them an interesting scent to follow in another direction . . ."

"What will you do?"

"I'll make a sweep to the south, crossing their paths before they get to the parachute, and I'll lead them to it. My own scent and R——'s. Then I'll head away over the mountain. The soldiers have no reason to suspect R—— isn't alone."

It made good sense to me.

"I have to go," he said. "I can hear them. You should circle back the way you came—"

"Don't worry about me. Just be careful yourself." I started sprinkling the vile substance, holding my breath. It looked yellowish in the air but left only wet patches on the stone. I felt sorry for R——, under the floor. Surely, the odor would reach him there, and he had no hope of fresh air.

Mr. Girandole lingered at the top of the stairs. "You and M—— will have questions to answer. Is she all right?"

"Yes, she's fine. She's having lunch with the major."

Mr. Girandole gave me such a look that I would have laughed under different circumstances.

"She didn't *want* to," I added quickly. "She had to go along with him so I could get away."

He nodded uneasily and was gone.

I finished the room, taking care not to get any of the terrible stuff on me, then worked my way down the stairs. It was hard going, moving backward and with only one hand to grip the steps. I'd already discovered the liquid came out more freely with the second stopper removed; both hung on strings from the gourd's neck, so I didn't have to put them into my pocket.

I dosed the stairway, jumping down the last stretch to escape rivulets of the potion. Then I sprinkled the terrace, being sure to hit the benches we'd used. I splashed both stairways leading up to it, backtracking so as not to walk through the stench I'd laid down.

By the gourd's heft, I figured just over half the contents remained. Far off behind the whispers of leaves, I thought I could hear the dogs, a chorus of barking on many pitches. I worked through the garden in a clockwise circle, apologizing to each statue as I contaminated its base and the earth before it. I fanned a liberal dose at the grove's entrance nearest the parachute. By the time I got to the mermaid, the gourd was mostly empty. I poured the last few drops onto her inscribed slab.

Then I looked at the empty gourd, thinking hard. It wouldn't do to take it with me. I didn't want any dogs later to have the same reaction to me or to Grandmother's cottage that they had to the garden. The only place this container might be overlooked was here, in the grove that reeked the same way.

Looking around, I decided on the thicket south of the mermaid, behind the tortoise, a tangle of vines and thorny bushes so dense that I doubted even a rabbit could pass through it. The bushes stretched all the way to where Heracles towered above them, the creepers clinging to his waist.

Mr. Girandole hadn't said what he wanted done with the gourd, but I couldn't believe it would ever be usable again. I dashed around the stone wall to the tortoise, pulled back my arm, and threw the gourd deep into the morass, aiming for Heracles. It fell far short of him but plummeted through the leaves into wiry depths from which there could be no returning.

Leaving the grove by the mermaid's clearing, I descended the slopes rapidly, stopping often to listen. I was sure I could hear dogs on both sides of me now, though both groups seemed to be higher up. I prayed Godspeed for Mr. Girandole. I'd arrived at the grove not a moment too soon.

I met no one. When I came to the meadow above the village, I guessed it could be no later than two o'clock. For the benefit of anyone who might be watching, I did my best to cross the ground aimlessly, as if enjoying the summer day: I went out of my way to follow a trickling stream in a marshy place, then stopped to lie down in the grass and study the clouds.

The exhaustion of my morning's efforts caught up with me. Among the fragrant stems, with grasshoppers using me as a step-stone, I could have fallen asleep with no trouble, but the breeze had picked up, and a mist veiled the sun. I remembered the talk of the morning, how everyone had been predicting rain.

Rain. What would that do, I wondered, to the trails of scent? I doubted anything short of a flood would wash away the stench from the monsters' grove.

I returned to find Grandmother entertaining two ladies in the back garden. Before I stepped into sight, I heard them plying Grandmother with questions about Major P———. "Was that *all* he said?" one of them asked. "And how were his table manners?"

"It's unnatural," said the other, "for a man of his age and position to be unmarried."

"He *was* married, wasn't he?" asked Grandmother. "I believe his wife died about four years ago."

"Then all the more reason for you to steer well away from him, M———," said the first woman, who I now saw through a gap in the hedge was Mrs. C———. "Why, if he had propositioned *me* in front of the police office—"

"He didn't *proposition* me, E———," said Grandmother patiently. "Unless you read a great deal more than I do into the hotel's mackerel."

I rustled the grass with my feet and rounded the hedge.

"Why, there he is now!" cried the other, Mrs. D———. "And just look at the little vagabond! Burrs from head to toe!" But she grinned at me, bunching her plump cheeks, and beckoned me toward the table, pointing at the tray of fresh cookies and crackers spread with liver-paste.

The ladies must have been desperate to hear about the major; the hour or so after lunch was usually nap time if we were home and Grandmother wasn't otherwise busy—it was much too early for tea.

"I don't for the life of me know why you let him roam like that," said Mrs. C———, shaking her head.

"Boys will be boys," said Grandmother, studying me carefully, her gaze taking in the carpet bag. "That's one thing that doesn't change with the generations."

I gave her a smile which communicated, I hoped, that things for the moment were going as well as they might be. At the sight of the crackers, I noticed how hungry I was.

"Go and wash your hands and face, and comb those seeds out of your hair," Grandmother said. "Then in the kitchen, you'll find a sandwich waiting for you, from the hotel."

"Courtesy of the Army!" said Mrs. D——— with a theatrical sweep of her arms.

Mrs. C——— *humph*ed in disgust.

Excusing myself, I obeyed the orders to wash and decided the burrs on my trousers could wait until after I'd eaten. I sat at the kitchen table, and while I was thinking of it, I took from my pocket the money Grandmother had given me earlier and left it on the tabletop. The sandwich lay wrapped in white paper stained with oil.

I said a quick but heartfelt grace and devoured it, finding delight in the crunchy roll, the meats and cheeses, the crisp lettuce and cucumbers, and the spicy green mustard. The overcast sun through the garden's leaves filled the kitchen with a greenish murk, and I could feel the rain coming. Talk drifted in at the open window— talk of Major P—— and what he might be playing at; then Mrs. D—— and Mrs. C—— discussed news from the war front. Some reports said we were gaining ground, and some said we were losing it.

I wished desperately for a letter from my papa. I thought of my mama, too, and suddenly, unexpectedly, I missed them so intensely that my eyes filled with tears. I was glad I was alone in the kitchen.

When the guests had left and Grandmother and I had told each other our stories, Grandmother advised me to make a decoy notebook; very soon, soldiers might be asking to see it. She found me a cheap, age-yellowed one from which many of the pages had been torn. While she took her nap, I set to work copying parts of my notes into it: the inscriptions, but not all of them, and the poem in a garbled form—I freely reworded the lines and composed new ones. Then I updated the real notebook with information on Aldebaran and the Pleiades, using the books from the shelf. When Grandmother reappeared, she put the actual notebook away in her cedar chest, and I left the fake one on my night table.

We picked a few tomatoes, pulled some weeds, and pruned back the purple germander, which grew so fast in the sunny areas that we could practically see it spreading before our eyes. One of the dirt-clods crumbled to reveal an earthworm, gray-pink and writhing at the unexpected touch of sunlight. I scooped a soft bed for him under the hedge and gently covered him up again. Grandmother was gathering a clutch of gaillardia for the kitchen vase when we heard an ominous yipping and baying from the field.

"Here they come," Grandmother said, straightening her stiff back. "I'd better put the kettle on." She took the bouquet into the kitchen, and I busied myself with carrying uprooted weeds to our drying-pile. I tried to stay calm as jitters ran through me.

Soon enough, I saw them emerge from among the arbors: four dogs straining at their leashes, noses to the ground, and soldiers with rifles. I dropped the weeds into the pile, brushed seed-tufts off my hands, and shielded my eyes against the sun. I counted nine men. Though I wanted to run inside, I forced myself to walk to the back gate and watch them, like any curious boy would do.

One of the men waved at me, and I waved back. The dogs seemed to catch my scent directly, and they barked with more fervor, nearly pulling their handlers off their feet.

Of course Papa was not among the men, but still I could not help checking each face. I didn't recognize any from the ferry, either.

They all came right up to the gate. I shrank back as the dogs leaped and pawed the fence and pushed snuffling noses against its base. They whined and raced from side to side, colliding with one another and tangling the leashes. A shiny black nose shoved through a knothole just in front of me. The barks were like gunshots. A soldier was talking to me over the fence, but I couldn't hear a word he was saying.

Finally, the soldier yelled and gesticulated to his companions, and the four dog handlers led the dogs back up the field. Being dragged away did not sit well with the dogs.

Grandmother crossed the yard, leaning on her stick.

The lead soldier tipped his hat. "Madam," he said, skipping any niceties, "have you or the boy been up in the woods?"

"Well, yes, of course," said Grandmother, in the same tone as if he'd asked if we'd ever been to the grocery store. "That's where we get firewood, and go berrying, and take walks . . ."

The soldier looked extremely irritated, and two of the men behind him exchanged a look that said, *Can you believe we're here wasting our time?* Up under a tree, I saw one man speaking into the radio telephone that another carried on his back, like I'd seen in the village. The one using it turned a crank, which I knew was to build up an electric charge. My father had explained them to me.

"What is all this?" asked Grandmother, peering uphill.

"Madam . . ." the soldier said, wiping sweat from his face with his shirt sleeve.

Grandmother suddenly looked worried, and she gazed around the garden in alarm. "You don't suppose that ⸺ is somewhere nearby?" (She said the name of R⸺'s people.)

"No, madam, I doubt it."

"Right outside our windows, looking in at us while we're asleep . . ."

"No. It's not likely."

"The tomatoes!" Grandmother's eyes were getting wider and wider. "He could be raiding our gardens for food!"

"Madam."

Grandmother hurriedly unlatched the gate. I dodged out of the way as she swung it open and seized the officer by the arm, pulling him forward. "Sir!" she said urgently. "You are one of the major's men?"

"S——, Madam. Captain S——."

"Captain, I beg you—you must have a look in my attic. Won't you? The thought that he might be up there, eating tomatoes— I know I've heard sounds—I'm a widow, you see. Oh, how can we sleep tonight? But if you take a look, I'd be so grateful . . ."

The men in the background exchanged glances again. One turned and paced off toward the others, batting his hat against his leg.

"Please," said the captain, shaking off Grandmother's arm. "Yes, I'll look in your attic. But it's not the ——." (He used an epithet that was less kind.) "What the dogs smell is you and the boy. Are you the only two living here?"

"Yes, just the two of us, and he's only here for the summer. My grandson. Oh, I do hope you're right! Would you care for tea, Captain? Or perhaps something cold?"

Captain S—— declined any hospitality. He informed us that he would bring one dog into the garden and watch its reactions. At his orders, a soldier came with a single hound, which barked furiously and pointed at Grandmother and me. The dog showed no interest when led up to the back door of the cottage, but he pulled his handler in agitated circles around the garden, following his nose from the flowerbeds to the clothesline pole and back to the fence. This puzzled the soldiers, since the hound had located us but wouldn't give up on our backyard. I guessed the truth: that the dog had caught the lingering scent of Mr. Girandole. I was grateful that dogs couldn't talk.

"The enemy hasn't been here, Madam," said the captain when the dog had been withdrawn again. But at Grandmother's insistence, the officer came in through the back door (first carefully scuffing his boots on the mat outside). He climbed the narrow stairway, pushed through the trap door, and had a look around the attic. The steps of his boots thumped slowly here and there over our heads, and the boards squeaked.

Clumping back down to us, Captain S—— reported that all was clear. "There are no signs," he said, "that anyone has been in your attic for a long time."

Grandmother's acting façade slipped a little because the comment piqued her. "I do my best to keep the *entire* house clean," she said. "But it's much harder for me to get up those stairs than it used to be."

He mumbled an apology, saying he'd meant only that nothing had been disturbed, and that the single window was securely locked.

"Well, that's a relief," said Grandmother. "I do feel much better. Thank you ever so much, Captain S——."

"There's some lovely furniture up there," he remarked.

"Thank you. My husband was a carpenter."

He stood for a while in the back garden, scowling at blossoms, looking as if he still had a grievance against us but wasn't sure how to frame it in words. Clearly, it annoyed him that he'd spent the day tracking us. But when it came down to it, Grandmother was a very difficult person to scold.

The captain was spared the need to say anything by the arrival of a car in front of the cottage. A soldier in the side yard waved to someone. Car doors slammed, and in another moment, Major

P—— himself stepped around the house, flanked by two more of his men. All the soldiers behind the cottage saluted him.

"Well," said the major, "this is quite a party." He looked weary and bemused, but I also thought I saw a dangerous flicker in his gaze as he eyed Grandmother and me, then strolled past us, examining the garden.

"Major P——," said Grandmother carefully, "I am deeply sorry our fondness of the woods has inconvenienced you all."

The major laughed by expelling air through his nose. "It's been good exercise for us, hasn't it?"

He was looking at Captain S——, who said, "Yes, sir!"— though I doubted the captain would have called it "good"—nor did I think the day had brought much "exercise" to the major.

"Lovely," said Major P——, admiring Grandmother's bougain-villea. "Mrs. T——, if we continue to meet like this, people will begin to talk."

"Oh, believe me, Major, they already are." Grandmother settled onto a bench. "Won't you sit down?"

The major handed his hat to his aide and sat facing Grandmother across the garden table. Captain S—— and the men who had arrived with P—— stood at attention nearby. Though I didn't want to be anywhere near the major, I couldn't leave Grandmother without support, so I perched beside her on the bench.

"Oh, dear," said Grandmother, making a quick count. "I'm afraid I don't have enough teacups for everyone. But would you care for something, Major? Returning your hospitality is the very least I can do."

"In a moment. First, I should like to know a few things, and you must pardon my directness."

"Of course." Grandmother laid the stick across her knees and folded her hands on the table. "When I think that we've unwittingly drawn time and manpower from your work . . ."

"Worry no more about that," he said. "We'll have our man soon enough. If we don't catch him, then Major B—— will. The trail heads that way, toward —— across the mountains, just as I suspected all along."

Grandmother did a good job of looking relieved, though she must have felt as worried for Mr. Girandole as I did. "Well," she said. "At least, I'm glad not all your dogs have been following my grandson and me."

"But several of them have been." The darkness had returned to the major's expression. "More than one scent trail leads to your gate. Whenever the situation involves those abandoned statues in the forest, it also seems to involve the two of you."

Grandmother smiled and touched my arm. "This boy loves the grove . . . just as his father did before him. Just as I did, when I was a little girl."

"A picturesque place, to be sure," said the major. "And yet, despite the known danger of this past week—an enemy soldier, likely armed, possibly injured, certainly desperate—you've seen no need to avoid the place. According to a report I received this afternoon, the boy was there, alone, yesterday." His eyes turned directly upon me. "Weren't you? And I suspect you were there again today, after you left us. Isn't that right?"

I nodded, feeling faint.

"You were there, even though my men yesterday ordered you not to come back. What's so important that you defy common sense and Army orders? What do you do in the grove?"

My head swam, and I feared I might faint. I took a few deep breaths before I managed to squeak out, "M—monsters."

"What?"

"The . . . the monsters. They . . . There's nothing like them where I live."

"His time here is all too short," said Grandmother, coming to my rescue. "Childhood, Major, is all too short. I've shown him the grove because I believe that something of the soul of our village is there—something most people have lost and forgotten—something we've even come to fear. There are things one learns in school, sir, and in life afterward. But there are things, too, that grandmothers must teach, or no one will. I'm trying to do my duty, Major, before the chance is lost. I know he's not in danger. Not in our sacred woods."

I sat in silence, staring at the medals on Major P——'s uniform, staring at the shiny black holster of his sidearm. I could hear by her voice that Grandmother wasn't acting now.

The major sat unmoving for a long time. When I ventured a glance at his face, I saw that most of the anger was gone.

"There are qualities that I admire," he said at last. "And you, Mrs. T——, possess most of them. Courage. Devotion. A love of the arts, learning, and of our country. But one more virtue this boy must learn is respect for authority. Troubled times demand such, if one is to survive."

Grandmother nodded meekly. "You are right, Major. Some qualities are best taught by men."

"Oh, come, Mrs. T——, there's no need to patronize me. We both know you are quite capable of teaching anything." He tapped his fingers on the tabletop. "Now, if the offer of a drink still stands . . ."

As Grandmother stood up, the major looked at me again. "Have either of you noticed anything strange in that grove of statues lately?"

I thought about it and shook my head.

"The whole place is strange," said Grandmother. "But what do you mean, Major?"

"Have you seen anyone there? Anything out of the ordinary? Have you, say, *heard* or *smelled* anything?"

I nodded. If I pretended not to know about the bad smell, he'd know I was lying. "I noticed a bad smell," I said.

"Oh, yes," Grandmother said offhandedly, heading toward the back door. "There are bad smells that come and go all through the woods. It could be geothermal, I suppose."

"How long has the smell been there?" the major asked.

Grandmother stopped to listen.

"A few days, I think." I had blurted the lie before I thought about it, wanting badly to distance the smell from today's manhunt.

The major looked to Captain S——, who shook his head and said, "Lieutenant N—— didn't smell it yesterday." S—— returned his gaze severely to me.

Grandmother tossed up her hands. "Smells in the woods," she muttered, and went inside.

The major leaned close to me. "Is there anything you have to tell me, man to man?" I could smell his hair tonic or his shaving lotion. Whatever it was, it was too strong an odor.

"No, sir."

He peered steadily at me, and his face tipped to one side. "I heard of a curious little notebook you had in the grove yesterday. I'd like to see it."

FREDERIC S. DURBIN

"Yes, sir," I said, glad that none of the men now present were those who had caught me then: they would have seen at once that my decoy notebook looked nothing like the real one. I hurried to my room, snatched up the fake, and took it to him.

He spread it on the table and turned the pages. "The words from the statues," he murmured in recognition.

"Yes, sir."

"And this poem?"

"Oh . . . I made that up. I wrote it there, in the grove."

"H'm. I thought you were an artist. Don't you draw pictures of the statues?"

"I've tried, but . . . I didn't like how they came out."

"H'm."

Grandmother returned from the kitchen with a bottle of wine and several glasses. I was certain that it was kept for moonlit nights, when Mr. Girandole came to the garden. At the sight of it, Major P—— brightened.

"Now," he said deliberately, gazing at me until I squirmed, "now, I will add a part to your education that your father doubtless would, if he were here." With a swift, ruthless movement, he gathered the three notebook pages on which I'd written, and ripped them cleanly from the spine. As he held the pages between us, staring me in the face, my vision swam. In his eyes I saw the bear's eyes—the bear from my long-ago nightmare, its face slashed and bleeding, watching me from the midst of the fire.

The major tore the pages into pieces no bigger than a postage stamp. He deposited the shreds into a pile on the open notebook, where a breeze stirred them and blew some of the scraps onto the ground. Crossing his legs, he sat back and watched me calmly.

I looked down, breathing through my nose. Around us, the other men stood without speaking or moving. Grandmother paused, motionless, as he was tearing up the paper. After a long moment, she set the tray down and began to pour the wine.

"Good," the major said to me. "You will make a soldier yet."

That night, the rain came. Flashes of lightning lit the cracks around the shutters, casting stark leaf shadows in the garden when we peeped out through the back door. Thunder crashed. We kept our hands busy since we could think of little else but Mr. Girandole, probably somewhere far from his home, and R——, huddled in that pitch-black space in the leaning house. Grandmother sewed and I drew sketches. From memory, as best I could, I drew a map of the grove of monsters, labeling each statue. Instead of my sketchbook, I used a two-page spread of my notebook—the real one.

As the rain fell in sheets on the roof, gurgling in the downspouts, we filled the big iron tub and took sponge baths. Grandmother's cottage was old enough that it didn't have pipes and a water heater like our city house did; we pumped the water from a well in the indoor kitchen and heated it in a kettle.

The next morning was Sunday, and even though a drizzling rain still fell, we made the forty-minute walk to the church up near the abbey. We didn't pass through the main part of town—church was the other direction—but we knew the soldiers had gone again. Major P—— had sent most of them over the mountain on Mr. Girandole's trail, and the major was confident his business in our town was finished.

Grandmother's church was a fortress of massive stone blocks, dim inside even on the brightest days. Light filtered through tiny, ornate stained-glass windows; each window told a story, but they were set so high in the walls that I couldn't see much.

Unlike the priest at my parents' church, who shuddered the pews with his sermons, the priest here was a small gray man with dark circles under his eyes, who flitted about the shadowy altar like a ghost, and whose soft, short messages would never disturb anyone's day. When he spoke, I could hear only occasional words, the ones he would pronounce deliberately, looking suddenly up at us from his notes. These enunciated words of his, followed by dramatic pauses, seemed to be chosen at random—but probably weren't, if you could hear them in context.

Today, I'd brought along a folded scrap of paper and a pencil, in case I had any inspirations about the garden. When the sermon began, I pulled the paper from my shirt pocket and—to give myself something to do—wrote down each word the priest said clearly.

Grandmother eyed me critically, but since I appeared to be taking notes on the message, she left me to it.

"IF," the priest said, nodding solemnly before falling away again into a murmur. "ONCE," he said later, holding up a finger. Over the course of the next few minutes, I collected "YOU," "BUT," "YOU (again)," "WERE," "CONTINUE," and "NOW." This "NOW" was his parting syllable. I couldn't make heads or tails of the unassuming little cadenza of words that had preceded it, but it sounded more like joyous Gospel than a command.

As the offertory stretched on, I looked at my paper again and read the words: IF ONCE YOU BUT YOU WERE CONTINUE NOW. Tapping the pencil against my lip, I began to rearrange the words in my head, shuffling them like cards. Spreading the paper on my hymnal again, I wrote: IF YOU WERE BUT ONCE,

CONTINUE YOU NOW. Frowning, I crossed that out and changed it to: NOW YOU CONTINUE BUT ONCE, IF YOU WERE. I didn't like that, either.

I almost missed the offering basket when it came down the row. At the last second, I scrambled to fish my coins from my pocket, and I dropped my pencil onto the floor. Grandmother gave me a long-suffering look.

When I had the pencil again, I wrote:

ONCE YOU WERE...BUT NOW...IF YOU CONTINUE.

That seemed to make the most sense to me, even though the thoughts weren't explicitly stated, and I drew a star beside it and underlined it.

When the organist was well into the postlude and the people were beginning to file out, Grandmother leaned toward me and said, "That was a good sermon."

I glanced toward the priest, wondering if Grandmother had actually been able to hear him. "Was it?" I whispered back.

"I meant yours," she said.

In the narthex and on the church steps, Grandmother faced a barrage of questions about what the soldiers had been doing at our cottage. Mrs. C—— complained that she'd pulled a muscle in her neck trying to see the back of our property from the arbors behind her place, and she came close to blaming Grandmother for her discomfort. Mrs. D—— asked if the rumor were true that, because of her education, Grandmother had been enlisted by the Army as a special consultant for help in capturing the enemy fugitive.

"The only help they enlisted from me," Grandmother replied,

"was in getting an advance on supper at half past four." She confessed that the dogs had followed my scent—apparently, Grandmother felt the porch of God's house was no place for "camouflage." Although she left her own scent out of the story, I still thought the admission was large-spirited of her: she got no end of tongue-clucks and I-told-you-so looks from Mrs. C——.

But Grandmother also made much of how Captain S—— had searched her attic from corner to corner for any signs of intrusion. At that news, everyone recalled again the unlatched garden gates, footprints, doorknobs rattled at night, lurkers-behind-fences, and the cigarette-end Mrs. D—— had found—which, in fact, she produced again from her handbag, still wrapped in its handkerchief, and showed to the priest for his opinion. If he had one, I didn't hear what it was.

We walked home under our umbrellas, stepping around the puddles. After lunch, while Grandmother took a nap, I tried applying what I'd done in church to the words from the sacred woods.

I used scratch paper from the decoy notebook for this, because even if I were on the right track, it would require a lot of trials and cross-outs. I played with the inscriptions one by one, rearranging the order of their words again and again. I tried it with the poem, too, but quickly saw that I was getting nowhere.

We would have to go back soon to the garden to take care of R——. Mr. Girandole might not return for a while yet.

All day, Grandmother and I were both practically climbing the walls. The rain pattered endlessly. We would gladly have braved it, but after the soldiers had been to our cottage, we were under too much scrutiny. We couldn't risk anyone seeing us climb the meadow: on a day such as this, we couldn't possibly be gathering firewood or much of anything else except mud. So, there was nothing for it but to turn in early and start out the next morning before the sun was up. I wondered aloud if R—— could survive for so long, trapped in the blackness of the compartment.

"He has water and food," said Grandmother, but she looked worried too.

For the rest of that rainy Sunday, we swept and dusted to keep ourselves busy, and we took naps in the late afternoon. I emptied the ice box's pan. For supper, we had chicken-and-rice soup, rolls from the bakery, and vegetables from the garden. Thinking of R——, I felt guilty to have so much light and freedom of movement, to have warm food.

Grandmother nudged me awake in the pre-dawn hours, when the world was dripping and all was quiet. We were both too sleepy to eat anything. Grandmother put on her raincoat and rain hat, which made her look like a fisherman. She dressed me in a waterproof poncho with a hood. It smelled musty, but it covered me like a cloak and hung down to my ankles all around. We left the umbrellas at home. Mr. Girandole had the lantern, so we'd have to do without it. Since he also had the medicines and the shears, we could do little else for R—— but take him food. Instead of the carpet bag, which would quickly become drenched, Grandmother loaded a rucksack with provisions, and I slid a pencil and my notebooks into it—both the real notebook and the false one, from which the major had ripped pages.

The rain had become nothing more than a mist. Through the hedges, Mrs. F——'s house was entirely dark. The tall grass soaked my pants' cuffs in no time, and the footing was slippery. Grand-mother chose her steps carefully, prodding with the stick, clutch-ing my arm. Twice, I slipped and landed on one knee. It took forever just to reach the edge of the woods. With no lamp, no light from the moon or stars, I wondered if we'd be able to find the grove at all; but Grandmother never doubted the way. Fallen limbs and dead trunks presented the greatest obstacles. I remembered the mushroom fairy-rings and hoped we weren't blundering through them—or if we were, that any fairies still in this human realm would understand our purpose and forgive us.

The blackness was paling to gray shadows on the outskirts of the sacred garden. Grandmother pulled me to a stop and whis-pered, "You go on up there first. Don't make a sound, and keep your eyes open. I wouldn't put it past the major to have left a few men here to spy on us. You'll do a better job of seeing them than I would."

She sat on a log, and I crept forward. The rain had stopped altogether, but as I'd seen before, a white mist floated between tree trunks. Birds warbled. I pushed the hood off my head.

This was a dramatic hour at which to enter the garden. In this light, looming from the mist, the statues might have been more than sculpted stone. I half-expected the dragon's neck to turn; I half-expected to hear its roar, the crunching of Heracles's foot-steps. In the pre-dawn, Apollyon's hair and robes might be flying in the wind.

Despite the rain, the odor from the gourd still lingered. I held my breath where it was worst. Keeping close to the bushes, I tried to see ahead before I advanced. The stone house leaned stark and black in the gloom. The tranquil lower glade stretched away; I made a slow circuit, checking behind the house (Apollyon was standing still, though as always, his gaze seemed to follow me), beyond the mermaid, inside the screaming mouth. I climbed to the temple and searched the hilltop; I went out of the ravine by the sleeping woman and re-entered by the square pool, which was now almost full to the brim—the new rain had mixed with the brackish dregs, creating a soup of leaves and twigs. Inside the leaning house, the stench was nearly unbearable. Grandmother couldn't stand the perspective of the building itself; I could imagine what she'd say now. I crawled up to R——'s chamber, wondering if he could hear my soft footfalls crossing above him. But I didn't dare call out a reassurance until I'd mounted the corner ladder to the roof, where I'd never been. The stone rungs were dank and rough.

Pushing open the hatchway was the moment of truth: if soldiers were camped on the roof, I would give myself away. Holding tightly to one cold rung, I put my other arm up against the hatch and pushed. It rose with a ringing scrape. I'm sure my eyes were round as two full moons as I peered up over the hatchway's edge.

Only a scattering of leaves and sticks occupied the roof.

The view from the top was breathtaking: arches and trees, tangled thickets and aprons of mist, figures of myth and dream in the heart of a deep forest at dawn. As I looked around, something told me this was one of those eternal moments, a memory I would carry with me forever—recalled at odd moments, for no particular reason, for the rest of my life. I looked everywhere, trying to absorb every detail—the glistening bark, the sudden flutter of a bird, the smells of wetness and newness mingling with the ancient stone beneath me and the taint of the potion I'd poured out. It would never again be this morning, this summer. In a few months, my age would have two digits, and it would have two digits until I died or reached one hundred. This was my last single-digit summer.

With a deep breath, I closed the hatch above me and hurried back to Grandmother. She was waiting contentedly on the log, admiring the view. When we moved into the garden, she wrinkled her nose and fanned at the smell. "Girandole," she muttered. "He never does anything halfway."

On the inner stairway, she coughed and made such a face that I doubted she'd go any farther. "If I had three wishes," she said, "I'd use one to wish we could keep R—— anywhere but here."

"Why not use it to wish him back to —— where he came from?" I asked, lending her an arm.

"That's right. In this stink, I can't think straight."

I reminded myself that, while Grandmother attended to R——, I'd have to keep watch. Without Mr. Girandole to listen to the wood's voices, it would be much easier for someone to sneak up on us. It was also harder getting Grandmother up the steps without Mr. Girandole's help.

When at last she'd struggled into the chamber, Grandmother rapped on the floor with her stick. "Are you in there, R——? All is clear for the present."

R—— cried out something in his own language. He seemed to be laughing and sobbing.

I looked questioningly at Grandmother.

"I believe he's thanking God," she said.

We turned our attention to the floor. "Well," said Grandmother to me, "open it up."

I gave her a blank stare. Mr. Girandole hadn't shown me which two holes to stick my fingers into to trip the hidden catch.

"R———," said Grandmother, tapping again with her stick. "Do you know how to open the floor?"

It was hard to hear his muffled response through the slab, but I thought he'd said, "Wait! Wait!" along with more mumbling. I explained to Grandmother about the holes, but there were hundreds of them.

When one occupies the prison, however, one pays more attention to the lock. R——— had watched Mr. Girandole convert the chamber again and again. Even in the dark, he knew where to begin searching. After a few minutes, we heard the click, and the floor shifted.

Planting my feet, I tugged with both hands, and R——— used his good arm from below. The floor trundled back, revealing the compartment.

Foul as the odor I'd sprinkled was, the reek of the makeshift toilet was worse. Pale and wild-eyed, R——— looked ready to jump up into our arms, injuries or not. The water bucket was nearly empty, and the pan of waste was about to overflow.

"Out!" said R———, clutching my ankle, since I was nearest. "Please! I go out now!"

Grandmother hunkered down and nodded. "That's a terrible pit you're living in. But it's still dangerous outside. The Army might come back. Someone from the village might come."

R——— shook his head in desperation. "Out! Please! Smell. Too dark—no room, no breathe, alone. I am crazy, crazy!"

The first business, Grandmother told me, was to get that wastepan out of there.

I nodded and took off the rain poncho. Having slid down into the well, I lifted the pan deliberately to the upper level, trying not to breathe.

"The stream is that way," Grandmother said, pointing. "Empty the pan in the woods, not the stream, then wash it out well. Whatever you do, don't fall down the stairs."

She stayed and spoke with R—— as I saw to the task. I took the pan far outside the garden before I dumped it. The stream chattered, swift and clear, in purple shadows. I balanced on a smooth rock and rinsed the pan thoroughly, scrubbing it with handfuls of pebbles and sand; then I washed my hands, enjoying the water's piercing cold.

It was daylight now, the gloom shifting to an emerald twilight that would grow deeper and richer throughout the day. Insects chorused, birds chirped and cawed, and from far away came the cannery whistle.

Next, I brought the bucket and filled it with clean water. After that, Grandmother had me assist in the compromise she'd reached with R——: taking great care, we hoisted him out of the well and onto the floor beneath the window. He could breathe the fresh air, and standing briefly as we supported him, one on either side, he gazed out at the grove. He gaped at it like a man beholding a new world, but then he nearly passed out; he hadn't stood in a long time, and his injuries were far from healed.

I think he had barely survived his time locked beneath the floor. He'd told Grandmother that, several times, he'd tried to get out, willing to take his chances on being discovered; but he'd simply been too weak and injured to move the floor. He'd been convinced we weren't coming back, that he was already in his grave.

We laid him down on the upper slab with one of Mr. Girandole's blankets beneath him and another folded under his head for a

pillow. I left Grandmother to check his wounds and bandages, and I went out into the grove to stand vigil. I tried to imagine what I would say if a stranger ever came here—a soldier, a person from the village, or some prying friend of the major's—he had mentioned an artist who wanted to see the statues.

Though I kept my ears wide open, I saw no harm in going down to the dragon and dogs and wriggling through the bushes there until I found the inscription on the dragon's base, which I copied into my notebook. It said, *All is folly and you search both high and low in vain.* I didn't like that one—especially since the grand original entrance arch stood just south of the dragon. This beast was the first statue the duke's visitors would see; this was the first inscription they were meant to read—well, more accurately, the second, after the one on the arch about observing the garden piece by piece and judging whether it was all for deception or for art.

Grandmother had said that "deception" had once carried the additional meaning of "magic." But what if the duke had intended no more than "deception"? Art is deception, after all (though I'm not sure how fully this thought formed in my nine-year-old mind): art makes us feel and imagine things that have no substance; paint and chisel-marks, ink and vibrations evoke in us what is beautiful and stirring, but all is illusion.

I floundered through the bushes around the sea serpent's base and came out soaked and scratched, but I found no inscription there. What I'd thought was a horn on the serpent's head proved to be a castle or tower with a crenellated parapet. When I looked in on Grandmother and mentioned this oddity, she said it was probably intended to be the duke's castle; putting it atop the monster's head showed the power of the duke's family.

"Truth be told," Grandmother ventured, "there may be some meaning to this tilted house, too. I've been thinking it over."

"What do you suppose?" I asked eagerly.

"Noblemen of the duke's day often used towers in their gardens or on their family seals to represent their wives, who stood faithful, especially when the men were away at war. Our duke loved his wife G—— very much."

"But why is the house leaning?"

"It could be to show that G—— endured hardships, but she kept standing steadfast. Or . . ." She dabbed at R——'s injured neck, and he winced. "Or it may be his acknowledgment that nature, in the end, overturns all the works of human hands." She grinned up at me. "Or both meanings—or neither."

Studying my notebook as Grandmother used a wet rag to rub R——'s hair, I jumped up suddenly, a thrill of inspiration shooting through me. "Fourteen!" I said. "Twice seven. *Words among the trees in stone.* Fourteen is the number of inscriptions there are!"

R—— cocked his head, probably wondering what I was carrying on about.

Grandmother looked puzzled, too, though she didn't stop working.

"*Find twice the number Taurus follows with his eye!*" I quoted. "Taurus keeps his eye on the Pleiades, right? Seven sisters. Twice that number—fourteen! We just needed the number. Not fourteen women, but fourteen *inscriptions!*"

She smiled. "I knew your father's handiness with numbers must be in you somewhere."

I was thinking that I could have spared myself that last hunt through the brambles. "I've found them all: twelve from the garden, the one from the entrance arch, and *Reason departs* from this room."

"Good," said Grandmother. "Now fill the bucket again."

We stayed until past noon, hoping Mr. Girandole would return. R—— ate and talked on and on about his home city and places he'd been and movies and movie stars he thought we should know. It was rather painful without Mr. Girandole to translate. Mostly, R—— spoke to Grandmother, because I kept going outside to watch and listen. Once when I returned to the chamber, he beckoned me closer and showed me a magic trick: reaching up with his good hand, he stuck his finger in my ear and mysteriously produced a coin. He claimed he'd pulled it out of my ear, though I thought I'd have felt it if it had been there. He wanted to give me the coin, which was from his country, but Grandmother said I'd better leave it here.

R—— told us he played the piano and the flute, and he was forever moving his fingers on an imaginary keyboard or in the air beside his face, his lips blowing across a pretend mouthpiece. He talked of meeting a certain famous composer of our country before the war, and that subject interested Grandmother more than anything else he'd said. I left them chattering about conductors and concerts (they had some differences of opinion, it seemed), and I went out to stand guard and think about *My answer is in three and seven*, the words from inside the screaming mouth. The complete line was *Round and round the dancers go and my answer is in three and seven.*

These dancers, I reasoned, could be the same as the Pleiades in the poem: "Sisters dancing in the water and the sky"—not stars or sisters, but the fourteen inscriptions. They danced "round and round" the garden—the inscriptions were scattered all around the grove. I was sure I was on the right track.

Turning to the map I'd made, I counted the statues. If you left out the leaning house and considered the four women at the pool as one sculpture, there were ten in the lower garden: the dragon, Neptune, the sea serpent, Heracles, the boar, the pool, the elephant, the tortoise, the statue of which only feet remained, and the Angel of the Bottomless Pit. Ten: three plus seven. Did that mean the riddle's answer was contained in the lower garden?

In the upper garden, I counted seven structures: the sleeping woman, the centaur, the Announcing Angel, the bear, the screaming mouth, the mermaid, and the temple. Seven . . . *My answer is in three and seven.* On the one hand, it could mean that the upper grove was false and insufficient, lacking "three"—whereas the lower grove, with seven and three—ten—was complete and held the answer. But on the other hand, it could mean that I needed the upper garden for the seven, and then three of something else. Could I isolate three of something in the lower half?

Seven urns on the terrace railing—that couldn't be an accident, could it? My head was spinning. Seven women: four at the pool, one asleep, one a mermaid, and one vanished but for her sandaled feet.

It was overwhelming. For the moment, I'd have to stop thinking about numbers. I paced around the leaning house, listening, clearing my head. I passed the beautiful feet (*Behold in me*) and along the border of the central, impenetrable grove. As I neared Apollyon, the Angel of the Bottomless Pit, I looked away with a shiver—and stopped. Slowly, I turned back to face that terrible angel with the keys and the chain.

Why had I not seen it before? My fear of the statue, perhaps, had made me skip over a close investigation without intending to—but now that I looked, it was quite obvious: Apollyon's base had an inscription, too.

So much for the neat number of fourteen I'd found. This made a fifteenth:

The path beyond the dusk

I copied it down and jotted the location with a hand that trembled. The angel glared at me from beneath his frozen, wind-streaming hair.

Grandmother and I had to go home; we'd eaten no breakfast, and it was past lunchtime. But R—— refused to be shut again in the secret compartment.

"If someone comes," Grandmother told him, "you'll never be able to scramble back inside by yourself and close the lid—not without tearing loose all your stitches and making enough noise to raise the dead. And all this work will be for nothing."

All this deception will be purely for art, I thought, my mind still numb from too much puzzling.

R—— shook his head.

"Stay hidden until Girandole gets back," Grandmother said. "When he's here to watch, you can stay out all you want."

But R—— would have nothing of it. The cramped, black space with its tilted floor was driving him mad. "And want hear fairies," he added. "Hear no good there." He pointed at the sunken compartment. "Fairies sing in night."

So, he was still hearing fairy music, either in dreams or when he was awake.

"I can't imagine it's good for you to be hearing them," Grandmother told him. But she eventually saw that persuading him was a lost cause. "You're not our prisoner, R——. Stay out, then. But if the fairies steal you away, or the soldiers return, or someone from the village comes to see what all the fuss was about, or if wolves eat you, don't come crying to me."

R—— said he wouldn't; and that, I supposed, was true enough.

Step by step, I helped Grandmother down from the upper room. On the way home, I asked her if there were really wolves in the forest.

"I've never seen one," she said. But not liking the look of relief I gave her, she went on: "You know Mrs. O——, with the thick eyeglasses? She claims in all her years of gardening, she's never seen a single snake. I can't believe snakes go out of their way to avoid her garden. The truth is, she's just not seeing them."

After a remark about how she'd missed nap time, she left me to my thoughts.

A little farther along, I asked her, "Do you know if there's an inscription on Heracles's base?"

"I'm fairly sure there's not," she said. "The bushes around him weren't so thick when I was young, and I remember thinking that doing all those labors of his must have left him no time for words."

We took a roundabout way getting home, crossing from the woods behind V——'s ice house. Mrs. F——, if she saw us arriving at our front door, would think we were coming back from town.

After lunch, we both needed a long nap. The sky clouded over again as I was helping Grandmother in the garden before supper. Near

dusk, another shower hissed into the leaves, making puddles along the fence row. "Well," said Grandmother, gazing out from the back doorway, "every raindrop washes a little more of that stench away."

"Do you think Mr. Girandole will come here first or go to the grove?" I asked, mostly because I wanted to say his name and wished he were back.

"The grove, I'd imagine." Grandmother shut and locked the door. "That's where he knows what to do."

"He always knows what to do, doesn't he?"

Grandmother shuffled into the kitchen, her stick clicking on the wooden floor. "Well, you saw him at a loss on the night R——arrived."

When we'd washed the supper dishes, Grandmother asked to see my notebook and settled in her chair by the lamp to study it. My mind was still worn out from all the thinking I'd done about the statues, counting and recounting . . .

Numbers. I still hadn't copied down the numbers from the stairway in the leaning house. I would have to do that first thing.

"I'm going to hold down the fort tomorrow," Grandmother announced, rubbing her eyes. "For one thing, I can't run up and down mountains every day. For another, we can't be gone all the time. The garden needs tending before the germander runs it over, and people come to the door sometimes. And for a third, I have to pay some visits to people myself if I don't want to be rude. You go on up there if the sun comes out, and see if Girandole is back."

We were just getting ready for bed when I suddenly thought of the mailbox outside the front door. While I was here, Grandmother had turned over to me the task of bringing in the daily handful of flyers, notices, and the occasional bill. I usually did this in the hour before supper. Today, I'd completely forgotten about it. I unlocked the heavy door, stepped out into the fragrant, drippy darkness under the porch roof, and opened the lid of the cast-iron box. Inside was a single letter in a small envelope.

In the patch of light angling from the back room where we sat at night, I recognized my father's handwriting. The letter was addressed to both of us. I re-locked the door as fast as I could and raced back to Grandmother.

"Open it!" she said, handing me her letter-knife. She sat on the edge of her chair with her hands in her lap and told me to read it aloud.

Like all my papa's letters, it had been opened once and taped shut again. The Army did that to make sure the letter didn't say anything that shouldn't fall into enemy hands. My own hands trembled with excitement as I knelt in the warm light beside Grandmother's chair and unfolded the cream-colored paper. It was dated months before, on the precise day I'd arrived in the village. We'd gotten four letters from Papa that he'd written later. I wondered what this one had gone through before it finally found its way here. It said:

> Dear Mama and G——,
>
> I hope you are well and are enjoying the chance to get to know each other at last. I hope you will both forgive E—— and me for not making it happen sooner. It seems we go through our lives thinking that such-and-such will be easier when thus-and-so happens. But in all this moving and listening, fighting and mostly waiting, it's come home to me

that we shouldn't put off anything good. Anyway,
I don't have to ask how you're getting along. I know
you both quite well, and I'd guess it will be a real
struggle for E—— and me to separate you two at
the end of the summer.

G——, the village is a wonderful place, isn't it?
What did I tell you? I love the way time passes there,
and what the people talk about, and the way the
arbors whisper, and how the sun makes the tomatoes
ripen, and how the woods glow with their green light.
I'd bet it has changed hardly at all since I was a boy.
I find that very comforting!

Here, it's more of the same. I know you want
some news, but we're not supposed to say anything
about operations, and there's really not much to
tell—nothing real, in the way that the village is real
and families are real—what we're doing in the war is
the bad business of another world. I'll be glad when
I can come home to the real one. But I'm well, and I
think of you every day and every night. Sometimes
the light falls just right here, too—like now, in fact,
as I'm sitting in the corner of a little garden behind a
farm house, and the sun is shining down through the
leaves of a brave old oak tree; and the tree is telling
me that it knows the bad business will be done
someday, maybe before very long. When I'm under a
tree like this, I feel—no, I know—that we are just in
different corners of the same sacred woods.

Well, speaking of woods, do you go up there,

G——, to the forest above Mama's cottage? If she
hasn't shown you the Grove of Monsters yet, that's
what you have to do. Don't you dare leave there
without seeing it.

And speaking of the monsters in the grove:
there's a surprise I've been saving for you, G——,
an interesting mystery of sorts. The monsters'
garden seems to be a big puzzle, which I was always
trying to solve when I was a boy. It's full of words
and images that make you think. There's something
I remembered a few years ago that I'd completely
forgotten for a long time. I'd hoped we might visit
Mama together and have another crack at the riddle,
and we may still be able to do that, but I wanted to
give you a head start, since you're there now.

When I was about your age, I found something in
the grove that I kept secret—I didn't even tell you,
Mama, because I felt in a way that I was stealing, and
I was afraid you might tell me not to fool around
with property that wasn't mine. You see, I rather
thought that the garden and all the monsters were
mine, because no one else seemed to want anything
to do with them. They were all alone in the woods,
covered with vines and overgrown by bushes.

Reading those lines, I felt sorry again for my papa: he'd had
neither Grandmother nor Mr. Girandole with him in the garden,
not ever. How different—how lonely—it would be to have no one
to share it with.

In the grove, there's one statue that's scarier than all the others—a terrible angel with a ring of keys and a chain. The keys are held against the angel's side, touching his robes. Why I tried this I'll never know, but I discovered that when I fiddled with those keys, one of them slid sideways. The statue's stone key was a kind of lid, and underneath it, in the robes, was a key-shaped depression. And in that depression was a REAL KEY made of brass.

I looked high and low in the garden for years after that, all over the walls, the arches, the statues and their bases, but I never did find a keyhole that the key might fit. Nor do I have any idea what a locked door in such a place might conceal, but I was always intrigued by what the words on that frightening angel's base said: *The path beyond the dusk.*

As your father, I'm not sure if I should be telling you this or not. But I know Mama is with you, and she won't let you do anything too dangerous.

At this point, Grandmother laughed aloud, and pretty soon I joined her, until we were both wiping our eyes with our sleeves. When I got control of myself, I continued:

In fact, the key is still there at the cottage. In the sitting room, you know the funny little corner beside the built-in bookcase? Level with the bookcase's top, there's a strip of trim cut to fit that odd, short wall in the corner. If you slide that strip upward, you'll find a space behind it, inside the wall. (I guess I was always pushing and pulling on things to see if they opened.) In there, you should find the key hanging on a nail.

I figured this was a good time to tell you both about it. Think of it as my summer present to you. If you're of a mind to try solving a puzzle, perhaps you'll do better than I did. Just be careful. And please don't go anywhere that you can't come back from!

Well, duty is calling me to stop writing now. I'll write again as soon as I get the chance.

I love you both very much. Mama, I'm wearing the socks you sent me. They're holding up well, and a good thing—we're on our feet a lot. Thank you!

I remain your adoring son and father,

A——

Intrigued as we both were by the last part of the letter, neither of us sprang up at once to run to the bookcase. We wanted to read and re-read the letter's first half, with its talk of trees and sunlight and how we were all together in the same wood, and how he thought of us day and night.

"He writes good letters," I said at last.

"He always has," Grandmother answered.

Grandmother had me hold the lamp, and she handled the exploration; it was her house, after all. Sure enough, the narrow board in the bookcase corner popped out of place with a bit of tugging. It slid upward as if in a track and then came loose. Behind it was a cobwebby gap between joists, a vertical shaft formed by the rear wall of laths, the upright braces, and the paneling of the sitting room. And straight before our eyes was an ancient-looking key, suspended on a nail by its ornate head. Grandmother let me get a close look before she touched it. Then she reached in and carefully lifted it off. We both knew that if she dropped it, it would fall behind the wall.

I breathed again when the key was safely out in the room. Grandmother carried it over to the table, and I brought the lamp close. "By all the saints in glory," she murmured. "I never dreamed this was hanging back there all these years. That little rascal! What if we'd remodeled the room, as your grandfather talked of doing?"

At her instructions, I fetched the damp cleaning-rag from the kitchen, and Grandmother found her kit for polishing the silverware. She soon had the key shining like new. It was half again as long as my hand with my fingers extended. There were no markings or writing on the key—just a broad, ornamental head, a strong, heavy shank, and elaborate flanges for a lock. I laid it on a page of my notebook and drew lines to indicate its dimensions, making special note of how big a matching keyhole would need to be. (I saw at once it was far too big to fit into any of the holes in the leaning house—I was glad we wouldn't have to try those one by one.) I'd decided to leave the key here at the cottage until I found a use for it. On the page, I wrote "Papa's Summer Present." I didn't write anything about a key, just in case my notebook was ever confiscated.

"I'll write a letter to him tomorrow," Grandmother said sleepily. "You can add a page or two before we mail it. For now, you'd better try to sleep and leave before sunrise again. I'll wake you up."

So, that's what we did. I put the key into the drawer of my night table, among the seashells from Wool Island, looked for a long time at our photo, at my parents' happy faces, and lay in the dark, listening to the insects and the trees rustling. I felt deliciously tired. My father had given me two other presents, I thought, both better than the key itself: one was sending me here to Grandmother's house for the summer, and the other was the message that we were together in investigating the garden's mystery. At last, Papa had us to share the garden with. I felt as close to him now as I ever had, though I was here and he was somewhere in a tent or a barracks far away.

As she'd promised, Grandmother gently shook me awake in the dark hour before dawn. I covered my eyes at first, not wanting to leave the pleasant dream I'd been having, though already I'd forgotten what it had been about. I thought that if I stayed in bed, I might slide back down into the dream. But I remembered R——— and Mr. Girandole and my eagerness to return to the grove before I ran out of days.

I stepped onto the cool, clean floorboards, checked on the key—to make sure that it hadn't been part of my dream—and stumbled off to the bathroom.

"I don't expect you feel like breakfast yet," Grandmother said. (The fact that she still wore her nightgown told me she planned to go back to bed when she'd sent me off.) "But there's plenty in this bag for you to eat, too." She'd loaded a bag with rolls, cheese, crackers, plums, tangerines, and a bottle each of milk and water. "Drink the milk early," she advised. "It'll be hot today."

Going out the back door to check the weather, I could see the last pale stars in a sky of deep blue. A soft wind riffled the hedge. The scent of the tomato vines tickled the back of my throat.

I held my notebook, wondering if I wanted to risk taking it along, tucked beneath the fake one. Yes—there was nothing in my notebook that couldn't be replaced. Grandmother and I knew the poem by heart, and everything else was written in stone, as it had been for close to four hundred years.

As I picked up the bag, Grandmother gave me an appraising look, and I guessed she was considering something with care. "I don't think R—— is dangerous," she said finally. "But he's getting his strength back. Remember that, for one thing, he is an enemy soldier, and for another thing, he's a man we know nothing about. The less he knows about us, the better. Don't feel you have to entertain him. Be wary around him, and if he does or says anything you don't like, you just run away. He can't run after you yet."

I nodded soberly.

"Be back in time for supper."

Again, I had the joy of watching daylight arrive, tremulous and misty, in the sacred woods. Again, I trekked silently all around the garden to check for strangers or anything amiss. The foul scent was fading from the glade itself, but it was still almost palpable on the stairs. I hoped we hadn't ruined the leaning house forever. Long before I entered it, I knew Mr. Girandole wasn't back yet. He would have heard me coming and met me somewhere outdoors.

R—— was dozing under a blanket, but he opened his eyes at my appearance and struggled to sit up. It occurred to me that we'd forgotten to move the padding from his old pallet up to the chamber floor where he now lay.

"Oof! Ah!" he complained, contorting his face as he slowly propped himself up against the wall beneath the window. "Hard bed. Bad smell hard bed."

"Good morning," I said, unpacking the food. Grandmother had sent along two old, chipped cups from the back of the cupboard, and I poured us each some of the milk. I was hungry now, after my hike. Still, the reeking chamber made swallowing anything unpleasant.

R—— thanked me and ate whatever I pushed his way. He seemed to be faring all right. At least, he hadn't been caught by anyone or eaten by wolves.

"Did the fairies sing last night?" I asked him, suddenly thinking that he'd done something remarkable, something wild and perilous: he'd spent a night in the garden outside the shelter of the compartment. What might have transpired in the moonlight just below his window?

He nodded. "Sing like angels. I want go fairy country. Later, I strong again, I go with them. Yeah? Fairy country."

His expression held such longing that I felt a pang in my chest. "If you go to their country," I said, "I don't think you can ever come back." At least, I thought it worked that way in the old stories.

"No want come back," he said. "No worry for me. Good there!"

I picked up a cracker but felt my stomach lurch. To eat in this malodorous place . . .

Seeing my plight, R—— showed me a trick: he tore two little pieces from a sheet of waxed paper that wrapped the crackers in the tin. Having wadded these into balls, he stuck them into his nostrils.

I thought it might be worth a try. It was uncomfortable to have wads of paper in my nose, but it made eating possible. The plugs I'd rolled jutted from my nostrils like tusks. R—— laughed at me, said "Elephant," and trumpeted, curling his arm in the air like a trunk. I couldn't help laughing and trying to imitate the sound myself.

We ate in silence for a minute or two.

When he was slowing down, R—— studied me. "She . . . grandma?"

"Yes," I said, pulling the papers from my nose. "She's my grandma. My grandmother."

"Good. Good lady. Kind."

I nodded. "Thanks."

"Mother? Father?"

I hesitated, remembering that I wasn't supposed to tell him much. But I didn't see any harm in the question, so I explained as clearly as I could that my father was away fighting the war, and my mother was working hard and taking care of my baby sister.

R—— declared that this, too, was "good."

He said, "Maybe you father shoot me. Shoot plane." He made an explosion gesture with his fingers and an accompanying sound, then grinned.

"No." I smiled back, guardedly. "He's not a pilot."

"Oh. Good. You, me, we friend, then. Yeah?"

I only smiled and left the food where he could reach it. Then I noticed that I'd better bring him a fresh bucket of water and empty his toilet again.

Pointing at me, R—— pretended to swing something—some imaginary tool, perhaps?—and smacked his fist into his other palm and pretended to catch something. It was a question. I had no idea what he meant—some sort of work?

"I don't have a job," I said. "I'm a kid."

"No, no! Baseball!"

So, that was it. I'd heard of it and seen pictures—a game played in other countries, involving funny hats and baggy pants.

R—— waved rapidly at me, as if telling me to back up. I looked around in confusion. Then he curled a hand in such a way that I realized he was supposed to be holding up a ball. He tossed the "ball" up, made a show of swinging with his invisible club, and made a cracking impact sound.

"Go! Go! Go!" he cried, waving me backward. Next, he said "Catch! Catch!" so fervently that at last I put up a hand half-heartedly, feeling like an idiot.

"Ff-tumpf!" R—— cupped hands over his mouth and made a catching sound. "Here! Here!" He held up his hands again. "Home! Home!"

Smiling awkwardly, I made a limp throwing motion.

"Out!" he finished in triumph, pulling off his "hat," throwing it into the air, and giving me a thumbs-up.

I wondered which of us had "won." It seemed a bizarre game, but I couldn't help chuckling at him as I picked up the bucket and the pan and carried them carefully down the stairs.

When I returned, I established from him that he hadn't seen Mr. Girandole recently, and R—— looked worried about him, too. As I was getting out my notebook and pencil, he had another question for me: he said "grandma" again and made a cigarette-smoking gesture with two fingers.

"No," I said. "She doesn't smoke." He wanted cigarettes.

"Beer?" he asked. "Wine? Whiskey?" Those words he knew just fine in our language.

"I don't know," I said. "I'll ask her."

He seemed to understand—or else he took it as a promise that I'd bring him some—and again he gave me a happy thumbs-up.

I turned my attention then to copying the numbers from the staircase. As I went along, I prodded and thumped on each riser to see if it might conceal a hollow space, and I was always on the lookout for a keyhole. R—— asked what I was doing, but I didn't know how to explain it to him. The numbers, in order, were:

5, 12, 3, 10, 7, 13, 8, 6, 1, 14, 11, 2, 9, and 4.

They were all of the same size and carved in the same style, but the 12, 7, 14, and 2 were upside down. I copied them that way.

Taking my notebook out onto the terrace, I pondered the numbers. When I counted them, I wasn't surprised to find that there were fourteen of them. That number again: fourteen. Twice seven.

On a blank page, I added up all the numbers and got a total of one hundred and five. The total of only the right-side up numbers was seventy. The total of the upside down numbers was thirty-five. I noticed at once that thirty-five was exactly half of seventy. I tapped the pencil on the notebook. Did any of it mean anything?

My answer is in three and seven. Among these numbers, the 3 was right-side up, and the 7 was upside down. That reminded me of a mirror again. This garden always came back to mirror images.

But if "three and seven" meant ten . . . Ten of the numbers were right-side up. That could mean that the answer was contained in them somehow, and I could forget about the upside-down numbers. But numbers were only numbers, cold and uncommunicative. Perhaps they were only here for decoration. *Reason departs.*

It seemed pointless for me to hunt all over the garden for a key-hole. My father said he'd done that for years and found nothing. I wished he were here now. I imagined him taking one quick look through my notebook, laughing, and pointing out how simple the answer was.

Or . . . maybe he wouldn't. A puzzle shouldn't be unsolvable, but it shouldn't be too easy, either.

With a sigh, I looked back at the page. Absently, I let my finger-tips walk across the four upside-down numbers.

Four.

The four in the garden that came readily to mind was the number of women with water-pitchers around the square pool. Could each upside-down number represent one of those women? Following that assumption, could each of the fourteen numbers represent a different statue? No, there were more than fourteen statues in the garden.

I shut the notebook and stood up, not sure what to do next.

At that moment, a voice spoke close beside me, and I nearly jumped out of my skin.

"Well, I'm back," said the voice.

It was Mr. Girandole.

I felt such relief that my eyes watered. Without thinking, I flung my arms around him, pressing my face against his lapel. He stood woodenly at first, but then he hugged me and patted my back. The long, bedraggled coat smelled of swamp water, and his shoeless hoofs were plastered with drying mud. He still wore his hat, but the ruck-sack was gone from his shoulder, and I saw no sign of the flak vest.

"Are you all right?" I asked.

"Yes. Just in need of a long sleep. How is everyone here?"

I assured him that Grandmother and R—— were fine. "But R—— refuses to stay in the compartment any more. He sleeps out on the open floor up there."

Mr. Girandole scowled.

"What happened with the dogs?" I said.

"They're making dogs more persistent these days." He sat wearily on a bench. "I went first to my cave, put that sack of gear there, and sealed up the entrance so you'd never know it *was* a cave. I had more dog-bane on my shelf—"

"The stuff in the gourd?"

"Yes. I doused the approach, then doubled back and laid my own scent trail in another direction, still dragging that jacket of R——'s. I led them over the mountains to get them far away from here. As I drew near to the villages on the other side, I left the vest in a barn and stowed away on a freight train. That took me through another arm of the mountains; I got off at a place where I knew I could use a river to come a long way back toward home without leaving a scent."

At the mention of a train, I wondered if it might have had the engine that my father had designed. I liked the idea of my father helping to save Mr. Girandole. "You swam?" I asked.

"Mostly floated, hanging on to a little raft."

I shook my head in amazement at his ingenuity. "How do you know the country so well?"

"I've explored a lot. And I've studied maps."

"I'm so glad you're back! We were worried."

"I was worried about you, too. I guess you've done well."

I told Mr. Girandole I had something to show him. "Not far away at all," I added when he looked worried. (He seemed to be on his last legs, about to collapse from exhaustion.) I led him down the terrace steps and then directly behind them, to the Angel of the Bottomless Pit.

"Did you know about this?" Summoning my courage, I eased through the weeds at the statue's base, reached out, and took hold of one of the stone keys hanging against the angel's side.

It wouldn't budge. Mr. Girandole stood quietly, looking over my shoulder.

I tried the second key, and it grudgingly slid back to reveal the key-shaped space behind it—which, of course, was now empty.

Mr. Girandole's bleary eyes widened, and he leaned close. "No, I didn't know!" he said. Cautiously, he touched the depression with his long fingers, felt around the edges, and tried pushing it like a button. Then he stood back, resting his chin on a palm. "It looks like it was made to contain a real key."

I grinned, relishing the moment. "It did. We have the key at Grandmother's."

"Extraordinary!" He beamed at me. "How did you find it? Clues from the inscriptions?"

Now I felt a bit sheepish—he was so proud of me. I told him about my father's letter.

He nodded, and a faraway look came to his eyes. "I remember those years when your father used to come here. I . . ." The subject seemed to embarrass him suddenly, and he fell silent.

"I know you kept hidden when he was here," I said. "Grandmother explained it to me."

"Oh." Now he looked even more embarrassed. "Well, I sort of

kept watch over him; not that there was much danger here in those days. If you don't mind my saying, you are so much like him—the same walk, the same eyes, almost the same hair. It's as if time has turned backward . . . though it never does."

"I don't mind."

"But I must not have been watching when he found this."

"Can you guess what it might open?"

He smiled faintly, studying Apollyon. "The door we're looking for? I *hope* it's not just for locking that compartment in the house, or the spare key to the duke's castle." Stooping, he examined the statue's base, where the mighty carven chains bound the door to the bottomless pit.

"I rather hope, too, that there's not a keyhole in this platform," he said. "Wouldn't you be reluctant to go sticking a key into the lock on the Bottomless Pit? No, I don't much care for the duke's sense of humor in making us use Apollyon's key. It's too much like asking us to open Pandora's box. That did not go well at all."

He shivered then as if with firsthand memory.

As we returned to the leaning house, I gave him a quick summary of my recent progress and thoughts about the garden. It came out mostly like gibberish, and I thought later how good it was of Mr. Girandole to listen so politely in his present state. But I did ask him clearly what he made of the number seventy.

"'The days of our years are threescore years and ten,'" he answered. Seeing my blank look, he said, "That's what Moses said. Seventy years is a human life."

"Moses?" I asked in surprise, crawling after him up the steep steps. "Do you read the Bible?"

He stopped, gazing down past his elbow at me with a serious

face. "Do you suppose that the Elder Folk don't know who makes the trees grow? We've known Him since the beginning." Climbing again, he added: "I would never disregard a book simply because it was so new and so concise."

Mr. Girandole's mood turned cranky when R—— greeted him with an exuberant "Mr. Satyr!" But after taking stock of the patient's condition—and commending me for keeping things clean and in order—Mr. Girandole climbed up to the roof to take a nap. I told him I'd stay around in the garden and keep my eyes and ears open, for which he was grateful.

I did more pondering and puzzling as the sun climbed to its zenith. Returning again to the great stone tortoise and then to the wild boar, I searched their slabs once more for inscriptions that I'd missed, but neither harbored any words at all. One foray through the sea serpent's brambles had been enough for me, but I did shore up my resolve and thread my way into the thicket where Heracles stood. I traversed the roots of a giant old tree and yelped as a black-and-yellow snake shot away from my feet. I wondered if Mrs. O—— would see a snake if one came *that* close.

When the icy tingles of the encounter had passed, I edged forward again, avoiding webs where fat spiders hung and shook their forelegs at me. The spiders, too, were patterned in bright yellow and black, as if all the thicket's denizens were in uniform. Heracles stood partly in a patch of sunlight; the dense brake beyond the tree-shade's edge was steamy and stifling. Dark purple berries shone like jewels. A prickly herbal odor hung thick, and mosquitoes buzzed. Something scrabbled through the bushes, some animal alarmed at my bumbling.

I hoisted myself onto the pedestal between Heracles's enormous

feet and sat cross-legged to rest on a bare expanse of stone, shaded
by the statue. Some creepers looped across the pedestal like oily
ropes sprouting leaves. As I'd noted from a distance, vines coiled
around the legs of the colossus, giving him a pair of leafy trousers.
Even so, I could see that his sandals, toes, and bulging muscles
were all carved in minute detail.

Moving all around the base, I hung down over its edge to push
back the foliage. But Grandmother's memory served well. Nowhere
did I find any engraved letters.

When I'd made my way back to the open glade, I observed the
arches: the northern pair, bare of any carvings, and the southern
pair, adorned with faces.

I peered up at these carvings one by one, bearded men crowned
with leaves . . . angelic faces of great beauty . . . weathered faces
that might have been animals . . . frightening faces with horned
brows. There were—as I'd come to expect—fourteen faces in all:
seven on the left arch, seven on the right.

Hungry, I returned to R——'s chamber for lunch. He had his
eyes closed but opened them when he heard me rummaging, and
was obviously glad I was still around. I peeled a tangerine and used
some of its skin to block my nostrils this time. R—— taught me
the words for "tangerine," "cracker," "cheese," "bread," and "water"
in his language. Then he pointed upward, whispered "Mr. Satyr,"
and taught me another word, smiling and nodding as I repeated it.

Mr. Girandole's hearing was sharp indeed. His voice drifted
down to us through the open hatch: "That doesn't mean 'faun' or
'satyr.' Forget that one!"

R—— slumped against the wall, laughing.

I pointed at R—— and said the word again, whatever it meant.

He laughed harder, holding his side. Then I took the pieces of tangerine peel from my nostrils and threw them at him one after the other.

R—— had an inspiration then and, with words and gestures, got me to retrieve four twigs from his old pallet in the well. He had me take these to the threshold and arrange them on the floor in a square. This outlined box became our target, and we sat beneath the window, throwing bits of tangerine peel across the open pit. R—— used his notebook to keep score. We laughed, and I thought it was like playing in the cabin of a sinking ship: a very *smelly* sinking ship.

As Mr. Girandole clambered down the ladder from above, I leaped to my feet and looked out the window, ashamed to have been neglecting my guard duty even for a few minutes. R—— aimed a fragment of peel at him, but Mr. Girandole wasn't amused.

"I'm sorry," I said, my face burning. "You're trying to sleep."

"I haven't been trying to sleep since you came in for lunch," he said. Strangely, though his tone was soft and grave, he didn't seem to be scolding us as we deserved. Rather, his eyes looked sad. Throughout the rest of the day I wondered why.

Back at the cottage, I told Grandmother about how R—— had said he wanted to go to Faery. I expected her to disapprove, but after some thought, she said, "That's probably a good place for him. If we find a doorway that goes there."

I spent the time after supper writing a long letter to my father, answering his, thanking him for the key, and bringing him up to date on our adventures and discoveries. (Again, I left out any mention of R—— or Mr. Girandole.) Near our usual bedtime, as he'd told me he would, the faun tapped on our back door. Grandmother pulled him inside, shut the door, and caught him in a long embrace.

Seeing the relief and bliss in his face, I understood at last why he'd been so determined to come despite the risk. During his far-ranging adventure with the dogs, he must have been even more worried about us—about Grandmother—than we'd been about him. (Or than *I'd* been, anyway; I couldn't speak for what went on in Grandmother's mind.) Though he'd learned from me that Grandmother was safe, he'd needed to see her with his own eyes.

Seventy years . . . the length of a human life, Mr. Girandole had said, quoting Moses.

How old was Grandmother? She'd mentioned her mortality the other day.

The older I become, the more I understand Mr. Girandole's look of sadness and what he must have been thinking then. These games with tangerine peels . . . the times of little wide-eyed girls arriving on the terrace, and boys with notebooks . . . none of it lasted for more than a breath. Time never turned backward. Summer gave way to winter, and summer came again, and year by year, the vines lengthened, and the sharp detail faded from the statues—scales becoming ripples, passion becoming tranquility. Each time Mr. Girandole saw Grandmother, he looked at her like we all ought to look at one another, every time.

Grandmother heated soup and brought out cheese and meat and bread. We sat around the kitchen table while crickets fiddled steadily in the night, and the world to me seemed as right as it ever gets. When Mr. Girandole had eaten his fill, Grandmother poured glasses of wine—mine a smallish one—and we retired to the sitting room.

"Oh, I forgot!" I said. "R—— asked for cigarettes and wine or beer or whiskey."

"Ha!" said Grandmother. "Then he'd better just check himself into the hotel."

Moving closer to the lamp, Mr. Girandole asked if he might see the poem in my notebook; R——'s poem. "These lines haunted me while I was away," he said as he re-read them. "I made some connections that had not at first occurred to me. I've been away for so long that I wasn't thinking of the poetry of Faery."

"What do you mean?" Grandmother asked.

"The Elder Folk have special names for nearly everything, used often in songs—'sisters dancing' refers to leaves—the leaves of trees."

"So, we're looking for *leaves*?" I asked with a frown.

"No, there's more to it. In Faery, it's difficult for us to comprehend the idea of death, though we know it's something that happens to mortals before they come to us. There's a song I knew once, though I'd all but forgotten it—a fairy song that describes death as 'sisters dancing in the water and the sky'—yes, the very line used in R——'s poem. The image, you see, is of leaves that fall from the branches to the water . . . leaves that are plucked from the boughs and borne away by the wind. The water and the sky are not where the leaves began, but they dance there—do you see? That's how we try to understand the mortal journey."

Grandmother put her elbows on her knees. "So, the poem tells us to look for fourteen, or twice seven, and it tells us to look for death."

Mr. Girandole sipped his wine. "I'm not sure *what* the poem tells us, but mortality seems to be a part of the garden."

For a short while, we listened to a soft orchestral piece on the radio. When it finished, Grandmother turned it off.

I pulled my knees up, rested my head on the arm of the couch, and must have drifted off. But at some point, I was awake again, warm and comfortable and listening to the two of them talk. I felt a pang of guilt—it was a personal conversation. And yet it seemed that were I to stir and alert them to my wakefulness, I would be doing a greater disservice, shattering a fragile thing. So, I lay without moving, and listened.

"A confession, Girandole?"

"Yes, of sorts. You recall the day I spoke to you of my first love, the woman I left my people for?"

"How could I forget?" said Grandmother dryly. "It was the day you told me in no uncertain terms that I should leave the garden without looking back and marry some good man of the village. The day you broke my heart." Grandmother spoke gently, not with bitterness.

"Yours and mine," he answered. "But what I said then was not entirely true. I abandoned my people indeed for a woman—but not for one I'd already met."

"What do you mean, Girandole?"

"I've never explained to you about the broken statue—the one of which only the feet remain. Tell me what you know of that image, M——."

I nearly opened my eyes.

Grandmother spoke softly. "You said once that you had never seen it, that it was already gone when the fauns came to the sacred woods. I told you, you'll remember, what I read about in the capital, that it was very likely an image of G——, the duke's beloved wife. The woman he built the garden for. *Behold in me,* the inscription reads. The duke must have 'beheld' in her *everything*: the reason the moon climbs the sky; the purpose of the dawn and the rain; the meaning in his breath itself. Listen to me!" She laughed at herself.

"Go on," said Mr. Girandole. "Everything you know about it."

"Well, she died," continued Grandmother, "and he could not bear to look at the perfect image of her when the woman herself was gone. In his grief, he had the statue destroyed. The garden, like his life, would never again be complete. He left the feet and the pedestal, according to the legend, to express the brokenness, the hole left in the world." Grandmother seemed to think for a moment. "And then he went through the fairy door, didn't he?—to be with her again. That's why he disappeared from this world. Mortality is a part of the garden, as you said. Its paths go round and round on life's journey, but then, at the end, one path leaves the garden and ascends."

"Up to the temple, yes." I heard Mr. Girandole set down his glass. "Well, I told you what I told you because I knew it was the only way you would leave me and have the life you were meant to have—a life among your kind, where time passes. You left me when I'd convinced you that I'd loved before and might love again—that you were the second love of my life. If I'd told you the truth, you wouldn't have gone."

Grandmother seemed at a loss for words. "But . . . you left your people. What could make you do that, if not—"

"I saw only the feet that remained. Only the pedestal where she'd

stood, and those words in the stone. I didn't know about G——
and the duke yet, but I understood—perhaps with the intuition of
a faun, for we are creatures of the heart, even as our satyr cousins
are creatures of the flesh. And once I understood, the music and
the dancing could no longer fill the emptiness in me.

"I knew that humans have a gift that is not granted to us in
Faery: this gift of giving the heart in devotion to one other soul,
and walking together through days of a limited number. This love
of which your people are capable . . . It's warmer than the warmest
hearth in winter. It's like a meteor, lighting the sky before it passes
beyond.

"If I couldn't have that with you, M——, I wanted it *for* you.
With your young human heart, I thought, you could forget me,
and find your love where you were meant to."

Grandmother was weeping now. "Oh, Girandole. You dear,
foolish man."

"The truth, M——, is that there was no 'first' woman. There
were only the feet, G——'s feet, and what they represented. I knew
I would find her, somewhere in this world. I wanted to touch and
hold such a gift in my own arms, even if I couldn't keep her. One
single moment of that would be better than an eternity without.
And I *did* find her—only once. I regret nothing. I've been blessed
to watch her son grow up, to know her grandson, and I've been
close to her for longer than I expected."

"Girandole," Grandmother said huskily. "Do you think for a
moment that you'll ever lose me?"

The couch moved then, and I knew Grandmother was getting
up to go and sit beside him. I took the opportunity to roll over
with my face to the cushioned back, so they wouldn't see my tears.

*   *   *   *

I awoke in my bed, with bright sunlight streaming through the curtains. I was wearing my pajamas, so I must have made my way in there at some point, but I had no recollection of it. From the way my mouth felt, I could tell I hadn't cleaned my teeth. No one occupied the sitting room, front room, or kitchen. I saw by the kitchen clock that it was past nine o'clock. As I grabbed my toothbrush and the powder, I heard Grandmother chatting with someone in the garden. At first, I wondered if it might be Mr. Girandole, though I doubted he'd remain here in the daytime, but then I heard another lady's voice. Peeping out through a window, I saw that it was a friend of Grandmother's I'd never met.

I cleaned my teeth, got dressed, and discovered the rucksack from yesterday packed and waiting for me on the kitchen table. A note beside it said, "Milk in the ice box." In the top section, next to the dwindling chunk of ice, I found the same milk bottle, not quite full; Grandmother was sending the last of it with me. By force of habit, I dropped to all fours for a look into the pan beneath the ice box. It was in no danger of overflowing before evening. I slid the bottle into the bag, went back to my room for my notebook, and took one more look at the key in the drawer.

Passing toward the back door, I glanced into the sitting room, thinking happily of the time we'd spent last night. I saw the mythology book lying open on Grandmother's footstool. I crouched beside it and found the entry about the Pleiades. Reading through it again, I noticed something that I had glossed over before: of the Seven Sisters, only six were said to be visible in Taurus. One of them, named Merope, was the "lost Pleiad." The book explained that she was ashamed to show her face because she married a mortal.

I stood and stretched. After a while, I ventured out to the garden and was introduced to Mrs. J——, who, like so many others, said I looked like my papa.

"I'll mail our letter, and I have to go to the store," Grandmother told me. I offered to help, but she said she only needed to get a few things, and she'd rather I went and gathered some wood for the stove. "Did you see the lunch for you to take?"

I nodded and thanked her.

"He's such a good boy!" exclaimed Mrs. J——.

I had reached an impasse with the grove of monsters. Though Grandmother and Mr. Girandole helped me, the mystery seemed to recede before us like heat waves shimmering on far fields. The more we probed, the more the answer crumbled beneath our fingers like the wood of a rotten log.

Grandmother wrote down the identity of each statue and spent hours poring over books from her shelf; she read about centaurs and Heracles, Neptune and mermaids. Mostly in the evenings, I joined her in this reading. We stacked the kitchen table high with books and pushed them back and forth, showing each other passages we wondered about.

I got into the habit of carrying a book or two to the garden each day, comparing illustrations of fantastic creatures to the statues there.

R—— confronted us at last with the question I'd been dreading: "What you do?" He pointed at my notebook. "All this, all time . . . what for? Why you hard think?"

I bit my lip, wondering how much to say.

Fortunately, Grandmother was there. She sighed and explained in a low voice that we thought the garden's statues and words and numbers were all part of a riddle that concealed a door into Faery, and we were trying to solve it. R—— gave a joyous whoop, but Grandmother shushed him. "If we're caught," she said, "you're going with the soldiers, not the fairies."

For a while, I grew obsessed with maps, supposing at first that the grove might be laid out in imitation of the classical city of Rome on its seven hills, each statue corresponding to a famous building of antiquity—but in the end, I couldn't make the theory stick. I wondered for a time if the grove's central thicket were shaped like the sea, and the statues around it the seaports and capitals of the ancient world. In desperation, I added all the garden's trees to my map, postulating that the duke had woven nature into his enigma—but Mr. Girandole gently pointed out that most of the present trees were much younger than the garden, and there had likely been different ones standing in the duke's era. So much for my idea that the seven major trees of Heracles's thicket might be the Pleiades.

We reviewed from the Gospels and Revelation and Genesis every account we could find of angels. Contemplating the elephant, we read about Hannibal and the Punic Wars. Grandmother even opened a heavy bestiary and studied tortoises, boars, and bears. I wasn't sure what research might be done on the four unclothed women with water jars, but I kept my eyes open for similar images.

Recalling what Mr. Girandole had said about the fairy poem— that "sisters dancing in the water and the sky" was a metaphor for death—we revisited every place in the garden that suggested mortality. The sleeping woman, I conceded, might well be dead. The soldier in the elephant's trunk appeared lifeless. Grandmother pointed out that the screaming mouth resembled a tomb. The hilltop temple (*I am a gate*) clearly led visitors Heavenward and anticipated the afterlife. But our searches yielded nothing new. Mr. Girandole also spent a long time reexamining the base of the missing statue and the interior of the leaning house. *Reason departs,* he mused to us, implied insanity. Did it refer to the duke's state of mind after his wife's death? Could it also be a direct reference to G——, since her death meant the departure of the duke's *reason* for existence?

Grandmother took to falling asleep in her easy chair with a book in her lap; I would nudge her awake so she could go to bed. She, in turn, would poke me in the early hours so I could begin my hike up the mountain. Having made her neighborly rounds of all her friends' flower gardens, she came with me more and more as the days drew nearer to the end of my visit. Mr. Girandole tapped more often at our back door after supper, and we talked and read, laughed and speculated on those hot late-summer nights, with moths beating against the screens and moonlight blazing down on the trees and hedges.

Our days in the sacred grove were both timeless and fleeting. In the morning, when the shadows were vibrant and blue, when the light was pink on the stone, I would sigh happily at the prospect of an entire day in this place, with these people. In the late afternoon, with the sunlight heavy, thick, and deepening from gold to red, I would wonder where that long day had gone while my back was turned.

Mr. Girandole brought a clear glass jar from his cave. It was huge, like the jars from which drugstores sold candy. He filled it with water, added certain dry leaves and herbs, and left it on the open hilltop, by the Greek temple. The sun shone down and brewed a rich tea scented of mint, which we drank with our meals in the grove.

I made the rounds of the monsters, scrutinizing them from every angle, tapping and poking and searching for any numbers hidden among their carved features. Mr. Girandole engaged in his own explorations, focusing more on those impassable tangles of vegetation where more secrets might still lie hidden. He wriggled into hedges and came out covered with burrs and spores and spider webs. Grandmother methodically dug up the weeds and soil from all seven urns on the terrace rail, sifting through the muck and examining each urn inside and out. (It was ideal work for her, since she could take sitting breaks or naps on the benches.) But there was nothing to be found. With our help as haulers, she refilled the urns with fresh earth, and we scattered the old snaily mulch in the bushes. In time, the forest would replant the urns with the seeds of its choosing.

In just a few days, unquestionably R—— became our friend. Grandmother laughed at his antics and seemed to enjoy impressing him by saying things in his language. Even Mr. Girandole forgot to be disgruntled at him when R—— spoke of the fairies' songs, which he heard every night—and of his recurring dreams of "satyr-men," which Mr. Girandole determined from his descriptions were in fact fauns. R—— spoke again and again of how he wanted to go to Faery, not back to his homeland.

One afternoon, when Mr. Girandole and I were doing our best to explore the central thicket, I asked, "Why does R—— hear and dream these things, and not the rest of us?"

Mr. Girandole looked back at me through thorny branches, his hat dusted with seeds. "He was there. Once a mortal has been on the borders of Faery, its voices can always reach his ears."

We couldn't penetrate into those unyielding bushes at the grove's heart. The tangle might harbor nothing more than thorns and roots and trunks from one side to the other, or it might conceal wonders; either way, it was closed to us. As we picked leaves from our clothing out on the open ground again, Mr. Girandole said he supposed it was fitting that the garden's very middle should be beyond our reach. "Like Eden," he said. "The Tree of Life, and the Tree of the Knowledge of Good and Evil, not to be touched."

Standing there, we were only a few steps from the pedestal of the missing statue—the image of the duke's wife, G——. I couldn't help moving closer to gaze in wonder at the small, sandaled feet, exquisitely crafted in stone.

Mr. Girandole watched me curiously, but his gaze, too, was drawn to the pedestal.

Without thinking carefully, I said, "The day I met you, you talked about Cinderella. The prince went to search far and wide through the land for the girl with the beautiful feet. He knew he'd find her."

I closed my mouth, realizing I'd probably said too much. I felt him staring at me. I finished lamely, "These are beautiful feet, I've always thought."

Taking my notebook, I climbed to the roof of the leaning house while Mr. Girandole patrolled the garden. Grandmother was snoring softly down on the terrace, and R—— was looking through a book of piano music we'd brought to amuse him.

I leaned back against the parapet and held the notebook in my lap. On a clean page, past all my notes and diagrams and scribbles that were swiftly filling it up, I copied out every inscription again so I could study them free of explanations:

You who enter this place, observe it piece by piece and tell me afterward whether so many marvels were created for deception or purely for art.

My steps fall softly like the rain

Or a thousand cheeses times a thousand if you give me days enough

Hurry now to find me draw near but not inside

I am it is very true

Round and round the dancers go and my answer is in three and seven

The Mermaid

Or walls or ivied garden porch or doorstep have we none

Behold in me

You have we have all have though perhaps home

Narrow

Reason departs

I am a gate

All is folly and you search both high and low in vain

The path beyond the dusk

Fifteen inscriptions. Some made an odd sort of sense; some made none at all. They had no punctuation, except for the one Grandmother had given me. I'd never seen it for myself; I wondered if she had added the punctuation, though I didn't guess it mattered much. Idly, I began to play with the punctuation of another:

I am. It is very true.
I am, it is: very true.

This was pointless. *You search both high and low in vain.* My father had spent years looking for a keyhole. I could spend years pushing words around on paper, counting trees, and reading books.

For deception, or purely for art.
A thousand cheeses times a thousand.
If you give me days enough.

There's no meaning here at all, is there? I asked the duke. Rising to my knees against the balustrade, I put my chin on my arms and watched Mr. Girandole pacing near Neptune, his hands clasped behind him. No meaning at all. The purpose is the search—to make discoveries, each one whetting your appetite for more. It's the perfect puzzle, because it never ends, from year to year, generation to generation. There is no disappointment, because the solution is always just ahead, growing more wonderful with each theory that fails.

I stood up and took a good look around. The filtered sunlight shifted with the breeze—shafts of light, as from the high windows of a cathedral. Green vaults receded among the trees, each an entrance to the secret avenues of the world. A plane was passing somewhere; I rarely heard planes anymore, here in our garden.

As my gaze slid over the mass of bushes between the square pool and the sleeping woman, I did a double-take. Once again, I saw something I'd never seen because I'd never been looking for it. In the middle of that thicket, against the ravine's west wall, there was a distinct gap in the foliage, a place where no bushes grew. Only my high vantage allowed me to see it. Perhaps it marked an outcropping of stone . . . maybe a pit or well . . . maybe a natural, muddy hollow where rainwater pooled. Whatever it was, I would have to go and find out. Again, my heart was fluttering—that was the effect the garden had.

As I climbed down the ladder, R—— sang, "Da dum dum daaa, da dum dee deedle-dee dum!"—his nose buried in the piano score, his hands playing a keyboard that wasn't there.

Grandmother went right on with her nap. Mr. Girandole noticed me hurrying down the terrace steps. I waved him over, pointing toward the thicket where I was headed.

"There's something in there," I said, facing the green wall that stood three times my height, thorny and dark. A white butterfly wove among the bushes' pale blossoms.

"What do you mean?" Mr. Girandole asked, his nose testing the air. "Something moving?"

"No. Something big and oblong that keeps the bushes from growing."

Eyeing the dense brake, he adjusted his hat. "Well, then, here we go again."

Once more, we pushed and twisted, fighting for places to plant our feet and squeeze through. Vines tried to choke us; dead limbs cracked and rolled beneath my shoes. Invisible strands of web stuck to my face, and spiders jiggled indignantly. Parting the leaves, I squinted ahead.

"I think it's just a big rock," I said, glimpsing a gray shape too formless to be a statue.

"If it's a rock," said Mr. Girandole, "then it's a rock with teeth!"

We struggled through the last vines, and I stared into a mouth wider than my outstretched arms, the thicket's creepers flowing between rounded teeth like an expelled mouthful of seawater. Far back in shadows rose a huge, fluked tail.

"A whale!" I cried out. It was another statue on a rectangular base, lost here in the bushes. And sure enough, we found letters carved into the pedestal's side.

"Didn't you know about this one?" I asked as we worked our way along the leviathan, admiring the intelligent-looking eye, the flipper, the power in its massive shape.

"I'm no longer sure," he said. "If I knew once, it was years upon years ago. It's certainly been covered over since before I met your grandmother, and I didn't pay as much attention to the statues back then—they were just man-things."

It thrilled me to have made a discovery the others had missed—

to be seeing for the first time something that not even Grandmother in her long years had ever seen. This whale had lain here behind the leaves and branches, his eyes unblinking through rains and winds, summers and winters, mere paces away from the open glade but always hidden. Garlands of vine draped the sea-beast so thickly that I doubt he would have been recognizable from a short distance; the tail seemed almost to be a leaning tree. Step by step, leaf by leaf, we uncovered the inscription:

Yet one by one a herd may pass

We circumnavigated the base, hunting for other markings, tapping for hollow sounds, and especially looking for keyholes, since my father had likely never found the whale. Mr. Girandole boosted me up, and I sat on the creature's broad back. There was a shallow depression for the blowhole, from which a real whale would send up plumes of breath—but it was only a blowhole, not a keyhole.

"So," said Mr. Girandole, helping me down. "Another enlightening revelation."

"Now there are *sixteen* inscriptions," I said. "When does it end?"

Grandmother awoke as we sat on the terrace, pulling brambles from ourselves and tossing them over the railing. "What did I miss?" she asked, sitting up.

"A whale," I said.

That afternoon, we scouted from the house's roof and from the hilltop for any other suspicious openings in the thickets. Mr. Girandole climbed a few strategic trees and did some hunting in the brake southwest of the dragon, down by the old entrance arch. Near as we could figure, there were no other places where statues might hide—except, of course, for that central tangle. Even so, the leaning house overlooked much of that, and no break in the rolling bush-tops was apparent. It was always possible, though, that branches might be joined in a ceiling, hiding something beneath. We could never truly know.

Before we left for the cottage, R—— asked if there were reeds growing by the stream; he wanted to try making a flute. Mr. Girandole said he would bring a few back when he went to refill the water bucket.

Despite the fun we were having, as that glorious week drew to its close, a feeling of gloom and frustration settled over me. We were finding no more clues—no numbers, no inscriptions, and certainly no keyholes—and what we had gleaned seemed to lead in hopeless circles. Again and again I pondered my theory that perhaps the duke had intended the garden to be no more than an endless path, that no ultimate attainment could be better than the journey itself.

And yet three factors persuaded me otherwise. One was the key: surely something as specific and purposeful as a key would not have been made without a door that it could open. The second was the strange poem R—— had written in his delirium. And finally, there were the fairy voices that he continued to hear at night, and his dreams of fauns, who seemed to be waiting for him beside a road that stretched away in the starlight. R—— had no memory of writing the poem, though it was there in his notebook, scrawled in his own hand. He claimed he was not a poet and had composed no poetry since his school days—when, he said, love compels every youth to attempt it.

He was, however, a musician, and he succeeded admirably at carving a flute out of a hollow reed. It couldn't play as many notes as a real flute could, but R—— was most interested in playing the fairy melodies he heard. Sometimes, Mr. Girandole listened keenly to these and asked R—— to play on and on without a rest; sometimes, the melodies plunged Mr. Girandole into melancholia, and he would leave the chamber without a word and disappear into the forest. As the days passed, we all walked around with the fairy melodies in our heads. We'd catch ourselves humming or whistling them without realizing it. R—— sent the piano book home with Grandmother and me. In his own notebook, he drew a musical staff and wrote down some of the melodies the fairies sang. Intrigued, I copied these into my record. They were not like ones I'd heard anywhere else, and in the years since, I've never encountered their like in any songbooks or the works of mortal composers. It's difficult to explain *how* they are different, but if you heard them, you would agree.

I wandered about the garden with increasing aimlessness, gazing at the stone faces, running my fingers along the pedestals, climbing and descending stairs. I lay on the benches; I sat with Grandmother and Mr. Girandole as they watched the slow play of light through the leaves. I learned a song in R——'s language. Grandmother encouraged this as a diversion from the fairy music, which she said we oughtn't to become too familiar with; it was like the germander, she said: beautiful and fragrant, but it would take over everything if not kept in check. She did her best to get R—— to think carefully about his determination to leave the human world behind, but it was a lost cause. In the middle of a conversation, he would hear the trilling of a bird, or his gaze would fix upon a dapple of sunlight on the mossy stone, and his mind would journey far away.

During the times he was most awake and present in our world, we would get him to talk about planes or the shenanigans he'd pulled with his fellow pilots or growing up on a dairy farm near the city of ———. He improved the tangerine-peel game when he discovered how well cockleburs stuck to a particular cloth we'd brought. With Grandmother's permission, he drew a target of concentric circles on it, and we weighted its top edge so that it hung down against the wall of the sunken compartment. We tossed the burrs, aiming for the bull's-eye, which I said was Aldebaran, the Red Star, the Eye of Taurus.

And always, always, I studied my notebook, looking for meanings—for some way that the cryptic words and numbers might relate to the garden as it lay there, in deep shade, in spears of sunlight, in the bottomless night when we were gone and the fairies sang R——— to sleep.

One morning, R——— greeted us from his window and announced that he wanted to come down the stairs and all the way to the floor of the glade itself, outside the leaning house. He'd been able to gaze across at some of the statues, but he longed to see them up close. Mr. Girandole scowled at the idea, but Grandmother thought it would be good for R——— to walk a little—a body, she said, had to be *encouraged* to heal.

So, Mr. Girandole and I climbed up and got him. After checking on his healing progress, we steadied him as he sat on the top step and eased his way down, stair by stair. Mr. Girandole went ahead of him to catch him if he fell; I moved beside R——, ready to grab his good arm if need be. He rested on the terrace, gulping the air, looking around in bliss. "Isn't this far enough?" asked Mr. Girandole hopefully, but R—— shook his head and clambered toward the lower stairs.

At the bottom, he sat breathing hard and wiping away sweat with his sleeve, clearly delighted. Grandmother looked him over and nodded. "To the pool and back," she ordered. "You don't want to overdo it."

R—— gave her a military salute.

Mr. Girandole and I supported him between us, and Grandmother supervised, directing us to watch his leg and go slowly and look out for fallen branches. We advanced over the mossy earth. R—— winced now and then, and we'd stop at once, afraid we were tearing his stitches loose. But he'd nod and urge us forward again.

"Nice fellows," he said merrily, between hitching breaths. "This good, huh? Good rummies, good rummies! Three musket-men!" He squeezed our necks and planted a noisy kiss on Mr. Girandole's cheek.

"Do that again and you're on your own," Mr. Girandole growled.

R—— cackled and sang, "Yo, ho! Yo, ho!"

"Will you be quiet?" said Mr. Girandole.

"I come home from tavern like this," said R——. "Just like this!"

From the corner of my eye, I saw Grandmother looking exasperated.

"Riddle for notebook," said R——. "What beast have six leg, three head, smell bad? . . . Us!"

Mr. Girandole muttered something under his breath, and I'm sure we reached the pool not a moment too soon. We lowered

R—— gingerly onto the rim, and as soon as he was safely down, Mr. Girandole squirmed free and retreated in a huff, fanning his face with his hat.

R—— looked at me with such infectious humor that I couldn't help smiling. Then he gazed around at the statues of the four women and remarked about what a good place this was.

Grandmother pointed out the inscription to him with her stick: *You have we have all have though perhaps home.*

"Make nothing sense," said R——.

"As much sense as you make." Grandmother rapped him lightly on the head with her knuckles.

R—— settled down, catching his breath, and grew more serious. "One part only," he said, looking down at the carved letters. "No all here. Part of more big something."

Grandmother sat beside him and sighed.

R—— grimaced as he stretched forward and picked up a twig. He used it to poke and stir the murky water. I watched a striped lizard skitter along the pool's curb just beyond the nearest statue. Already the day was warming up, even here. I could sense the late-morning heat ringing on the leaves above us, baking the rocks that lay at the bottoms of sunlight wells. The air was wonderfully aromatic. R——'s twig made lazy splashes. The lizard vanished over the far rim. Grandmother began to look drowsy.

"Hey!" R—— said suddenly.

That woke Grandmother up, and when she saw R—— pointing into the pool behind her, she jumped to her feet and caught my arm for balance.

We watched a gray-brown snake, about the length of Grand-mother's stick, swimming across the pool toward us, gliding in

S-curves, its head just above the surface. R—— made a commotion with his twig, and the snake changed course, heading toward the pool's northwest corner.

"Is it dangerous?" I asked, feeling chills.

"No," said Grandmother. "It's harmless."

R—— started to say something, but at that moment, Mr. Girandole dashed closer, motioning for silence.

"Someone's coming," he whispered.

A new chill struck me. I peered around, looking for movement, but saw only the green vaults and sun-spears receding into the distance.

R—— raised his head, alarmed, and glanced toward the leaning house.

"No time," Mr. Girandole hissed. "On the ground. *Now*." He half-lifted, half-dragged R—— off the pool's rim.

R—— grunted in pain but looked to Mr. Girandole, awaiting instructions.

Mr. Girandole jammed his hat into place and crouched behind R——, putting his hands beneath the pilot's arms. "We'll be there, in the brush." He indicated the dense bushes where the whale hid, just north of the pool. Then he nodded toward the southern arch. "M——, you go that way, and make yourself obvious." To me he said, "You'd better close up the bedroom." At once, he began to drag R—— backward over the mossy ground, the pilot grimacing and flinching.

Grandmother had already pulled the medicine bottle out of her carpet bag and now thrust the bottle into my hands. "Go!" she said.

"Notebook!" I whispered back and started to rummage through the bag.

"Take the whole thing!" She gave it to me and hobbled away down the gentle slope.

I sprinted to the leaning house and up the steps, ascending to the upper room as quickly as I could go. Once there, I yanked R——'s pallet into the secret space, set the medicine bottle on the sunken floor, and lifted down the half-full waste bucket. When I'd cleared the chamber's upper half of incriminating evidence, I unloaded my notebook, climbed out of the well, and heaved the floor shut. I clenched my teeth at the reverberating sound. Bounding down the stairs with the bag over my shoulder, I hurried to rejoin Grandmother. I saw no sign of Mr. Girandole and R——; they'd successfully disappeared into the thicket.

I'd scarcely started across the glade when I heard Grandmother loudly calling my name. Approaching the arch, I saw her on its other side, standing in front of the dragon and dogs, apparently waiting for me. Just as I drew up with her, a voice called, "Good morning!"

On the slope leading up toward the parachute glen, I glimpsed someone advancing through the shade and sun-flecks. A military uniform.

I had a wild hope and shielded my eyes, squinting against the glare.

But it was the major.

"*Is* it still morning?" He checked his pocket watch. "Just barely." Striding down to us, he tipped his hat and smiled. There was a sprinkling of seeds on his shirt, and he'd loosened his collar. He carried his jacket folded over one arm. His pistol rested in its shiny leather case at his side. "I hope you're not leaving already?"

I looked around for other soldiers, but I saw no one else.

"Major P——," said Grandmother. "It is a fine day for a walk."

"That it is, Mrs. T——. And so here you are, and here am I."

"It's a very long walk from the garrison," she said.

"I only walked from the village. From your cottage, in fact, where I left my car."

"Your car is parked at my house, and neither we nor you are there. Major, you are clearly determined to start the most interesting rumors."

He laughed, swatting at a mosquito on his neck and examining the blood-smear on his fingers. "Just as you are determined to ignore any order or request not to come up here."

Grandmother looked startled. "Does that order still apply? Surely, any danger has passed."

The major examined us. "You are well aware, Mrs. T——, of the standing directive against interference with cultural treasures."

"Ah," said Grandmother. "The ban on art. We are not interfering, Major. This stonework has always been a part of our forest, and it will be here when the laws have changed again. I am a good citizen who loves her country, and I'm an old woman. Let me walk in my woods, sir."

The major's face was hard, his eyes unkind. I saw the bear in them again. He walked a few steps past us, toward the arch. "So, since nothing I can say will keep you away, I decided to pay you a visit. I was hoping you might show me just what it is you do here." He turned back and stared at us each in turn. "Come along. Share with me what is so intriguing about this place."

"Major," said Grandmother, sounding patient and instructive. "The sacred woods are here in plain sight. You've been to the grove quite a few times already, haven't you? You yourself said it was intriguing on the first day we spoke. Beyond what your own eyes can see, there's nothing I can tell you that will help." She looked at me. "Can *you*? Can you help the major understand why we come here?"

I shook my head.

"Sir, let me ask you this," Grandmother continued. "Suppose my grandson and I were to walk into your headquarters. Do you have a war room there, with maps and pins and telephones and reports, and a big black book full of secret codes? Do you believe that we could understand what you do there? Could you explain it to us in an hour or a day?"

The major regarded her, then raised a hand and curled his finger several times, beckoning. "Let's walk," he said. "Let's see this place."

"As you like," said Grandmother with a shrug. "We're not nearly as busy as you."

"Indeed? My own observation would suggest otherwise."

Grandmother gave a dismissive wave. "If one stops going and doing, one may as well be in the ground."

He offered Grandmother his arm, but she declined with a gracious bow. "There are a few rough and rooty places where I will gratefully accept, but on the whole, I'm less dangerous if left to my own devices."

This answer amused the major greatly. "Madam, I know of no one more dangerous when left to her own devices."

"What do you know of it, sir?"

"Enough to come armed," he said, "even if I come alone."

Now Grandmother rewarded him with a chuckle.

I tagged along behind them as they passed through the arch, and Grandmother launched into what promised to be a tour of the garden. Showing him the statue of Neptune, she pointed out the subtle carving of Scylla and Charybdis and made sure he knew the story.

"And this word?" he asked. "*Narrow?*"

Leaning on her stick, Grandmother angled her head and raised her brows. "A very narrow strait, I suppose. A narrow passage between the certain deaths on either side."

"H'm," said the major, eyeing Neptune carefully before they moved on.

After allowing Grandmother to explain to him the boar, the pool of the four women, and the Angel of the Bottomless Pit, he announced that he wanted to have a look inside the "tower," as he called it.

"It may make you queasy," she said. "It leans."

"And it has an unpleasant odor," he said, "I know." Excusing himself, he climbed the stairs, his boots clicking on the stone, and glanced down at us from the terrace before vanishing inside. I believe he expected to find something in the upper chamber that would solve the mystery for him, something that would condemn us beyond any doubt—though what he suspected us of is anyone's guess. He appeared briefly at the window, which meant he had edged along the catwalk beside the forward well. All the evidence against us was just beneath his feet; he'd walked across the top of a compartment filled with bedding and medicine and a bucket of R——'s pee. I was glad the stone house still reeked with the other stench.

After another minute, we heard the scrape of the roof hatch, and he stepped up to the crenellated wall. From atop the leaning house, the major surveyed us and the whole garden. He moved from end to end of the roof, studying all the ancient figures arrayed before him in their cloaks of moss and leaves—all the images crafted by those long-dead artisans at the bidding of the long-dead duke.

As Grandmother calmly returned his gaze, I understood that the sacred woods had defeated the major. The commander of men and trucks and dogs, he stood high above us, his pistol in its shiny holster. His jaw was clenched in anger. He had penetrated to the very heart of our world, this place of green stillness; it was all around him and under his boots. He looked upon the mystery, and it was opaque to him. Grandmother's face wore an expression that I later understood was pity.

When at last he left us, having insisted on escorting us back to the cottage, he shook my hand and bowed to Grandmother. "I wish you good health and good fortune," he said as he opened the door of his car. He'd come today without a driver. "But be reminded, Mrs T——, that no matter how clever we are, nothing is indefinitely sustainable."

Grandmother answered with quiet sincerity. "You mean that nothing lasts forever. Of that, Major, we are painfully and constantly aware."

He replaced his hat on his slicked hair. "The last word is yours, Madam."

Neither of them quite smiled as he closed his door and started the engine.

In our conversation that evening at the cottage, it was clear that Mr. Girandole liked the major even less than my grandfather would have. Before Mr. Girandole would stop grumbling, Grandmother had to apologize for serving the major lunch from the carpet bag on the terrace steps—the lunch she'd packed for us all.

When the mood had returned to normal, the three of us discussed what was to be done about R——.

"He's clearly getting better physically," said Mr. Girandole. "M——, you should have been a doctor."

"That's divine Providence," said Grandmother. "My sewing projects don't usually turn out so well."

"But what's he going to do," I asked, "if we don't find the door into Faery?" I was thinking that he couldn't stay in the leaning house during the winter.

"He's almost well enough to walk properly," Mr. Girandole said, pouring us each a cup of tea. "I can always guide him over the mountains to ——. From there, in a boat after dark, he could row to ——, which is enemy territory—friendly for him."

Grandmother frowned. "That's too dangerous for both of you. There must be patrols all up and down the coast."

"Well," said Mr. Girandole, "every other path looks worse."

"The war can't last forever," said Grandmother, settling back in her chair. "If it would just *end* . . ." She heaved a sigh and appeared to study the ceiling. "Suppose we *could* hide him in this attic . . ."

I nearly choked on a mouthful of tea, and Mr. Girandole set down his cup so abruptly that I thought it would break.

"All right, all right," said Grandmother. "I guess it wouldn't work. Mrs. F—— would hear him playing his flute, or he'd go tromping across the boards when I had company."

Mr. Girandole nodded, his eyes round. "You absolutely cannot harbor an enemy soldier here, M——. Promise me that." He lowered his voice to a whisper on "enemy soldier."

"I withdraw the suggestion," she said. Then, seeing that he still wasn't satisfied, she added, "I promise, I promise."

"But *you* could," I said, and they both looked at me.

Mr. Girandole shifted uneasily. "I could what?"

"You could harbor him in your cave, couldn't you?"

Now Mr. Girandole looked slightly ill. Grandmother failed to suppress a smile.

"I don't relish the idea. But . . . if it comes to that, I suppose . . ."

Grandmother touched his wrist. "The better alternative is finding that fairy door. It's what R—— wants, and it's what you need."

The next morning, it was Sunday again, and I didn't feel like getting out of bed. I was to leave the village on the following Friday. Though I wanted to see my mother and sister, and I longed for the day when my father could come home, I was already missing Grandmother and Mr. Girandole . . . and even R——. I had reached a way-marker on the path to adulthood—the first dividing of my heart. To live in this world, I realized, is to leave pieces of your heart in various places; and to move *toward* any place is to move *away* from another.

I groaned, covering my head with the pillow. I didn't want to get dressed up and sit among people and mind my manners—it was too much like going to school again. I asked Grandmother if I might skip church, since this was my last Sunday here.

"Skip church!" she cried, dragging off the pillow. "Shall we just cancel Christmas and next Easter while we're at it? Look," she said, prodding my back: "we're asking God to help us get

Girandole back to his people and keep R—— from a firing squad. You want two miracles, but you can't be bothered to pay God a visit?"

I blinked up at her. "Do you think God stays in the church more than in the woods?"

She dragged off the light summer blanket and began to tug on my arm. "I think He sends us messages in both places. And I think we need to start this week in the best way we can."

So, I tamed my hair and put on my starched shirt with the strangulating collar; I jammed my feet into the shiny, pinching black shoes that made me think of beetles' carapaces, and all the while, I wondered why showing respect to others required physical discomfort. When I grumbled about this to Grandmother, she reminded me that we lived in a sin-dark world.

On sunny days such as this, the small stained-glass windows blazed with their rich colors high in the gloomy vaults, telling stories of Heaven that we could just glimpse if we stood on tip-toes and squinted. I liked the glowing patches of color they cast on the old stern pews and the dank floor.

There was a traveling guest organist this morning, a pale young man with his hair combed straight back, who seemed to know things about the organ that usual organists did not. I imagined him learning to play in some towering castle-college, where all the turrets and corridors reverberated with sound. He unleashed some exceedingly low notes that drew a strange ringing from the altar area; he played a wild introit with crisscrossing scales that evoked stairways in my mind, endless stairways going up and down. I craned my neck to stare at the ranks of organ pipes, dull and glinting in the shadows behind the empty choir box. The pipes stood like a forest there, like many forests growing on slopes, and the organist seemed determined to use them all. At one point, I was sure I saw plumes of dust shooting from an obscure bank of pipes on the side wall.

At the end of a hymn, Grandmother cupped a hand to my ear and whispered, "Do you suppose his playing is for deception or merely for art?"

Grandmother's church was not much accustomed to music; it had no choir, and I could barely hear anyone singing, even beneath the subdued playing of the regular organists. Today, I saw some frowns when the music got too loud, or when the organist would pause between hymn stanzas to deliver thunderous interludes that scattered the melody, as if the hymn had been snatched up by a whirlwind. During one such magnificent interruption, I heard a lady behind us mutter, "He should have done his *practicing* at home."

I sensed relief all around me when it was time for the sermon, and the little priest ascended to the pulpit, gave us a kindly gaze, and delivered his soothing, mostly inaudible message. His whispery voice ebbed and swelled like the rhythms of the sea, and it was to such rhythms that the people here awoke and slept and spent their days. Today, the sermon was entitled "The Long and the Short of It." I gathered, mostly from reading the Scripture text, that he was telling us how all the Commandments boil down to just two, that we are to love God and love our neighbor. But the only words of the priest's that I was sure I understood were those of the title. After a susurrus of explanation, he would hold up a finger or throw his arms wide and announce, just within the range of hearing, "And *that's* the long and the short of it!" Near the beginning, when he was presumably telling us the Law, the sentence came out severely: we fall short, we are found wanting, we deserve to die—that's the long and the short of it. By the end, when he got to the Gospel, he was declaring it with joy, bouncing on his toes: we are redeemed; eternal life is ours—that's the long and the short of it.

Then the organ storm began again, and the congregation hunkered down like mountain-climbers on a bare saddle.

Afterward, people drifted out of the sanctuary, greeting one another and chatting. Mrs. C—— appeared from across the aisle and latched onto Grandmother, and their conversation gave me plenty of time to wander over to the neglected choir gallery.

At some time in the church's past, its congregation must have been wealthy and dedicated to musical splendor. Those long-ago people would have appreciated the pale young organist. The organ pipes towered over me, ranging from huge ones like factory smokestacks to some as tiny as a pocket whistle—and every size in between. I didn't know at first why they captured my interest. Perhaps it was because I'd been thinking of R——'s reed flute and hearing its voice hidden in the hymns, drifting behind the voluntaries. Maybe I was looking for that flute now, half-expecting to see it—or one like it—tucked among the proper metal pipes, abandoned there by some goat-footed piper who'd been lurking in the shadows, accompanying our worship with a wink and a dancing step. As I crept closer, I thought about how the organ pipes were like the statues in the sacred woods: the pipes occupied that great dark alcove behind angels and saints—once built with highest craft, now mostly forgotten . . . and frowned at when they thundered out their ancient music.

* * * *

In the heat of the late afternoon, Grandmother was taking a long nap and I was moping and drowsing on my favorite shady bench behind the cottage. A bee buzzed nearby; in the middle distance, a squadron of our country's planes followed the mountains. I sighed, feeling sluggish, and watched clouds floating in the endless blue.

With a suddenness that would have startled anyone seeing me, I sat up, and the notebook on my chest flopped to the ground. As clearly as if the priest had been beside me, I heard his voice say:

"And that's the long and the short of it."

Snatching up the notebook, I flipped it open to the latest, most complete list of inscriptions from the statues. Pressing a hand over my mouth, I stared at the transcription, not reading now, not seeing words—but seeing instead lines of gray pencil marks on the page.

A fact about the lines had always nagged me like a thorn in my sock, but it had never risen to my conscious mind. Some of the lines were very short; some were very long; and they ranged in all lengths between, like the organ pipes. But, unlike the pipes, my lines were not arranged in a neat, graduated rank.

My heart pounding, I began counting the words in each line. I leaped to my feet. Counting, I paced to and fro, unable to sit still. I collided with a wrought-iron chair and knocked it over. Ignoring the pain in my shin, I counted.

The shortest line, *Narrow*, had a single word. The next longest, *Reason departs*, had two. Sure enough, there was a three-word line: *Behold in me*. Then came *I am a gate*, with four. And so it went.

Kneeling at the garden table, I fished the pencil from my pocket and, in shaky letters, copied out my discovery:

1—*Narrow*

2—*Reason departs*

3—*Behold in me*

4—*I am a gate*

5—*The path beyond the dusk*

6—*I am it is very true*

7—*My steps fall softly like the rain*

8—*Yet one by one a herd may pass*

9—*You have we have all have though perhaps home*

10—*Hurry now to find me draw near but not inside*

11—*Or walls or ivied garden porch or doorstep have we none*

12—*All is folly and you search both high and low in vain*

13—*Or a thousand cheeses times a thousand if you give me days enough*

14—*Round and round the dancers go and my answer is in three and seven*

I could scarcely breathe, but I hit against two problems: one was that there came next a leap to twenty-six words in the inscription from the main gate. No, that was not a problem, I told myself—it was so different in count that it was clearly meant to be separate, an introduction to the garden.

A more troubling matter—the only thing that ruined the perfect pattern—was that I had an extra inscription of two words:

2—*The Mermaid*

How could there be two twos? If one or the other were not there, I would have the fourteen I'd been seeking all along.

But I was too excited to think any further. Nor could I keep this discovery to myself. For the first and only time that summer, I intruded on Grandmother's nap with an exuberant calling and hammering on her door.

"What?!" she cried back, probably thinking the cottage was on fire or that I'd hurt myself. "Open the door!" she shouted next, which certainly was quicker than waiting for her to struggle off her bed and across the room.

She'd managed to sit up by the time I raced to her side and thrust the notebook into her hands. It took her a while to comprehend, because I think she'd just been awakened from a deep sleep, and I couldn't stop babbling.

"But there are two twos," I said at the end of my breathless explanation. "See? Why are there two? Maybe one's not important, but which? *The Mermaid* is only a plaque in the ground. It just tells us what the mermaid is—maybe the statues all used to have plaques, and most are gone now. But *Reason departs* is in the leaning house, not out in the garden—maybe that's the one that doesn't belong with the fourteen."

At last Grandmother saw the pattern I'd found, and she'd counted enough of the words to convince herself it wasn't just wishful thinking. For a long time, she looked at me, and her eyes shone. Then she hugged me and said, "Very good. It can't be by chance."

I was giddy and happy, and my thoughts still hadn't stopped spinning. "It has to be the numbers, right? The numbers from the stairway!"

Grandmother nodded, locating the page where I'd written them. She flipped back and forth between the numbers and the last page, where I'd numbered the words per line. "Well," she said, "there's the solution to your 'two' problem." Taking my pencil, she made an X after five of the lines:

> *The Mermaid*—X
> *Reason departs*—X
> *My steps fall softly like the rain*—X
> *All is folly and you search both high and low in vain*—X
> *Round and round the dancers go and my answer is in three*
> *   and seven*—X

She was grinning, but I hadn't caught up yet.

"Why did you do that?" I asked. "What are the X's for?"

"We can forget about those lines. Toss them out. That rascal! He had us scrambling all over to hunt for threes and sevens, but that was all sleight of hand. Three and seven mean nothing at all." She turned to R——'s poem and read aloud:

> Heed the words among the trees in stone
> Though not all words are true.

I blinked at her, still not quite getting it. "The X lines aren't true?"

"False clues," she said.

"But how do you—?"

The moment she turned back to the list of numbers from the stairs, I had it: the 2, the 7, the 12, and the 14 were upside down. She pointed at those inverted numbers one by one, her gnarled finger moving down the page. It had to mean that the inscriptions of those word-lengths were lies, added simply for mischief.

"That's how there can be two twos," Grandmother said. "They're both horsefeathers. And since we're rid of that twelve, we know that all is not folly, and our search is not in vain.

"Now"—she handed me back the notebook and the pencil—"I need a cup of tea. While I put the kettle on, you take those lines that are left over—the ones with numbers right-side up—and write them out in the order from the stairway."

Unfortunately, the result of my modified recopying was no lightning-strike of revelation. In the stairway order, the lines read:

> The path beyond the dusk
> Behold in me
> Hurry now to find me draw near but not inside
> Or a thousand cheeses times a thousand if you give
>   me days enough
> Yet one by one a herd may pass
> I am it is very true
> Narrow
> Or walls or ivied garden porch or doorstep have we
>   none
> You have we have all have though perhaps home
> I am a gate

"Curious," said Grandmother. "It almost seems to make sense, but not quite. We're still missing something. Are you sure you copied these numbers properly, and that no more of them were upside down? I'd like to be able to throw away a few more of these lines."

I knew I'd copied the numbers with the utmost care. More than anything right now, I wanted to show our findings to Mr. Girandole.

I hoped he could see something that we were overlooking. We seemed to be so close . . . But it was too late to climb the mountain. Already the trees were casting long shadows, and the light on their crowns was deep golden.

"Girandole will be here after dark," Grandmother said as if reading my mind. "Give me a hand with supper."

We had plump noodles covered in cheesy sauce, eggplant from our garden, and a wonderful tomato soup garnished with herbs. Before washing the dishes, we carried our teacups outdoors and watched the fireflies winking in the hedge. Slowly the meadow flooded with dusk, and the leaves whispered of coolness and rest. Night birds called from the arbors and were answered from the forest. Vine-covered fence posts faded to silhouettes, and the arbors might have been the ruins of old fantastic castles. One by one the stars came out. It was a glorious ending to the day of our great breakthrough.

We put the kitchen to order and were waiting for Mr. Girandole on a garden bench when he opened the back gate.

"You're both smiling," he said, and I wondered how he could see our faces in the dark.

"Because you're here," said Grandmother.

When we were inside in the lamplight, we sat him down in front of the notebook and overwhelmed him with the day's findings. He gazed at us in awe, shaking his head. "It's not the time you have," he said at last. "It's what you do with it. I've spent three or four mortal lifetimes in and around that garden, and I've never made this connection. But it's so simple, any child might figure it out."

"The best puzzles are," said Grandmother. "That's what makes them elegant."

"This poem—or whatever it is—still doesn't make sense, though," I reminded them. I looked hopefully at Mr. Girandole. "Can you see what's wrong with it?"

Fingering his short beard, he bent over the page, leafed back to my list of numbers, and smiled. "You've gotten it backward, is all. I could say those stairway numbers from memory. You wrote them from the top down. Try going from the bottom up."

It was easy enough to read the lines from the bottom to the top. But I wrote them out the right way, and this is what I got (after Grandmother added punctuation):

> I am a gate
> You have, we have, all have, though perhaps home
> Or walls or ivied garden, porch or doorstep have we
>   none.
> Narrow
> I am, it is very true;
> Yet one by one a herd may pass,
> Or a thousand cheeses times a thousand, if you give
>   me days enough.
> Hurry now to find me; draw near but not inside.
> Behold in me
> The path beyond the dusk.

"Ten lines," I said. I had developed the habit of counting everything. "So, maybe *my answer is in three and seven* isn't a *complete* lie. *If* the answer is here."

But Grandmother and Mr. Girandole were lost in thought. The lines did indeed seem to make up a poem, though it didn't rhyme.

"A gate without a garden," Grandmother murmured. "Without walls, without a house."

"A narrow gate," said Mr. Girandole, "that an entire herd can pass through, one by one. And all those cheeses!"

"A gate we 'all have,'" said Grandmother.

Suddenly, they both burst out laughing. Grandmother looked expectantly at me.

I blinked, trying to think of all the farm enclosures I'd seen in my life, the different kinds of fences with swinging or sliding gates. But what did farms and herds and cheeses have to do with the garden?

Mr. Girandole snorted. "Well, it's one gate or the other—we know it's one of two!"

"Don't be crass," Grandmother said, dabbing at her eyes. "You're a faun, not a satyr." For my benefit, she asked, "Why do we keep herds? Why do we make cheese?"

"For food," I answered.

"And what 'gate' do we send food through?"

At last I got it. "Our mouths!"

"Exactly! And where in the garden can we find—"

"*The screaming mouth!*" My mind filled with a vision of the stone face that was also an entrance—the yawning mouth that led into a chamber with a table and benches.

"Or the pictures of the screaming mouths inside the stone house," said Mr. Girandole. "We shouldn't discount those just yet."

"There are a lot of mouths in the garden," said Grandmother, "but that big one seems the most likely to me. I always wondered why the duke was satisfied to build nothing more than a single room behind such an impressive opening."

"Do you think there's a tunnel?" I asked, dancing around the table. "It must be behind that plate on the wall, with the angels!"

"Possibly," said Mr. Girandole. "But what do you make of 'draw near but not inside'? How can one pass *through* without going *inside*?"

Grandmother picked up her teacup. "That's a question we can only answer on the premises."

If I'd had trouble waiting for sundown, the wait for early morning was many times worse. I tossed in my bed as the crickets and tree frogs shrilled on and on. Perhaps I dozed now and then, but I know I was already wide awake when Grandmother stirred in the darkness before dawn, leaned into my room, and said, "Shall we go?"

When I asked Grandmother if I should bring the key along this time, she said yes. We threaded a sturdy twine through its head, tied the loop around a handle of the carpet bag, and nestled the key inside the bag, beneath our supplies to take to R——. I put my notebook in, too. "You can run ahead of me if you want," Grandmother said, "but it's still as dark up there as it is down here." I stayed beside her, moving at her pace. We'd long since gotten the lantern back, and our many trips to the grove had begun to wear a trail, even in the lush meadow. That wasn't good, I thought: it would lead curious wanderers to the garden. No one would need dogs to see where we'd been. I mentioned this to Grandmother, and she said it didn't matter much, that the summer was almost over, and nature would soon wipe the slate clean.

I asked her, as we passed beneath the trees, if she thought she'd come up to the woods much after I'd gone back to the city. She said she didn't think so—that she even planned to start paying Mr. H—— to bring her firewood.

"The grove is really no place for an old woman," she said. "Especially not once all the menfolk are gone."

The idea of Grandmother alone made me sad. "But if we find the door, Mr. Girandole doesn't have to go through it now. He could wait until—" I faltered.

"Until I die? I suppose that's what he'll choose, the old dear. As if there's any good in watching me totter along and turn into a prune."

"Besides," I said, "I want you both to be here when I come back. I'm sure I can come again next summer!"

"You should never say you're sure about the future."

"Well, if I have anything at all to say about it, I'll be back. Maybe even at Christmas."

I saw her half-smiling in a ray of moonlight. "We've had a good time these several months, haven't we?"

"The best," I said. After a while, I added, "I'll bet the garden is quite a sight in the winter, too. You've seen it then, haven't you?"

"Yes. It's quite a sight in the winter, too. But winter is a rainy time, good for resting."

The garden was coming to life as we approached it in the hour of translucent mist and bird songs, the lingering pools of night lightening to purple between the trunks, and soft pink and yellow in the sky. A woodpecker knocked on a tree somewhere as if reporting the breaking news by telegraph.

Grandmother had blown out the lantern, but it was still too hot to stow in the bag.

Mr. Girandole met us while we were some distance from the dragon. I could see ruffles in the weeds where he'd been pacing about, leaving swaths through the silvery dew. He was hare-hoofed and had his patched trousers rolled up to his goat's-knees to keep the cuffs dry; he seemed tense, and I thought I understood. For me, the day was a culmination of one summer, but for Mr. Girandole, solving the puzzle would bring change to a life that never changed. This was a momentous hour of a momentous day.

Once we'd said our good-mornings, I asked if he'd been to the screaming mouth.

"Not yet," he said. "I thought we should go together." Hands joined behind his back, he fell into step beside Grandmother. Carrying the carpet bag and the lantern, I led the way, barely able to restrain myself from breaking into a run.

"How is R——?" asked Grandmother.

"Sleeping. He was making music with the fairies all night and hardly slept a wink. I took some extra things back to my cave and had a nap there."

"You've never heard these voices he hears?" asked Grandmother.

"Not since leaving Faery."

At Grandmother's suggestion, we turned right before we reached the garden and circled around to its east side, "to let R—— get his sleep," she said—though I suspected she didn't want to deal with his ebullience as we explored the chamber of the open mouth. We came up behind the mermaid with her twin tails, passed through her sequestered yard, and entered the upper clearing by the gap in the low wall. To the southwest I could just see part of the leaning house, steeped in early-morning shadows. But as we followed the stone wall northward, the central thicket quickly blocked the building from view.

So, we arrived in that wonderful young light before the face, its round window-eyes, nostrils, and mouth looming black. Neither human nor animal, it howled silently from the bank of earth and mossy stonework. Still the slender birch grew up alongside the left eye; still dead leaves drifted on the furrowed brow, around the ears-or-horns, and clung to its beard-or-mane. I counted eight steps leading up to the mouth. Behind the face on the slope, an age-pitted urn stood atop a short pillar.

Grandmother and Mr. Girandole hung back, looking things over. I preceded them, moving cautiously up the steps. A small animal scurried in the brush to my left. I paused halfway up, listening and watching. Above me, the round eyes were hypnotic in their emptiness. It was easy to believe this bizarre cave was an exit from the world.

I peered inside, then stepped across the threshold. The stone table and benches waited within the narrow room, illuminated by the grove's filtered daylight through the eyes, nose, and mouth. Above the frieze on the rear wall were the chiseled words of what we now knew to be a false clue. Except for the sentence on the entrance arch, this one, at fourteen words, was the longest in the garden:

Round and round the dancers go and my answer is in three and seven.

Such was the duke's sense of humor: a picnic table inside an ogre's mouth, and an elaborate deception inscribed in the chamber to which the other clues led. Yet even the duke's falsities had an impish ring of truth. The "dancers," I thought, might be visitors to the garden, all those who had admired the wonders and pondered the mysteries. And after all, if the answer truly lay here, it had been

reached through "three and seven"—the ten true inscriptions, properly arranged, that directed us to seek a mouth. A garden where lies
contained the truth: it boggled the mind and made reason depart.

I had thought of the metal plate as a frieze when I first saw it,
but now it looked all the more to me like a door of some sort. It
seemed much too simple to be an ornament, its only decorations
the three angels—one on its right edge, one on its left, and one
near its top—leaving its center featureless. Moreover, each angel
had an arm and a finger slightly extended. Before, I'd supposed
them to be pointing at one another, but now it occurred to me
that they were all pointing at the smooth, empty expanse of metal
in their midst. Their gestures formed a triangulation—a set of
imaginary lines that intersected in the middle of the plate. It *must*
be a door.

I touched its surface lightly, wondering if my fingers would
pass through into another world. No: it was as unyielding as it
looked—cold and sticky with a dusty residue. I examined my finger-
tips and rubbed them together. Whatever the dirty coating was, it
made them black. I wished I had a pair of gloves.

Grandmother entered behind me, her stick tocking on the
cobbled floor. Mr. Girandole peered across the threshold but said
he thought one of us should stay outside at all times, in case the
room contained some kind of trap. Grandmother seemed unfazed
by the notion, but I glanced nervously at the domed ceiling and
into the dim corners.

"Did you ever sit here and have a picnic?" I asked, kneeling to
study the undersides of the table and benches.

"Heavens, no," said Grandmother. "There are far more pleasant
places for that."

I warned her about the grimy film on the metal plate.

She prodded it with the tip of her walking-stick. Then she rapped harder, as if knocking on a gate. The sounds echoed in the confined space. "It doesn't sound hollow," she said. "But I suppose it might be a very thick door." Opening the carpet bag that I still carried, she pulled out a rag and used it to grip the angel on the left. The figure stood out in low relief from the surrounding surface, like the keys at Apollyon's side.

Remembering the key-shaped compartment my father had found, I hurried over. "Does it open?" I asked. "Can you slide it right or left?"

Grandmother applied pressure in every direction, including pushing straight against the figure as if it were a button. Finally, she shook her head. "It's solid." The rag came away soiled, like my fingers. Where she'd gripped the embossing, cleaner patches of the metal showed through—a dark bronze, barely lighter than the patina of grime. She tried the right-hand angel with the same results.

I climbed onto the table, took the cloth, and experimented with the top angel. I felt no give or play.

Grandmother sat on the left bench and looked around from that vantage. I helped her feel along the edges of the table and seats—and I checked the table's supporting block—for any hidden catches. Finding nothing, we faced each other across the tabletop, and she pronounced the situation "curious."

Mr. Girandole had been studying the place from the outside; now and then, I'd see him stalk past the doorway with his head cocked to the side, or with a twig in his hand, or focused intently on the ground. Suddenly, he appeared at the threshold and said, "R—— is coming."

I looked out to see R—— waving cheerily, far away by the arch to our south. He limped toward us. The motion seemed to pain him, but he was able to move pretty well.

"Good morning!" R—— called. "This wonder place! Wonder!" He paused to lean on the stone wall, staring at the mermaid.

"Stop shouting," Mr. Girandole advised. "And you shouldn't walk too far all at once. You'll wear yourself out."

R—— shook his fists beside his ears as if to demonstrate how strong he'd gotten.

Grandmother looked out from the mouth.

"This door?" R—— moved toward us again, gazing in delight at the monstrous face with Grandmother framed in its maw. "You find?"

"No," said Mr. Girandole. "We haven't found anything."

R—— mounted the steps with care, leading with his good leg. Partway up, he seemed unsteady, so I offered him a hand. He bowed to Grandmother and had a good look around the chamber himself. Easing down onto a bench, he asked about the inscription, and I explained it to him.

Grandmother eyed him curiously. "How did you find us, R——?"

"Hear tap, tap, tapping. You look for fairy door." So, he'd heard Grandmother pounding on the wall. "But I think, 'Maybe soldiers,' so I go like dog and look first." He indicated his hands and knees and squinted his eyes. He meant that he'd been creeping in the bushes.

"I'm glad to see you're getting around so well," Grandmother said.

Nudging my arm, R—— put his fingers and thumbs together to make an oblong shape. "Hole for key. I dream of key and hole for key. You got key?"

We had said nothing to him about the key from Papa. Grandmother sat opposite him and fixed him with her gaze. "Yes, R——, there's a key. You really want to go to that other world forever?"

He smiled at her, and I thought his eyes were misty. "Here, nothing. There . . . beautiful. I see it."

"You were on the border once," said Grandmother. "You think they'll let you stay this time?"

R——'s smile broadened, and he clutched Grandmother's wrist. Glancing at Mr. Girandole, who watched from the doorstep, R—— spoke in his own language.

When he'd finished, Mr. Girandole watched him for a long time and finally said, "Thank you, R——."

Grandmother asked what R—— had said.

Mr. Girandole looked confused for a moment, forgetting that we hadn't understood the other language. "He said that he might have stayed in Faery the first time. But they sent him back to help me get there, too."

Grandmother patted R——'s hand and added her thanks.

R——'s dreams and poem had convinced us to try and solve the garden's puzzle, and his hearing fairy music had inspired us along the way. We believed we'd been helping him, but he had come to help us.

So, now we all worked together to scour the chamber inside and out, searching, tapping, vigilant always for a keyhole. The table and benches were anchored in mortar and could not be moved. I crawled on hands and knees, hunting for any stone in the cobbled floor that might be loose. Mr. Girandole climbed over the exterior, prying and probing. Once, his face appeared at one of the eye-holes, looking in.

I joined him outside for a while. Grandmother came out, too, to sit on the steps and rest. I investigated the stone walls on both sides; scrambling up the bank, I examined the urn. Centuries ago, it had held flowers, I supposed; now it housed a tuft of weeds.

Mr. Girandole seemed most interested in the mossy open ground in front of the face. He positioned himself here and there, on the steps, near the steps, and back by the thicket, always peering toward the sculpted entrance. *"Draw near but not inside,"* he muttered. *"Behold in me the path beyond the dusk."*

"Do you see anything?" Grandmother called to him.

He shook his head.

I wandered back inside.

In his broken speech, R—— pointed out something intriguing about the metal plate. It seemed indeed to be set in the wall, like a jewel in a ring, but it stood at a curious angle: the left edge emerged farther from the wall than the right edge—not a great difference, but measurable—*as if the plate were a door that had not closed all the way.* Moreover, to a lesser degree, the top edge protruded just slightly more than the bottom edge. But there was no discernible crack around the plate, as one would expect around any door; not so much as a knife blade could be inserted beside it.

"Maybe someone slammed it closed and it jammed," I suggested. "Or maybe the hillside has settled over the years, and the building isn't straight anymore."

"Or maybe," said Grandmother from the threshold, "the duke wasn't satisfied with just *one* skewed building."

R—— clawed and shoved at the angel carvings. At last, he sank back onto a bench in exasperation, wiping his hands on his clothes. More of the original color peeked through the grime.

"What is this sticky stuff, anyway?" Grandmother scratched at one of the handprints on the flat metal surface. "It can't be tree sap, under a roof."

I saw what interested her: the color of the "clean" patch on the plate was different from the angels' bronze. She dug in the carpet bag, which I'd put on the table. "Run and bring that water bucket," she told me, "and any rags you can find. There's enough dirt on this thing to plant a garden. Let's see what's under it."

I didn't mind being given the order. I was ready to stretch my legs. Cautiously, I trotted around to the leaning house. The bucket was full of water; I guessed Mr. Girandole had filled it before dawn. Gathering up an armful of rags, I gazed fondly about the awful, tilted room. Even the last lingering reek had fond associations now.

When I returned through the arch, Mr. Girandole was fairly jumping in place, pointing at the ground and waving at me to hurry. Grandmother and R—— hobbled down the steps, and I'm not sure who was helping whom.

I rushed forward, sloshing out some of the water.

"However did we miss them?" Mr. Girandole. "All these years . . ."

So, yet another feature had been hiding under our noses. As I drew up beside him, I saw that he'd scraped away an earthy mat of leaves, twigs, and moss. Beneath, on the landing of stone just at the bottom of the eight steps, were two large human footprints— a left foot and a right, as if someone had stood there barefooted when the masonry was soft. Ornamental spirals were etched in the toe marks, the heels, and the balls of the feet; the footprints were centered just before the middle of the lowest step, as if whoever had left them was ready to begin climbing.

"Ah, haaa," said Grandmother thoughtfully. R—— squatted

with effort and ran his fingers through the shallow impressions.

"Near but not inside," said Mr. Girandole. "This is where we're supposed to stand."

"Brilliant!" said Grandmother. "You've done it, Girandole! But what can you see from there?"

Mr. Girandole shook his head, looking perplexed. "Nothing."

R—— elbowed him aside and stood with his worn flight boots on top of the footprints. He squinted hard at the stone face, but apparently there was nothing to see. "Maybe you have to be my height," I said. I stepped up next. Unfortunately, no miraculous visions unfurled. Not to be left out, Grandmother tried looking too but fared no better.

R—— said a word that Mr. Girandole translated as "pickaxe." R—— wanted to use one on the metal plate.

Grandmother rolled her eyes and muttered, "Thank goodness you didn't come with grenades, R——." She told me to bring the bucket and rags, and to try not to spill any more of the water.

Inside the chamber, she supervised as Mr. Girandole and I washed the metal plate. "Don't put the rags in the bucket, clean or dirty," she said. "R—— drinks out of it." We got the rags wet by pouring water over them. Wiping and folding, we used the cloths one by one until they were all black.

"I can't tell if this is just dust," said Mr. Girandole, "or if it's been deliberately applied."

"Nothing else in the garden is covered with it," I pointed out, working from atop a bench.

"True. But nothing else is made of this same material, whatever it is. Things don't all get dirty in the same way or at the same speed. Have you noticed how black the ceiling is in here?"

I hadn't, but looking up, I saw what he meant.

"I think someone must have built a smoky fire in here once—maybe many times—before the fauns came; it wasn't us." He looked at his rag. "This could be smoke residue."

I had a mental picture of the screaming face viewed from outside at night, a fire in its gaping mouth, its eyes and nostrils ablaze with red light.

The angels were tooled in far greater detail than had been visible through the coating of grime. With the proper polish, Grandmother conjectured, they would gleam. The plate itself was smooth as a sheet of ice, very hard, black, and shiny.

"Stone?" asked R——, gazing over our shoulders.

Mr. Girandole nodded, rapping it with his knuckles. "Yes. It's some kind of stone."

I jumped down from the table for another rag. "Now that we're cleaning it up, I can see my reflection in it."

Mr. Girandole stopped washing. He waved his arm back and forth in front of the plate, and slowly he turned to look at me, then at Grandmother.

Grandmother's eyes widened.

A *mirror*.

All the grove's suggestions of mirrors whirled through my mind.

"Not 'come inside,'" Mr. Girandole breathed, "but '*behold* in me.' We're not looking for a doorway in this room. We're supposed to see something reflected in the mirror—something out there." His rapt face turned outward, peering through the distorted stone jaws.

I bounded from the doorway, my pulse pounding. There was nothing to see but the central thicket, filling the entire view—the tangle of giant trees and interwoven bushes, locked with thorns and chained with vines, the haunt of lizards, snakes, and spiders. The door into Faery must lie somewhere in there. Perhaps once it had been plainly visible, though disguised. My spirits sank. Clearing even a narrow path would be a task of many days.

"Wild place," said R——, behind me. "Fairies like wild."

"Finish the job," Grandmother said. "Get the mirror clean, and we'll see what's to see."

My feet dragging, I went back to work. "The mirror will just show us the thicket," I said.

"Perhaps," said Mr. Girandole, dumping the last of the water over the cleanest of the rags and squeezing it out. We'd gone through all the cloths and had resorted to searching them for tiny clean patches to use. Dirty water puddled around us. "Now we know," he said, "why the mirror isn't set straight in the wall. It's tilted to line up perfectly on something when you stand down there in the footprints."

Grandmother gave R—— a withering I-told-you-so look and muttered, "Pickaxe, indeed!"

Although we left a few smudges and streaks—especially down near the floor, when our rags were too dirty to do much good—we got the mirror clean. We all hurried to the bottom of the steps.

R—— made for the footprints, but Mr. Girandole barred his way. "As keeper of the notebook and breaker of the code," Mr. Girandole said to me, "the honor should be yours."

I grinned at him. His gravity seemed a bit much for the moment— it wasn't as if I were stepping *through* the door into Faery. I was only looking into the mirror, and unless it was itself magical, I knew what I would see.

"Do you think I should take my shoes off?" I asked, looking at the footprints.

"Perhaps it would be best," said Mr. Girandole.

R—— sighed impatiently.

I untied my shoes, pulled off my socks, and stepped into the cool impressions, still moist from their long blanketing. The carved spirals felt pleasant beneath my soles.

I peered up the stairs, through the gaping mouth, and into the stone's black surface. As I'd expected, the leafy light and sundapples showed me a reflection of the trees and bushes. It was as Mr. Girandole had said: the mirror was angled to reflect the thicket, not us.

I felt a rush of emotion. It wasn't anything I saw, but the fact that I stood on the threshold of the puzzle's solution. With my feet set here, I had reached the end of the clue path; I was gazing into the face of the duke's secret. I'd accepted his invitation to examine the garden piece by piece, and now I could have told him "whether so many marvels were created for deception or purely for art."

But . . . such grandiose thoughts presupposed that there *was* actually a fairy door somewhere in the verdant sprawl.

"Can you see anything?" Grandmother asked.

"The thicket," I said.

"What about it?" asked Mr. Girandole. "Look carefully. Where do the angels' fingers point?"

Taking a deep breath, I studied the reflection and its framing figures. At the very center was . . . was an imposing vertical shaft—grayish-white, and cloaked in green—that old, dead tree, the giant trunk without limbs or crown, overgrown with vines.

The puzzle's final piece had fallen into place. Of *course* the door would be in some natural location—a rock wall, a bank of earth . . . *or a tree.* Most of the garden's light was filtered by leaves; they whispered in the music of Faery. This stump—the remnant of one of the grand trees, those that now provided the roof of leaves— was easily old enough to have been here before the duke's time. There could be no mistake. The top angel's arm and finger were dead center on the trunk, pointing straight down its length. The other two angels pointed at it from the sides, and they smiled their enigmatic smiles.

But with the triumph came a new worry. What if the doorway required the tree to be alive? What if the portal we sought had died long ago?

"It's that dead tree!" I stepped out of the prints so the others could see.

"That old rampike!" Mr. Girandole stared at it, taking off his hat. "I've walked past it so often. A day or two ago, I even said to it, 'I wish you could talk, old friend, and tell us of what you've seen'!"

"I remember it being there when I was a girl," Grandmother said. "It seemed halfway between a tree and a statue. I wondered if all the statues had grown from trees, or if all the trees had started out as statues."

Grandmother and R—— didn't remove their shoes, but they seemed to place their feet respectfully enough. Our different heights didn't matter: we all saw the vine-clad stump at the mirror's center.

Mr. Girandole clapped his hands. "*Sisters dancing in the water and the sky!* The fairy metaphor of death—here death stands, amid all the garden's life, a trunk without limbs—the 'dancing sisters' of its leaves are long gone, dancing far away."

My worries about the door's functionality dissolved. It was fitting that the garden's answer lay here—in a mouth like a tomb, a lifeless tree, and a path leading on beyond the world to where there was no more death.

But I was too nervous to go farther. I could only watch as Mr. Girandole and R—— crossed to the thicket, moved through the first brambles to the trunk's base, and began to search among the vines.

Grandmother and I sat together on the steps. She laid her stick across her knees.

"I think we've found it," she said.

"I think so."

"I wonder what your father would have done," Grandmother said, "if he'd found a keyhole in this stump when he had the key. He might have disappeared into Faery, and I would never have known what became of him. I'd have been wrong about how the garden was a safe place to play."

I nodded. Probably, my papa had never suspected a *tree* of harboring a keyhole. He would have assumed the key opened something built by the duke.

"Do you suppose the duke made the key," I asked her, "or that the fairies gave it to him?"

"I have no idea," she said. "Girandole might."

Mr. Girandole and R—— vanished around opposite sides of the trunk, picking their way into the brush. After several moments, by R——'s wild whooping, I knew they'd found something. Soon, they came hurrying back, R—— elated and Mr. Girandole quiet and serious.

They'd discovered, at about waist height on the tree's far side, a keyhole.

"It's not framed by any metal," Mr. Girandole explained. "Not carved. It's just right there in the wood, as if it grew there. It has to be magical; most holes in tree trunks will swell shut or change shape."

R—— spoke earnestly in his own language, and Mr. Girandole translated for us.

"R—— wants to go through the door. He knows that I plan to wait. Obviously, R—— can't wait for years, and shouldn't have to. He can be a test pilot, he says—he'll establish for us that the key works, and that I can use the door when I need to. He says he's no good at prolonged good-byes, so he wants to leave soon."

"No want good-bye," R—— said. "But here, can't stay. No place. No want good-bye, but tomorrow and tomorrow, more, more hard. I go today."

Mr. Girandole drew a long breath. "R——, there *is* a place for you here, if you'd like to stay. You can live in my cave for the winter, and through next year . . . for however long it takes until the war is over. Then you can go or stay as you please. You're our friend. *My* friend." He reached for R——'s hand and clasped it.

In a breaking voice, R—— said, "Thank you, Girandole." He pronounced the name badly, but it was the first time I'd heard R—— call him anything other than "Mr. Satyr." Again he spoke in his native tongue, and at the end, Mr. Girandole gripped R——'s arms before turning back to us.

"He's resolved to go."

Grandmother nodded understanding.

"But R——," said Mr. Girandole, "Noon is the worst hour to do this. You want to cross the border into Faery quickly, because the border is the most dangerous. It's thinner at dawn and dusk. Can you wait until gloaming this evening, when you won't have far to go?"

R—— agreed.

Mr. Girandole took off his hat and placed it over his chest as he faced me. I knew he was searching for the words to thank me, trying to take care of all the things that needed to be said. We'd found the door for him—we'd done it together. I shook his hand.

For lunch, we had a picnic on the terrace. We ate the food Grandmother and I had brought: crackers, sardines, cheese, plums, tangerines, and a few early grapes. Mr. Girandole fetched his jug of sun-brewed tea; we had no way of cooling it, but its flavor was summer itself. The long, warm afternoon stretched around us as R—— played fairy melodies on his flute, Mr. Girandole kept his tireless lookout, and Grandmother settled down on a bench for her nap.

"I'm not going all the way down the mountain and then back up before evening," she told me. "But if you have the energy, it would be good for you to make a trip down there and gather up what you can find in the kitchen. R—— ought to have supper before he goes."

"I can go hunting for the main course," Mr. Girandole offered.

"Then we'll have a proper feast," Grandmother said.

I was glad for a mission. The waiting was unbearable, and I was already missing R——. His music filled me with an indefinable emotion that was part sadness, but it included a yearning for something I could not name.

"What if some of your friends are looking for you?" I asked, thinking that it was unusual for Grandmother to be away from the cottage all day.

She eased her head back, using the carpet bag as a pillow. "Tell them we've switched today, and I'm off playing while you mind the house."

*   *   *   *

As I descended the meadow, I caught sight of Mrs. F—— taking down laundry in her back garden. She looked toward me between billowing sheets, and I waved. She may have tipped up her chin in a dour greeting, but it was hard to tell. I let myself in at our back door with Grandmother's shiny brass key. I was so used to village life that I was thinking of the ice man, who made his deliveries twice a week; tomorrow, whether we were home or not, we would have to leave the door unlocked for him. It was such a different world from the city . . . the city to which I'd be returning in only four days.

I collected what transportable food I could find and stuffed it into the other rucksack. Slinging it over my shoulder, I pulled the door shut and locked it. I bounded off the mossy step and raced toward the gate. But halfway there, I stopped so suddenly that I pitched over forward, landing on all fours.

A man was standing just outside the gate. He leaned with his arms folded on it, watching me from beneath the bill of his hat.

A policeman.

"Whoops," he said, commenting on the tumble I'd taken.

I floundered and scooped up two bread rolls that had bounced out of the bag.

"Good afternoon," said the policeman, and I returned the greeting as best I could, picking myself up, wondering what to do. It felt as if the air were being squeezed out of my chest.

"Where are we going?" He raised his head and sighted along his nose at me.

"Not, uh, far," I mumbled. "I mean . . ."

A second policeman strolled toward us from out by the arbors.

"What's that? Speak up," said the first. "Where's Mrs. T——?"

I opened my mouth with absolutely no idea what I was going to say. I hadn't been thinking about a thing except getting back up the mountain as quickly as I could.

But at that moment, Mrs. F—— appeared from around the corner of her back hedge. Her sharp glance took in the two men and me. "P——!" she cried pleasantly, calling the policeman by his first name and waving to his companion. I'd never heard such a cheerful tone from her. "A fine day, isn't it? What brings you here?"

Both men tipped their hats. "Making the rounds, Mrs. F——. Keeping an eye on things, now that the Army is gone." The man at the gate turned back to me. "Well, boy?"

I looked down at my shoes and sideways at the purple blossoms of the germander.

"Look up here, and answer my question."

Just when I thought I might faint, Mrs. F——, the last person from whom I'd have expected help, came to my rescue. "P——, you're scaring the boy. He's not a burglar. That's M——'s grandson, staying with her. He's been here since April."

Of course, the policemen knew I belonged here. They must have seen me with Grandmother a hundred times. But how was I going to explain where Grandmother was now, or where I was running to with an armload of food?

Mrs. F—— continued. "I'm watching him today, because M—— has an appointment."

I felt my eyes widening, but I kept my face averted.

"He just went over there to collect some things from the kitchen. I told him to hurry."

"Oh." The policeman straightened and patted the top of the gate. "Right, then."

His partner chuckled, thumbs stuck into his belt. "Burglars generally don't have keys, do they?" he said as if to me, and winked.

The first man unlatched the gate for me and held it open as I hurried over to join Mrs. F——.

"Take it on inside," she told me, and with a nod, I let myself into her back garden, where the laundry billowed like sails and circus tents. The hedge was dense, but I found a place to peep through. She stood and chatted with the two policemen for a long while.

Not wanting to go into her house alone, I sat down and pulled up my knees in a shady corner of the yard. A white stone cherub held a basket that sprouted pink fuchsia, its blossoms like lanterns.

Eventually, Mrs. F—— entered the garden and looked around until she spotted me. With a gesture she told me to stay put, and she went into her kitchen. She emerged soon after with a glass of cold tea that clinked and rattled with chips of ice.

As she handed it to me, I blurted my thanks. I was almost as afraid of her as of a policeman or soldier. I remembered Grandmother saying that Mrs. F——'s boys had been hellions. I wondered what exactly that meant, what kind of mischief they'd pulled. I still didn't know how to explain myself.

She held up a hand to cut me off. "The thanks will suffice," she said. "Whatever you're up to, I won't have M—— thinking I wrung the story out of you."

Mrs. F—— certainly knew my grandmother well. Crossing her arms, she peered down at me from beneath her straight hair—it was as gleaming white as her linens on the clothesline. "You'd better sit there and take your time with that tea before you go scampering up the field again." She glanced toward the hedge, indicating that I should give the police plenty of time to move on. To spare me the anguish of conversation, she turned her back, adjusted one of the sheets, and hobbled up the path to her door.

I clutched the sweating glass, sipping at the frosty, aromatic tea, and listened to the birds chirping in the trees and hedges. Slowly, my heartbeat returned to normal. The largest sheet above me inflated with the breeze, tugging at its clothespins, and it was like being on the deck of a ship; the colorful handkerchiefs and skirts were flags and pennants, and the vine-covered clothesline pole was the mast.

But the sun was forever moving, and I was itching to get back to the grove. I walked carefully among the flower beds to the path and carried the empty glass to the cottage door. Before I could knock, Mrs. F——'s face loomed in a window.

"You can leave it there, on the step," she told me. She was chopping some pungent vegetable on a cutting board. I could hear the knife going *zak-zak-zak*. The strong odor of the juice made my eyes water, even outside the window. It didn't seem to bother Mrs. F——.

"Thank you again," I said.

She nodded briskly and turned back to her cooking.

Pausing only to take a good look around for policemen, I hurried back up the mountain. Before I passed under the roof of treetops, I noticed that the sky was one of the best I'd seen all summer: bottomless, dazzling blue, with magnificent white cloud towers. They formed endless pictures, their shifting so slow that one hardly noticed it.

Then I followed the now-familiar path up the slopes, in the secret tree world that was like the beds of the deep sea. Mrs. F——'s laundry had started me thinking about ships, and I imagined having a ship that could glide on the rolling waves of the trees' crowns, the leaves whispering along the hull, the masts up among the clouds, and the anchor crashing down at times through these limbs to catch among the roots and hold the vessel in place. It would creak and rock up there where only green branches and blue sky were visible, and no village or smokestack could be seen anywhere. And maybe with the anchor keeping it steady in just such a place, the summer for those aboard the ship would never end; the leaves would never turn red; the cold winds would never blow; and there would be nothing but clouds and sun, moon and stars.

When I returned, I found R—— sitting alone on the terrace. He said that Grandmother and Mr. Girandole had gone for a walk. My first impulse was to run and try to catch up with them, but when I asked which direction they'd gone, R—— motioned for me to sit on a bench.

I did so, setting down the rucksack, and felt awkward and sad. I'd never said a real good-bye to a person forever. I knew I'd never see R—— again in this life.

"I close eyes," R—— said, pointing at his head. "I think . . . I try remember home." He frowned in concentration, shut his eyes, and sat still for a long time. "I no see, not see Mother, Father, Brother . . . wife, too. Baby, too—not see. You know?" He shook his head and laughed quietly, in a way that seemed sad. "Remember people, not . . ." With a gesture, he indicated his face. "Not faces."

I nodded. "I can't see my mother or my father clearly, and for me, it's only been about five months." I couldn't hear their voices in my head. How quickly those things faded from our memories. But the people were there . . . people without faces, without sound. I stared at R——, trying to memorize his appearance.

273

"I see . . ." he went on. "I see . . . the river. The tree. Old piano of my mother. Old clock, *tick tock tick tock tick tock—cuckoo! Cuckoo!*"

He watched me with a smile and brushed back his greasy, unkempt hair. He'd grown a scraggly beard and mustache and looked like a character from a book—a pirate or someone marooned on a desert island. He called me by name, pronouncing it pretty well, and I grinned back.

"You smart," he said deliberately, tapping his forehead. "You writing in book. Find fairy door."

"We all did it together," I said. "It started with your poem."

"I —— [his nationality]. You help me."

I watched him, thinking of what Grandmother had said, that the concepts of war and enemy had no place in the sacred woods.

"Thank you," he said, and held out his hand.

I shook it and answered, "You're welcome."

He handed me his flute and said, "You keep."

I felt my eyes beginning to burn with tears that might spill out, so I just nodded and took it.

But R—— wasn't content to *give* it to me; he wanted to be sure I could *play* it. For the next half hour or so, we had a flute lesson. The instrument was little more than a whistle he'd carved out of the reed. I grew light-headed from blowing and blowing, trying to find the angle at which my breath would coax sound from it. But when I could finally play three notes, R—— taught me the simplest of the fairy melodies.

At last we saw Grandmother and Mr. Girandole returning, and I slid the flute into my shirt pocket.

"You be good man, future," R—— said. It wasn't an order; it sounded more like a prediction.

During his walk with Grandmother, Mr. Girandole had managed to catch a squirrel, which he now took away to dress and cook. I wasn't sure exactly *how* he'd caught it. The image of him pouncing or leaping up to snatch it off a branch was unsettling.

Grandmother was satisfied with the kitchen gleanings I'd brought. I told her about my adventure with the policemen and Mrs. F——. She laughed at the end, at what Mrs. F—— had said about not wanting to wring the story out of me.

We waited on the terrace; Grandmother and R—— talked more about music, and we played a final game of pitching cockleburs at the cloth target, which I carried down from the chamber above. I found in my notebook a sketch of the leaning house—one of my better drawings of anything in the garden. I added the four of us, doing my best to capture our attitudes and postures with simple lines and shading. It wasn't perfect, but it was decent. Carefully, I tore the page out and gave it to R——. He looked at it for a long time, then folded it with great deliberation and put it into his own pocket. "Best present," he said. "I always keep."

When the shafts of light slanted deep golden from the west, and dusk was already gathering in the quiet places, Mr. Girandole returned with roasted meat on skewers. Our feast began with us all bowing our heads. Instead of praying aloud, Grandmother put one hand on Mr. Girandole's wrist and one on R——'s. The two of them took my hands, completing the circle. We all looked solemnly at one another, and then we prayed our own prayers in our heads. That was the beginning of a dinner party I would never have imagined when the spring began.

Grandmother leaned back against the terrace railing with her ankles crossed, sipping her tea. "Girandole," she said suddenly, "there is something I've been wondering about all afternoon. If the duke really went into Faery and never came back, why didn't he take the key with him? Why was it hidden in the statue of Apollyon? Did he have a second key?"

Mr. Girandole dusted cracker crumbs from his lap. "Fairy doors also open for certain words—poetry, spells, and the like. The duke probably knew the secret words if he was able to discover the door. If so, he didn't need the key; he meant it for others to find. We can hardly know all his reasons for making the garden, but two of them seem clear: for one, it points the way to his discovery. I would guess he made that key with magical art so that others who cared enough to find it could open the door. He found a way to go beyond the veil—beyond the shadows—and the garden was his unselfish act of gratitude. He made this place for others. He left hope in the world."

"And the garden's other purpose?" Grandmother asked.

"It was his tribute to G——, his monument to love that never dies." Mr. Girandole gazed toward the pedestal of the beautiful feet.

Watching him and Grandmother, listening to their voices, I felt my tears overflowing at last. Pretending to brush hair back from my forehead, I wiped at them. My chest ached with the happiness of knowing these two, of knowing I could come and visit on every holiday, and they would be waiting here, together, with their truest feelings confessed. Duties and sacrifices were behind them now; ahead were warmth and friendship. Before this year, I hadn't grasped the enormity of the gifts we receive through our loved ones. Whenever I came, Grandmother and Mr. Girandole would welcome me, and no matter what was happening in the world, we would have our own special place where the coldest winds didn't reach. So I thought; I was very young.

*   *   *   *

All too soon, the meal was over, and we put the dirty cups and empty tins back into the bag. I rolled up the cocklebur target and offered it to R——, too. "You can teach the fauns to play," I said.

R—— laughed, nodding, and tucked it inside his shirt.

Fireflies had begun to wink in the dusk around us.

"Well," said Mr. Girandole softly, "it will be dark soon."

"Yes," said Grandmother. "We'd better do this while you can still see the keyhole."

So, we stood up, stretched, and breathed deeply in the evening's cool. Grandmother brought the carpet bag. R —— preceded us; Mr. Girandole helped Grandmother on the eastern stairs—but I lingered on the terrace for as long as I could, peering in turn at each of the fantastic figures I could see: the tortoise, the elephant, a glimpse of Heracles, the sea serpent, the boar, Neptune on his throne, and the four women at the pool. Soon, I thought, the garden would be silent again, left to the birds, the small creatures, the leaves and moss, and the changing light. The monsters would all be here, slowly sinking again into the blankets of vines—but we would be gone as the summer passed away, and autumn settled in for a while with a riot of colors and a rattle of nuts. And then rainy winter would steal in like age. But then we'd come back. I had to keep reminding myself of that.

Grandmother stood for a long time before the pedestal of the sandaled feet. R—— trudged onward, but Mr. Girandole waited beside Grandmother, his hand on her shoulder. Finally, gazing once into each other's eyes, they continued walking, and I followed.

We made our way through the arch and up into the higher glade.

277

The mermaid regarded us somberly as we passed—wondering, I fancied, if we had any news of the ocean, which she could hear and smell away down the slopes but could never see.

I had the unsettling notion that the night's darkness was pouring out of the screaming mouth. I'd never been in the garden at such a late hour. Somehow, this time of twilight, with the sun vanishing, frightened me more than the pre-dawn dark when daylight lay just ahead. Tiny frogs sang in the trees and along the mossy stone wall. Crickets chorused in the thicket. On every hand the fireflies kindled their pale lamps. I wondered what I'd see if I ran after the fireflies and looked closely.

There was a breathless feel to the woods. The visible patch of sky above the hilltop, where the temple stood hidden behind the trees, had become a deep lavender; the stars were not yet alight.

"This is the hour," said Mr. Girandole. "The walls of the worlds are thin." He pointed to murky recesses in the bank's foliage, alignments of depth and silhouette where day and night commingled. I wasn't sure what he saw there, but I believed him about the nearness of Faery.

R—— pressed forward, approaching the limbless tree, a ghostly tower now beneath its garment of leaves.

Mr. Girandole clutched my arm and spoke quietly into my ear. "You see how eager he is to be there—to leave this world behind without a thought. That's what happens when the colors and voices of my land get into a mortal. Stand well back from the door, if you want to have any peace for the years that remain to you. In fact, the two of you should hold onto each other, and don't come close, no matter what you hear, no matter how badly you want to peek inside. The border is always dangerous."

"What about you?" Grandmother asked.

"I'll make sure he gets through the door safely, and that it closes behind him."

R—— had already floundered into the brambles, his hands on the bone-white trunk of the ancient tree. He called excitedly to us when he'd relocated the keyhole.

Twisting his hat more tightly onto his head, Mr. Girandole led us to the tree's foot. We sidled around it, the thicket black and tangled. To move even a step required planning and wriggling. Mr. Girandole positioned Grandmother and me to his right as he faced the trunk, with R—— on his left. There was scarcely room to stand. Branches poked our backs, and thorns tore at our clothes. The thicket was so dense I could no longer see the gaping mouth. It was steamy among the vegetation, even with the sun gone.

R——'s eyes were wide and expectant, but he came forward and embraced us one by one. He smelled of sweat.

"Kind, kind lady," he said, squeezing Grandmother's hands. I thought about what a long way we'd come since he'd been hanging in the tree and pointing his gun at us. Clearly, he was healing; his injuries were not going to kill him—nor was our medical treatment. Grandmother had done well. "You save me. I remember. I always remember."

"Yes, well," said Grandmother, "we'll remember you, too." She hugged him again and patted his face with both hands. "I'm glad you came to us. Be careful, R——, and be well."

He glanced a final time at me, and I touched the flute in my pocket. He grinned and gave me a thumbs-up.

Grandmother drew the key out of the carpet bag and used the shears to snip the twine that bound it to the handle. She looked at me. "This key belongs to you most of all," she said, and passed it to me.

I ran my fingers over its ornate head and handed it solemnly to Mr. Girandole.

Grandmother told him, too, to be careful. Then she clutched me with both arms, and we retreated a step, as far back as the thicket would allow us.

From my position, I could just make out the keyhole in the deepening gloom. R—— took his hands off the trunk and moved aside. Mr. Girandole drew a breath, held up the key, and slid it into the keyhole. It sank in almost up to the head. He turned it slowly, and there was a loud click from inside the tree.

Then the key was jerked from his fingers. The trunk pulled it in like a retracting tongue. Though the keyhole was too small to admit the head's flanges, I distinctly saw the hole widen like a mouth, suck the key inside, and then close, puckering in upon itself. In the next instant, even the keyhole was gone; only bare, hardened bark remained.

Mr. Girandole dropped to a crouch, clawing at the trunk.

But then a narrow door swung inward, a rectangular section of the bark just wide and tall enough to accommodate a person of average size. The receding portal tugged at the vines that covered its surface. Some were dragged after it; some tore loose and hung slack across the opening.

From our vantage, Grandmother and I couldn't see inside, but Mr. Girandole and R—— were bathed in a wondrous, changing light. At first, it was so blue-white and brilliant that they shielded their eyes. All the leaves behind them shone as if under the full face of the sun, and shadows were banished far back into the thicket.

Then the light softened and shifted to a silvery green. I thought at once of the reflection from one of my favorite Christmas ornaments, an old glass globe of my mama's that hung on our tree each year.

Staring into the light, R—— laughed, his expression one of pure joy. He thumped Mr. Girandole on the shoulder, pushed vines out of his way, and plunged through the door.

"Good-bye!" Grandmother called, but I doubted that he heard her. He was no longer listening to anything in our world.

Mr. Girandole remained sitting on the ground, his legs folded beneath him. Removing his hat, he gazed into the glow, his face touched by deep emotion. At once, his eyes widened, and he cried out as if in pain. Then he appeared to be listening. He nodded and pointed toward Grandmother and me.

Very slowly, he turned his head to look at Grandmother, and I saw a terrible sadness in his eyes. "M——," he said. Tears pooled in his eyes. "M——, the Lord and Lady summon me." He could barely force the words out. "They've let the door stand here this long for my sake, but no more. They will close it forever. The fauns are calling. The Piper on the hill—I hear him . . . I see him dancing. M——!"

There was panic in his voice, and he crawled toward us.

At first, I didn't comprehend. Then the realization crushed down on me. Mr. Girandole was leaving us too.

Grandmother ordered me not to move. Dropping her stick, shrugging off the carpet bag, she fell to her knees and caught Mr. Girandole in her embrace.

He cried her name again, pulling her close, weeping into her hair. "M——! The pain ahead . . . I've seen . . . I *understand* now. Oh, M——!"

She held and hushed him, and said it was all right. "If they summon, you have to go now," she said. "This is the way. I won't be far behind. Just be there, Girandole. Just be there."

They kissed, long and tenderly, in a radiance more sacred than a dawn. I was crying too, my vision blurred, so it was difficult to be certain of what I saw. But in that glow, Grandmother's silver-white hair looked black, and it hung down her back in lustrous waves. Just once, she glanced toward me, and the breath snagged in my chest.

For the Grandmother I saw was not wrinkled by years; the mischievous eyes were the same, only wider and exquisitely angled in a smooth olive face. This woman could not have been much past twenty, if that. I knew then how beautiful the face of the missing statue had been.

Mr. Girandole rose to his feet and helped Grandmother up. The smallness, the weight of the years and the mortal world were gone from him, too. A lightness beamed from him, as if he were the first faun in the first spring of the world. He backed away, holding Grandmother's hands for as long as he could, then touching her fingers, then stepping through the vine-draped doorway. At the threshold, he peered at me with what seemed renewed wonder and affection. Then he held Grandmother's gaze, and as he vanished, his weeping turned to a smile, then laughter. His hat lay in the weeds where he'd dropped it. The glorious light of Faery narrowed to a sliver, then a line, and the door closed with a ringing boom.

In the last of the daylight, I saw that there was no door, no lines to show where a door had been, no keyhole, and no key.

Grandmother picked up the battered hat. I gathered the carpet bag and rucksack, and I handed her the walking-stick. She received it in a hand that was wizened and knobby again.

Without a word, we left the garden by the nearest exit—the mermaid's yard, through which Grandmother had first entered as a girl. It was full dark now, and we did not look back.

Grandmother re-lit the lantern, and we did not speak a word on our way down to the cottage. We both knew that there was no place for words that night. No questions mattered, and no answers were adequate. We'd gotten R—— safely off to whatever awaited him. We'd lost Mr. Girandole, and in our humanity we would grieve for him as if he had died or left us. Drained of emotion and strength, I fell asleep quickly and awoke to the smell of breakfast cooking.

After eating, we washed the dishes, including those from the previous day's picnics. As Grandmother handled the four cups from which we'd drunk Mr. Girandole's tea, I knew she was missing him. She'd taken his lost hat into her room.

Another bright, golden day was gathering heat. We wandered out to the back garden and sat on a bench. Since Grandmother had made no announcements about what we'd do, I suspected she had no energy for working in the garden or walking around the village on errands. I wanted to say something, but I didn't know what it should be. The notebook in my hands was meaningless now except as a memento. We'd solved the puzzle, but instead of a sense of accomplishment, I felt empty and sad.

I listened to the sound of a car driving along the street. I contemplated getting up and peering around to see what sort it was; but just as I decided I didn't have the energy, either, it stopped in front of the cottage. The engine shut off. Grandmother and I looked curiously at each other.

FREDERIC S. DURBIN

Car doors closed, *thunk, thunk*, as Grandmother stood up, smoothing out her skirt and sleeves. Someone knocked on the front door, and a man's voice called, "Mrs. T——?"

I went and stood at the back corner of the cottage, from where I could see along the side yard, beneath the window of my room. The pear and plum trees cast dapples of shade over clusters of creeping myrtle and the magnificent fuchsia.

I caught no glimpse of the car, but a soldier appeared beside the rain barrel. Seeing me, he motioned to someone and said, "In the back." I hurried to stand with Grandmother and told her it was soldiers.

Such a thrill raced through me that I barely stayed on my feet. My heart beat madly. As sure as the sunlight on my face, I was certain that Papa had come home from the war. I knew in another moment he would come around the corner of the house, drop his pack on the walk, and throw his arms wide to embrace me.

But Grandmother waited, frowning.

My breath stopped as Major P—— appeared. His uniform was crisp and impeccable, his hair and boots shiny, his hat in one hand. Raising his chin in greeting, he came toward us, his boots clacking on the bricks. Two soldiers accompanied him. One was the aide who'd been with him on the ferry; the other was one of those who'd caught me in the garden, on the stairs to the hilltop. The major made none of his usual magnanimous greetings.

Strangely, Grandmother sat down on the bench, just when I expected her to say something. I backed up and stood at her elbow, beside the bench.

We were in some kind of trouble—the Army had discovered something about R——, but what could it be, now that both he and Mr. Girandole were beyond anyone's reach? We'd left nothing of consequence in the leaning house, and it was hidden in the compartment: the remains of the pallet bed, a few rags, the bucket and pan—what did the major know?

I thought next of R——'s gun as the men strode closer. Had someone on the ferry seen me throw it into the sea? What if the gun had somehow been sucked back into the ferry's engine? What if some mechanic repairing the motor had been shot by it as he tightened a bolt? The mind moves quickly. And some moments in all the years it never loses; it holds them for a lifetime, every scent, every stirring, the sound of every voice, the colors.

"Mrs. T——," said the major quietly. "Madam . . . I must speak with you privately. Lieutenant, take the young man for a walk."

"Yes, sir," said the third man and beckoned me.

But Grandmother said, "No." The firmness of her tone surprised me. She held the head of her stick in both hands. The look on her face scared me. "No, Major. Whatever you've come to say to me, my grandson should hear it, too."

The major cleared his throat and glanced at me, then back at her. The lieutenant dropped his hand and resumed a posture of attention. Something had changed about the major. In that moment I saw no arrogance, nothing of the fiery bear.

"As you wish," said Major P——. "Madam, it is with deepest sadness I must inform you that your son, Captain A—— T——, has made the ultimate sacrifice for his country. He was killed in action yesterday. He died under heavy fire, defending the approach to a field hospital until the forty-three wounded men inside could be evacuated to safety. Please understand the significance of his actions. He was a hero."

"Defending?" said Grandmother, her gaze far off.

"The reports tell us that the enemy seems to have been unaware of the hospital. They hit with everything they had. Your son, Captain T——, maintained his position, operating a tripod-mounted gun. He was the last one who could save the wounded men, and so he did. But, Madam . . . he was killed by an incendiary shell. I'm afraid his body was unrecoverable."

"No body," Grandmother repeated.

The major spoke on about honors and a medal, and how he'd wanted to deliver the message personally, but I wasn't listening closely anymore. I knew he was wrong. I wanted to tell Grandmother he was wrong, so that she wouldn't worry. He couldn't be talking about my papa. My papa wrote me letters, and they were never about tripod-mounted guns. He marched from place to place and camped. He looked at the stars and the sunsets and described the trees. My papa would be coming home soon.

Grandmother clutched her walking-stick and stared straight ahead, her shoulders slowly rising and falling with her breath.

Then I became certain that this was the major's cruel trick—a terrible revenge he was exacting. Fury ignited in me. Lunging forward, I made fists and shouted up into his face. "You're lying! You're lying! It isn't true!"

The major stiffened, and even in my anger I could see in his eyes the hardness, the coldness again.

I couldn't endure having this hateful man in our garden, telling such lies to Grandmother and me. Without another word, I dodged past him and ran to the back gate, left it swinging, and charged out among the arbors. When I found one screened from our cottage by a row of bushes, I sat down on a bench. Then I got up again and crawled under the bushes, through fragrant branches that touched the ground—I crawled into prickles and shade where there were dead leaves, and the bushes' stems were sticky with sap. I pulled my knees up to my chin and hugged them hard and waited. I would go back when Major P—— was gone with his men and his lies.

Through a gap in the branches, I could see the puffy white clouds hanging motionless.

A while later, I heard footsteps and saw Grandmother hobbling among the arbors, searching for me. She looked much older than she had during breakfast. I wriggled out from the bushes and went to her. She put her arms around me and we sank onto a bench beneath the ripening grapes.

"It's all a lie, isn't it?" I asked desperately.

Grandmother combed her fingers through my hair, kissed my forehead, and pulled me close. Shutting her eyes, she rocked us gently back and forth, back and forth.

Tuesday afternoon passed in a blur. We walked to the store where there was a telephone so I could call my mother; Grandmother told me to. She brought along the number in her handbag. When Mama and I heard each other's voices, all we could do was cry. She called me "Baby" and said she'd see me on Friday night, and she told me how much she'd missed me and that she loved me. I said I loved her, too. She asked to speak to Grandmother, and Grandmother hesitated when I held out the phone to her. But she took it and listened and said "Yes" and "That's right" a few times. "Yes, he did . . . Yes, he was . . . Yes, of course there will be, but I don't know anything yet." Then she looked at me and said, "He's a wonderful boy. He's been my right hand all this time." After a long pause, she said, "I know that, dear, and I say the same to you. You're in my heart."

In no time, it seemed the whole village had heard the news, and Grandmother's friends started bringing pans and bowls and baskets of food. By that night, my disbelief had turned to anger. If it wasn't Major P——'s vicious lie, then it was God's mistake. God had simply been wrong. He'd let the wrong person die. I knelt on the floor of my room and begged Him to take it back. My papa smiled from the photo on the table, his arm around my mama, his hand on my shoulder. He was there, so clearly there—such a force of life and joy couldn't be gone from the world; it was all wrong. In bed at night, my knees ached from all the kneeling, and I couldn't sleep.

Wednesday was more of the same: people coming and going, hugging and weeping. Grandmother got misty-eyed at times, but she never lost her composure—at least, not that I saw. The soft-spoken priest came and prayed with us. At close range he was easier to hear, but it didn't matter. He wasn't asking God to correct His mistake, so I didn't listen. A telegram also came from my cousin C——, saying he'd pick me up on Friday in a car so that I wouldn't have to take the train home. One of Grandmother's friends explained the situation to the stationmaster, and the money for my return ticket was refunded.

My friend the postmaster came and hugged me and said some kind things. His eyes were red. We sat in the back garden together and talked—I don't remember about what. He gave me a silver-bodied pen that looked expensive. "To remember me by," he said. "But mostly to write with. Keep at it, G——." And so I have.

Mrs. D—— couldn't stop crying. When each new person arrived, she would burst into another paroxysm of wailing and tears, so that people held her and fanned her and tried to console her. Once, a long time afterward, I talked about that scene with Grandmother, who said, "It was her way of honoring us. She knew *someone* should be carrying on properly, and you and I were still too numb."

I don't remember my numbness so much as my anger.

Mrs. F—— took charge of the kitchen, of getting everyone fed and served tea, of cleaning up, and of making sure Grandmother received all important messages.

Grandmother looked in on me during the night and saw that I wasn't asleep, so we went to the kitchen and heated milk. We sat there surrounded by the loaves of bread and pastries and piles of fruit, and finally Grandmother cried. I think I started it; I'm not sure. But soon we were gripping each other's hands across the table and bawling.

When we'd cried all we could for the time being, we carried the cups of milk into the sitting room. Grandmother settled me on the couch with my head on a pillow, and she stroked my hair. In a soft, husky voice, she sang an old song about a wanderer on a long journey. The wanderer rested on a mossy stone and longed for a maiden back home, with skin pale as snow and hair dark as the raven's wings.

I knew without asking that it was a song she'd sung to my father when he'd been small. At some point, while the crickets sang to us both, I fell asleep.

On Thursday morning the visits began again, and I could take no more of it. I asked Grandmother if I could go to the monsters' grove. She hugged me and said yes.

Everything seemed different in the sacred woods—the bird song, the light, the sighing of the leaves. A moment that I'd known would pass had passed. I was seeing the garden's statues now with older eyes. The leaning house stood empty and sad.

I climbed the precarious stairs and, armload by armload, carried outside all the debris of R——'s stay: the branches, leaves, and blankets; some dishes and cookware of Mr. Girandole's; the pan and the bucket; and the rags we'd used to wash the mirror. Before I left for the final time, I made certain the sliding floor was locked against the back wall, giving easy access to the ladder. Then I ascended to the roof for a last look around. "Good-bye," I whispered to the garden.

I scattered the leaves and branches and tied everything else up in a blanket. Before I took it home, I dropped it on the terrace and went to the upper garden, where the door into Faery had been.

As I drew near, it occurred to me that my father had died before we opened the door. He'd been there, somewhere on the portal's other side . . . maybe no more than a few steps away. Mr. Girandole had seen him—remembering the faun's reactions, I was sure of it.

Seeing the great, limbless tree, I drew a sharp breath. It had withered as with the passage of a hundred years or more since the other night. Caverns of rot yawned in the trunk. Any day now, it would crash down into the thicket or across the glade. I went no closer.

I headed west through the upper clearing. As I passed the stairway leading to the temple, I heard a noise. I froze and turned to my right. I didn't want to meet anyone here in our private, sacred place, but there was no time to run.

A man emerged between the bushes, coming down the steps. Tall, lean, and baked by many years of the sun, he was not a soldier . . . but not a villager, either. He reminded me somehow of an orchestra conductor. Around his neck hung an expensive-looking camera.

"Hello!" he called cheerfully. "So, your kind do come here! This place was made for you!"

My kind? Was this man another denizen of Faery? I glanced quickly at his legs, but they seemed human.

He laughed, striding nearer. "Your kind—children! This is the place for you, isn't it?"

"No one comes here, sir," I said. "People say the woods are haunted."

"You're a serious little fellow," he said. "Haunted? Are you a ghost, then?"

I didn't tell him that my father had just been killed. He offered his hand, and I shook it.

"'No one,' you say—but *you're* here. Do you play here?" he asked.

I explained that I'd played here for months, that I was visiting my grandmother. He nodded and said it's exactly where *he'd* play if it were him. We strolled past the Announcing Angel, past the centaur. I still didn't like finding a stranger here. But then . . . the garden had belonged to others before it was ours.

"Doesn't it spark your imagination, this place?" he asked me.

"Yes. I like to sketch it."

He stopped and shook my hand again. "A fellow artist! I draw pictures myself. And paint. And sculpt."

I suppose I still wasn't thinking straight, and that's why the realization had taken me so long. This was the friend of Major P——'s, the artist he'd spoken to about the statues.

The man paused before the sleeping woman, shaking his head in admiration. "That's why I'm here, you see. I had read something of this place, but I had no idea . . . But a soldier friend of mine was here recently on some sort of patrol—looking for a lost person, I believe—and he told me how truly remarkable it was."

FREDERIC S. DURBIN

A "soldier friend" . . . but this tall man seemed nothing at all like the major—I suppose because he was an artist. For starters, he had much kinder and warmer eyes.

"It's a magical place," the man said. "One can easily envision fairies dancing here—or just there, behind that arch!" He grinned at me. "Have you ever seen a fairy here?"

"No," I said. "Only a faun."

"Only a—" He raised his eyebrows and laughed with delight. "You know," he said in a conspiratorial tone, "I'm going to bring a crew and a moving-picture camera and make a film about this place. People should know about this garden. The poets, the historians, the seekers of mystery, the spiritual, and those in love—definitely those in love. And those like you and me. The artists."

We descended the root stairway and walked beneath the arch. I almost told him there was a whale hiding in the brush to his right, but decided against it. If he was serious about the garden, he'd find it himself.

On a sudden inspiration, he asked, "Would you like to be in my movie? You and—your grandmother, you say?"

I thanked him, but told him I had to leave the village tomorrow, to go back to the city.

"Oh—a pity," he said. "This grove seems to like you. Some people clash with the lighting of a place, you know. They throw back a place's light and don't fit in at all. But you—this is your home!"

I remembered how the major had looked on his visit here, and I thought I knew what the artist meant.

"Shall we take a picture at least, then? Help me take a picture or two. There, perhaps? With that grim Angel of the Bottomless Pit?" He knew Apollyon.

292

I shook my head. "Not that one." I glanced over his shoulder.

He followed my gaze. "Ahhh," he exclaimed. "A much better choice! You do have the eye of an artist."

And so, we went over to the square pool, and I had my picture taken next to an unclothed lady with a water jar.

"Can I trouble you to shoot a couple of me?" asked the man, and he showed me how to work the camera. I did, and for the first photo, he stepped up onto the rim of the pool and brazenly put his arm around the woman's waist. He had me take three. Two were more serious.

Some months later, when I visited Grandmother again, she gave me prints of two photographs—one I'd taken of the man, and the one of me. That artist had interviewed Grandmother as the local authority on the sacred woods, and I suppose he received her unique blend of the truth with prudent camouflage. Of course she'd seen me in one of his pictures and identified the serious little fellow as her grandson. In the photo, I looked shy and sad, standing there with my hands in my pockets. Grandmother showed me a portrait of the same man in a book from her shelf. Though I hadn't known it, the artist with the camera—the last acquaintance I'd made that summer, at the last possible moment—was none other than the great artist D—— S——. He was known all over the world; I'd seen his work in museums. He'd signed the backs of both photos for me. One of his inscriptions read: "For G——, with thankfulness for chance meetings." The other: "For G——, who has an artist's eye." I kept the photographs in an old travel-case of my mother's with my notebook from that summer, and the shells from Wool Island, and R——'s flute, and the letters from my parents.

But that day in the garden, the man and I parted ways. He was going to take more pictures of the statues, and I picked up my clanking bundle and trudged out of the grove by the way I'd come in. The last glimpse I had of it was the dragon rearing out of the bushes, forever keeping the dogs at bay.

And that was the end of my spring and summer in the village. Grandmother and I talked a lot more that night, when the house was quiet again. She let me read a letter that a soldier had delivered that afternoon, a report from my father's superior officer commending Papa and telling the same story the major had told us. Grandmother gave me the letter.

"Shouldn't you keep something?" I asked.

"I'm keeping everything," Grandmother said, and pointed at her heart, "in here. Besides, I have all the letters he's sent me for years, which will belong to you someday. *Also* besides, you need these things more than I do. You have a much longer way to go before you're done."

"You should never talk in absolute terms about the future," I reminded her.

"That's right," she said. Except, she added, there was one thing we *did* know for sure: that the paths joined up again, somewhere ahead. Bringing me a large, soft cloth with a pattern of sea horses and starfish, she helped me wrap up the seashells so they wouldn't break. "This cloth is part of a dress I wore when I was a baby," she said. "They named me after the sea, you know." I picked out the best shell for her to keep on the bookshelves beside her chair. Those seashells were always a treasure, for in the years afterward, whenever I put one to my ear, I could hear, amid the voice of the sea, all the sounds of the village—the waves and breezes, the gulls, the distant engines, and all the voices of Grandmother's friends.

I renewed my promise to visit soon, and to write often.

She told me to be patient with God. Before long, she said, I'd see that nothing He did was a mistake. And she told me how happy she was that I'd spent those months with her.

In the morning, we sat on the bench behind the cottage, waiting for Cousin C—— to arrive in the car. Grandmother said that with all the uproar of the last couple days, she hadn't picked the ripe tomatoes, and they'd be going bad on the vines. So, we went into the patch and hunted for them, their bright orbs peeking out of the spiky, aromatic leaves. Grandmother told me not to get my pants dirty and I said I wouldn't. Soon, she said, it would be grape-harvesting time, and the villagers would be making the new wine and dancing till all hours. When that happened each year, it was as if there were still satyrs and fauns about.

She said one more thing I recall: that she'd thought she could duck her head and let the war pass over the top, but she'd been wrong. The war wouldn't be ignored. It had come home to us, like it did, in one way or another, for everyone who lived in those times. But the war had brought us R——, too. We'd never have met him without it, and having known him was a gift.

As I watched her brown hands work, I thought for some reason of Mrs. D—— and of how much Grandmother had been upset when I'd told her about the setcreasea and fuchsia. For all the grief that weighed on me now, a warmth touched me deep inside. "You've always planted the garden for him, haven't you—for Mr.

Girandole? It's why we don't talk about the flowers until they come up. You wanted him to know about them before anyone else."

I imagined Mr. Girandole deep in the woods, catching a new fragrance in the air each spring as only a faun might, when the first blossom opened.

Grandmother made a sound that was both a "Hush" and a chuckle, and I knew I was right.

So, we ended that visit as we'd begun it, in back of the cottage with our faces close to the earth, and soil under our fingernails.

I remember looking up again at the clouds. Some things were almost always in motion—clouds, laundry on clotheslines, and the leaves of the trees. Some things, like the statues in our woods, were forever at rest. As Grandmother hunted tomatoes beside me, humming now and then, talking to me and to the occasional grasshopper, I sat back on my heels and watched the clouds for a long time. They billowed and stretched in the perfect sky, magical pictures that lingered for a moment and then changed, one morphing into the next.

Grandmother lived a long time. I wish I could say that I spent every summer with her after that, or many, at least. But the hard truth was that I had become the man of our house at age nine, with no more of a choice than Papa had been given in his going to the war. The war ended, but summers were no longer carefree. Summer's difference from the rest of the year came down mostly to the heat. I helped at home, worked as soon as I could, and went to school. We kept ourselves together; we always had a roof over our heads and food on the table, which was more than many like us had. My sister grew up to be a music teacher, and my mother was proud of us both.

I wrote to Grandmother and visited when I could, but things had changed for us. There was no mystery to solve, no patient to care for. There was no faun to rap on the back door in the moonlight. On every visit, after Grandmother and I had exchanged news, we had little to say. We would listen to the radio, and I would help her in the garden, digging or weeding quietly beside her. One good autumn, I re-roofed her cottage, which was the talk of the town. Once, I brought her a modern refrigerator, but she made me take it away; she couldn't abide its noise. I think, too, that she disliked how it had no blocks of ice to melt; it gave no water to the garden and thus did not really earn its keep. Usually, I would mend a latch or a fence for her. Then, in a day or two, Grandmother would tell me I should get back and look after Mama and N——, and I would go.

When in time the little cottage was silent and empty, I was the one who sorted Grandmother's things. My sister would have helped me, but it seemed right that I should do it alone. It was not difficult; Grandmother had lived simply and saw no sense in clutter. There were a few family treasures and some fine pieces of furniture that Grandfather had made.

In the bottom of the cedar chest was a letter, neatly folded in its envelope. Though it was in one way incriminating, she must have cherished it. It's entirely possible she'd forgotten it was there; but more likely, I thought, she'd wanted someone to find it someday, even before she'd known that the someone would be me.

The letter, brittle with age, its ink fading, had been written by Grandfather, its signature unquestionably his. The envelope bore no address, and I imagined him coming to Grandmother's door, putting the letter into her hand. It said:

My Darling M——,

 If you have it in your heart to forgive this fool his pride and stubbornness, please accept my apology for words spoken in anger. If there is anything I know about you with absolute certainty, it is that you are always true to your word; and if you say that this other whom you once loved is no man of the province and has been gone from your life since before we met, I believe you. Indeed, what right have I to blame you for what you felt in another time? I was angry only because I know you so well, and I see that you love him still; it vexed me that I must share even a part of you with another, though that part be only memory. You have assured me, too, that with him it was different—that what you mean for us to have is more complete. Most importantly, I know that you love me. At last I understand why you felt it so important to tell me of him, so that there may be no secrets between us.

 Dearest M——, will you meet me tonight at nine o'clock on the beach by the sea caves? The weather will be fine, and the view will be wondrous. I have a very important question to ask you. If you do not come, please know that I understand the fault is mine. Either way, I will love you: from near at hand if my dreams are to be fulfilled; from afar if it must be so. Please come to the sea caves tonight!

 Yours forever,

 B——

My car was loaded with the last of Grandmother's possessions. I chose to leave the cottage for the last time by its back door. For a while on that late-spring day, I sat in her old garden on the stone bench. No one had planted or tended the hanging boxes or the flower beds; they were trying to carry on by themselves, but they had fulfilled their purpose. I hoped a worthy gardener would move in.

Next door, Mrs. F——'s house had been torn down, her garden nothing now but bare earth. There were new wooden pickets in the ground with yellow streamers tied around them. A new foundation, I gathered, was to be laid.

Standing, I stretched my back, breathing, taking the fragrances deep inside myself. I let the sun warm me and fill me with light. Then I began to walk—through the gate and the high grass, past the arbors, into the wildflower meadow, and finally, into the cool green embrace of the woods.

ACKNOWLEDGMENTS

I wish to express my heartfelt thanks to my agent, Eddie Schneider, for never ceasing to believe in this book, and to my editor, Navah Wolfe, for finding a way to publish it, and for all her work, support, and commitment to helping the story find its best form. I send thanks to Tricia, Tammy, Steven, Gabe, Nick, Jeff, Ina, Lizzie, Catherine, Zana, Shelley, and Elizabeth, who read early drafts and offered sound advice. Thank you to Saga Press for bringing this book to light and for a cover that I love.

My deepest gratitude is due also to Pier Francesco Orsini, called Vicino, for building his *sacro bosco* (holy wood) in Bomarzo, Italy. Although the sacred woods in this story is fictionalized, it is inspired by the statues, structures, and alluring mystery of Vicino's lifelong labor; his legacy echoes here as it has in the works of other writers and musicians across five centuries.

To those who wish to know more about Vicino's garden, I commend the outstanding book *The Garden at Bomarzo: A Renaissance Riddle*, by Jessie Sheeler (Frances Lincoln: London, 2007). Finally, thanks must go to Janet Brennan, for her article "Monster Parks" in *Fate*, May 2008, which introduced me to the *sacro bosco* and was the first inspiration for this book.